WHY HE LIED

A MAK AND WILTON THRILLER
BOOK 3

ADDISON MICHAEL

PAGES & PIE
Publishing · Marketing Writing · Consulting

2024 Pages & Pie Publishing

ISBN: 979-8-9927544-0-7

Library of Congress Catalogue-in-Publication Data

Michael, Addison

Why he lied: a mak and wilton thriller/Addison Michael

Cover Design by Art by Karri

Editing by Tiffany Avery and Jayne Shaw

While set in real places, this novel is a work of fiction. All characters, events, and police agencies portrayed are products of the author's imagination. Any resemblance to established practices or similarity that may depict actual people, either alive or deceased, are entirely fictional and purely coincidental.

www.addisonmichael.com

PROLOGUE
TREVAN

Trevan Collins lay on the ground, face up, staring sightlessly at the ceiling with eyes that had begun to swell and bruise prior to his final exit from this world. His face was evidence that Trevan had put up a fight before he died. A trickle of blood ran from the corner of his mouth and dripped onto the tan carpet where his body lay motionless.

That little drip wasn't what caused the large stain of blood now soaking into the ground under him. The once oozing blood was coagulated in the grisly, open gash on Trevan's neck. It had left him gasping and sputtering until he finally gave up his life a few short hours ago.

Tonight—the last hour of his life—had started with a knock at the door. But that's not when the end began. It wasn't even when Trevan had gotten his hands on that fateful photo. No, that had just pushed the button on the count-down clock to his final days.

The beginning of Trevan's expiration was that fateful night over eighteen years ago. That night, they—Beth Donovan, Davey Stinnert, Greg Wilton, Jacob Greenly, and Trevan Collins—became the Delinquents, and they would never be the same. They were all in the wrong place at the wrong time. The outcome was a murder that none of them were charged with, yet they all paid the price for. An incident that had cost them their childhood and their innocence. Jacob had ended his own life less than a year later.

As a result, the Delinquents would cling to each other like a lifeline with a closeness no one on the outside would ever understand. They were bound by the toxicity of murder, then drugs. It was no life. It was slavery. Then they grew up. Minus Jacob and Greg, of course. Greg was a different story. He'd taken a bullet for all of them.

It was sheer, stupid luck that Trevan had found the photo. Adult Trevan now knew things teenage Trevan was too naïve to consider. The murder accusation had been just that—an accusation. The Delinquents would never have been charged. It had all been trumped up. The perfect opportunity to manipulate a bunch of high schoolers—popular, well-liked ones at that—into doing the bidding of the Corruptors, as they called them.

Trevan had swiped the photo that proved who killed Greg and had given it to Greg's little brother, a US Marshal. That's what Trevan was thinking about when he'd heard the knock at his door over the loud, rage-rock music he was playing that would serenade him to his death.

It was probably his duplex neighbor, Scott, knocking to ask him to turn down the music. For half a second, Trevan considered ignoring him. Trevan shook his head back and forth as he wiped his hands on a kitchen towel. He pulled chicken out of the oven and turned the heat off.

Can't a guy make dinner without getting interrupted? Trevan muttered, feeling edgy and irritable. He wore those feelings like the clothes he put on his back every day. He couldn't remember a day in the past year when those emotions hadn't dictated his mood.

For years, things had gotten better. Once they all graduated from high school, the Delinquents were off the hook. The Corrupters didn't seem to need them anymore. Until Trevan got the summons. He, Beth Donovan, and Davey Stinnert, the last Delinquents alive, all showed up on trembling legs to a secret, underground meet-up. If they didn't show, they knew what would happen to them. Just like that, the gang was back together.

There were three major players in the room when they arrived. Anthony Gerritt, Mickey Upton, and Boyd Allister had all stood in front of them, eyes dead and glaring, a trifecta of pure evil. That's when Trevan knew. His life was about to get so much worse.

The loud pounding at his door brought Trevan back to the present and he yanked the door open. "What do you want now, Scott?"

Only, the person who stood on the other side of the door wasn't Scott. It was the last person Trevan ever expected in this neighborhood, yet here he stood on his doorstep.

"Get in here," Trevan hissed, pulling the man into his house, looking around outside to check if anyone saw him. "What the hell are you doing here? It's not safe. What have I told you about that?"

The man clenched his jaw, a clear flash of anger. "We need to talk about this." His deep voice was low and deadly calm.

Trevan stared at what the man had clutched in his hand. Trevan wondered how he hadn't seen it when he'd pulled the man into his living room. Trevan froze, the color draining from his face. He didn't have to see it to know exactly what was in the envelope. He quickly weighed his options. *That damn envelope is going to be the death of me, one way or another,* he predicted.

"What did I tell you about coming here—to my home?"

Trevan said with a menacing growl of anger. "You're gonna get us both killed."

"Explain this," the man demanded, ignoring Trevan's threats.

"No." Trevan pushed the man. "You're gonna get the hell out of my house and hope that no one saw you come in. You're a stupid man. Suicidal. You know that?"

The man, who was angrier than he let on, pushed Trevan back. His light hair fell across his forehead. Trevan supposed some would find him attractive, but what did he know? The man wore a black hoodie, black jogger pants, thin black gloves, and black tennis shoes. The thought hit Trevan and made his stomach turn, ice flooding through his veins. The man did not plan to be seen. But that wasn't for Trevan's protection.

"Start talking!" the man growled.

Trevan shoved the man so hard the envelope fluttered to the floor. Trevan launched at the man, landing on top of him. He got a punch in before the man rolled Trevan to the side with such force that Trevan hit his head against the wall. For a moment, Trevan saw only black.

Then Trevan shook his head and came to just in time for a large, powerful fist to connect with his mouth. Pain exploded in Trevan's face, and he slid his tongue over his teeth, wondering if it had knocked any of them loose. He could taste the metallic tang of blood.

Rage overcame Trevan and he flew at the man, using his body weight to move him. Both of them hit the opposite wall. Trevan was pretty sure that hit left a mark in the drywall.

"We're on the same team, you piece of shit," Trevan raged as he attempted an uppercut, but the man launched to the side.

"Debatable," the man grunted. "If we were, you would explain how this came to be in your possession."

Trevan was on his feet now, but so was the man, which surprised Trevan. Trevan never would have expected this man to fight him, but he sure was knocking the wind out of Trevan at the moment.

"I don't owe you an explanation," Trevan said as he took a hit to his temple that knocked him off guard. A follow-up hit exploded into Trevan's eye socket. Trevan staggered back two steps into the living room, trying to keep his balance.

What he saw when he opened his good eye made him freeze. This guy was serious. He wielded a knife. It wasn't just any knife, either. It was a butcher knife, and Trevan could see that it was sharp. The man was advancing. Trevan looked around for a weapon. He came up short. He knew the back door was just behind him. If he could back up just a few more steps…

But the man was on him. He tackled Trevan to the ground. The knife was at Trevan's throat.

"Talk," the man commanded.

Trevan could feel the sharp edge stinging as it touched his throat.

"It never sat well with me how it ended. I thought—" Trevan dared not move or even gulp. It was hard enough to talk with a knife pressed against his Adam's apple. "I thought it would give me some good karma, you know? I'm a bad guy. I do shitty things. I needed to set something right."

"Bullshit," the man growled. He pressed the knife into Trevan's throat harder. The sting gave way to pain. "You're bringing on a lot of unnecessary attention and I want to know why."

"Man, I'm just tired," Trevan said, then he blinked a few times, feeling surprised by his own honesty. His life had never been his own. He was tired of playing puppet in someone else's theatre. When he heard about Anthony Gerritt's death, Trevan knew they would stop at nothing. No one was untouchable. Word had gotten around that Gerritt had turned snitch. Trevan didn't believe that. He did believe that Gerritt had made a mistake. That's all it took. One mistake and you're out—in a horizontal box. "I got nothing else to say. If this is it for me, then just do it."

The man didn't need any more coaxing. Trevan felt the sharp slice of the butcher knife blade as it slipped in quick and deep through Trevan's neck. Trevan gasped, trying to take back the air that left his windpipe in a whoosh.

Trevan could see the man watching him with no emotion in his eyes. He could feel the liquid that ran down his throat, slowly at first, then in spurts, until it became a pool of thick, viscous liquid underneath Trevan's now motionless body. Trevan's vision was fading.

Trevan lay gasping in surprise and pain. He actually thought his words would make the man reconsider. But before Trevan bled out on his own living room floor, Trevan wondered one thing.

Why didn't he ask me what he really wanted to know?

1

———————

WILTON

Stephen watched Beth Donovan as she barely stifled a groan, sat up, and swung her legs over the side of the bed. She wore a silky nightie with thin spaghetti straps. The skirt barely covered the round curve of her bottom. He sighed in contentment. From her impeccably polished fingernails down to her matching toenails, Beth was almost perfect.

Almost, Stephen told himself. *Because nobody is perfect.* But Beth was pretty close, in his estimation. With Beth by his side, the past four months had been pretty great. A nice distraction from all that was going wrong in his life.

He'd been attending US Marshal hearings to determine if he could go back to work. No matter how well the meetings went, his status remained the same. *Undetermined.* He was on leave until they decided who had killed Anthony Gerritt, a well-known criminal boss who had agreed to inform on a larger sex-trafficking organization. Before that could happen, Gerritt had been killed, leaving Stephen looking like the prime suspect.

It was all because Stephen had lost his self-control and beat Gerritt up after he'd agreed to cooperate. Losing his temper did not make Stephen a murderer. But the five US Marshal Service officials on the panel couldn't seem to agree on that and had kept him on leave. It hadn't seemed to matter that Stephen had attended multiple counseling appointments, had attended every Disciplinary Panel meeting, and had been completely honest.

What was the old adage about the truth setting a person free? Stephen decided it was BS. He wasn't free. He was unemployed. He'd made a mistake—granted, it was a big one —but he'd immediately owned up to it. He'd told the truth. Shouldn't that put him back on the good guy team?

Instead of working to clear Stephen as a suspect, Stephen thought they must be attempting to solve Anthony Gerritt's murder. Bitterness took root in Stephen's thoughts when he contemplated his profession these days. He felt angry as he considered whether he needed a lawyer and if he should have already gotten one. But he just kept thinking if he played nice and did all the right things, he'd get to come back to work.

What he hadn't counted on was the severe consequences for his actions from that night. That was the night he'd lost everything—his home, his partner, his privacy, and his girlfriend. At the thought of Alyah, Stephen's heart still constricted. No amount of time with Beth had lessened that wound. He frowned at the thought.

Feeling guilty for thinking about another woman, Stephen reached over and ran his hand down Beth's black, shoulderlength hair. She shivered a little and looked over her shoulder at him. Her vibrant blue eyes lit, matching the smile on her face.

"Good morning," she said. She turned and leaned over to kiss Stephen.

Stephen tried to pull her back down into bed, but Beth protested. "I have to work, Stephen," she laughed as she scurried backward and out of his grip.

"Jealous," Stephen grumbled with a frown.

"They still haven't given you a date to go back?" Beth asked as she slipped the nighty over her head, let it hit the floor, walked into the bathroom, and turned on the shower.

"No," Stephen growled.

Beth didn't know the whole story because it was classified, of course. But she knew enough. Stephen had admitted he'd taken down a dangerous criminal with excessive force and the marshals had put him on leave until they decided on a course of action. What he hadn't said were the words they used that rolled around his head, creating the source of his guilt and shame. *Abuse of power*.

"What do you have going on today?" Beth asked.

Stephen heard the shower curtain move to the side and knew Beth had gotten in. He got up, followed her into the bathroom, and grabbed his toothbrush. "Shopping with my mom. Anna is coming to stay this weekend—"

"Oh, that's right!" Beth peeked her head out, her silky hair dripping wet. "Are you excited?"

"Of course," Stephen said through a mouth full of foamy toothpaste. He spit, rinsed, and put the toothbrush in the holder.

After a few minutes, Beth turned off the shower, grabbed a towel, and dried off. Before she could wrap the towel around herself, Stephen put an arm around her waist and pulled her close.

"I'm gonna miss you this weekend," Stephen whispered into her ear as he pulled her against him.

"Stephen," Beth protested weakly. "You're gonna make me late to work."

"So be late." He leaned down to kiss her. Beth put her arms around his neck and kissed him back.

2

———

MAK

Mak reached across the table, grasped a tiny piece of wood, and straightened back up. It was the tenth time she'd done the exercise, and her back was aching.

She tried to push down the impatience she felt that such small movements still caused her such big pain. She hadn't hit her goal. She was four months into therapy, and no matter how much she begged, they wouldn't release her to return to the marshal service.

When doctors initially estimated anywhere from three to six months of physical therapy, Mak had pushed herself to return in three. And here she was at four, still not cleared to go back to work. Now her physical therapist, Richard, was telling her she'd be in therapy as long as it took to heal.

"Be patient with yourself, Mak." Richard was tossing a ball against the wall and catching it, switching back and forth with whichever hand caught it when it bounced back at him.

"Show off," Mak sniped. She wiped a wayward drip of sweat that slid down her forehead. *Seriously, this should not be this hard,* she thought.

"You're making good progress. Everyone heals at different

rates, you know. You'll be back to work in no time. In the meantime, enjoy the break. Plenty of people would love to take time off."

"I'm not plenty of people," Mak snapped.

Richard smiled that annoyingly bright smile and put two thumbs up in the air. "You're a winner, Mak. You've got this. Enough for today. See ya tomorrow."

"I hate that guy," Mak whispered as she walked away at a slower pace than she'd ever walked in her life. It took forever just to get out the door.

She had barely sat down in her car and was buckling her seatbelt when her phone buzzed with a text. She checked the screen, surprised to see that Deputy Director Rob Sikes was asking her to come in to the office. She wondered if he'd asked Wilton as well. She sighed. Probably not. She figured her partner was likely still on leave for a murder charge that he didn't commit. She had to admit, her situation was bad. His was worse.

Mak pulled into the station less than ten minutes later.

"Wow, that was fast." Sikes did a double take when she walked through the door.

"I was in the area." Mak tried not to walk so gingerly. The last thing she wanted was pity, or worse, for her boss to fear she was now incompetent to perform the basic functions of her job.

"You weren't waiting outside in your car, were you?" Sikes teased with a grin as they walked toward the conference room.

"No. I had PT. It's right down the street," Mak reluctantly admitted.

"Right, well, I know you're still on medical leave, so I won't keep you long. Just wanted to brief you on where we are with your case." Sikes waved a hand for her to take a seat.

Your case. His words warmed Mak's heart. They made her

feel included. Almost like she hadn't been gone for four months.

"Boyd Allister and Mickey Upton," Sikes announced while peering at Mak. He toggled his mouse, and his MacBook woke up. Two pictures flashed up on the big screen.

Mak's eyes shifted to where Sikes was pointing. One man was tall—easily over six foot five—and thin. Mak wondered how he kept his balance. The other man could not look more opposite. He was only five foot nine with a tubby belly. What a sight the two made together. Did they look familiar to her? Since her accident, the words *mild brain trauma* played in her head on a negative loop of fear that she might never be the same. She tried to shake it off. She'd also missed the wrap-up of the last case.

"Who are they?" Mak asked, her heart racing with excitement over the possibility of a new case. She knew better. She hadn't been cleared yet. Her back ached even as she sat in this comfortable chair. Yet here she was debating with herself over how honest she wanted to be with her boss about that.

"Remember the two men we originally believed were Anthony Gerritt's bodyguards?"

Did she remember them? Mak nodded her head confidently. In truth, she had very little recollection of that.

"Bodyguards they were not. They are now our prime suspects who we believe are heading up the sex trafficking ring that formerly belonged to Anthony Gerritt." Sikes gestured to the screen with his hand. "A few minor felonies, but nothing huge in their histories to indicate these guys are big-time criminals. The good news is we caught Boyd Allister transporting the missing women in our last case. He's still sitting in prison, where he will stay until he stands trial."

"Wilton told me some details but remind me…" Mak hated admitting her memory lapse. "How did we find out who these guys are, and how do we know they're involved?"

Mak tried to remember. Were these the guys at the diner with Gerritt when she first met him? Or were they his *bodyguards* at the racetrack when she ran into Gerritt?

Unfortunately, her accident had rendered her with an unwelcome side effect. The memory of the events leading up to the explosion were fuzzy at best. It was like some of it had been erased from her brain. Mak didn't exactly want to admit that to Sikes—or to anyone.

Sikes narrowed his eyes and paused. For a minute, Mak thought Sikes was onto her. He gave her a funny look and continued. "They're the men that Lacy Donovan helped us identify via the sketch artist. They, along with Gerritt, are involved in the trafficking ring."

"Wait, we're calling it a *ring* now?" Mak asked.

Sikes nodded. "I forget where you left off after your incident and hospital trip. Before Gerritt was murdered, he agreed to inform on a larger organization he had identified as a trafficking ring. Right here in this local southwest area. He confirmed that Allister and Upton were involved."

Mak's eyes widened. "Right under our noses?"

"Well, Gerritt indicated they were on the move. When we got as close as we did in our last case, it shook things up for the ring. They were looking for a new home base, and Gerritt was planning to tell us where they landed," Sikes admitted.

"Convenient," Mak snarked. "Gerritt gets let out on full immunity with only a little information—"

"He gave us the location of the three women," Sikes interrupted indignantly.

That, Mak remembered. "Fine, he gets out of jail free, leaves the station, then is found murdered?"

Sikes nodded his head. "Found him bleeding in a local rest stop in a bathroom. Gunshot to the head. Multiple stab wounds. Lots of blood at the scene."

"Right out in public," Mak mused.

"We think they—his criminal buddies—found out and wanted to send a message," Sikes said.

"You don't really think Wilton murdered him, do you?" Mak asked.

Sikes flinched. "I don't. The US Marshal Service Disciplinary Board isn't as convinced. They think there was no reason for Gerritt's people to turn on him. No way for them to know he'd made a deal. They're keeping Wilton on leave until they can determine who murdered Gerritt."

"What?" Mak gasped. "What happened to innocent until proven guilty? Wilton was with my family at my home. He has an alibi. If you wait until you find the murderer, Wilton may never come back!"

"Nice vote of confidence, Mak," Sikes said sarcastically.

"No offense to the PD around here, but it's not like you have me and Wilton on the case. If we were involved, we'd have found our traffickers and had them locked up by now," Mak smirked with overstated confidence.

"So, now you want to play detective?" Sikes shot back.

"Let's be honest, if the Attorney General tells us to investigate, we do it. There's always crossover," Mak spouted.

"No."

Mak felt surprised to hear the authoritative note in Sikes' voice. "Okay, why did you call me in here if you aren't planning to put me back on the job?"

"I am. It's a different kind of job. I need you to check on Wilton for me," Sikes lowered his voice though the conference room door was shut.

"What?" Mak snapped, feeling surprised.

"You know, go see him and let me know how he's doing." Sikes shrugged casually.

"You want me to spy on my partner and report back to you?" Mak's voice cut through the BS. "Why can't you do it?

You're his superior. Surely, the US Marshal Service board will let you check on him."

"He hasn't been answering my calls or texts in the last week. I don't want you to *spy*, exactly. Just—check on his state of mind. Make sure he isn't looking for another job—"

"He's pretty pissed. I can tell you that. I would be too if someone falsely accused me of murder and put me on a leave." Mak had a sore spot when it came to being on leave. She'd been put on a mandatory leave before, hadn't thought it was fair, and hated every minute of it.

"No one is accusing him of murder. They're just keeping him from getting more tangled up in it," Sikes defended.

"You tell yourself whatever you need to sleep at night. I'm not spying on my partner. If you remember, I'm still on medical leave." Mak got up to leave.

"Just check on him for me, please. He typically answers my calls. I'm concerned," Sikes tried again.

"Really?" Mak asked wearily.

"More or less," Sikes answered. "Also, I want him to be ready if his status changes and we have work for him."

"Do you mean in case you have work for both of us?" Mak bartered.

"As soon as you're cleared." Sikes smiled at her.

Mak groaned, knowing she couldn't lie to him about her physical progress. She hated that Sikes knew her so well.

3

———————

LACY

Lacy's fingers flew over the keyboard as she manipulated the web to the dark side. In the four short months in protective custody, Lacy had enrolled and started a crash course in computers and cybersecurity. Her online instructors had no clue she planned to use her training to access the black market with the intention of cyberstalking. She'd managed to find her own picture and her friends' pictures before *they* deleted them.

They were Anthony Gerritt, Boyd Allister, and Mickey Upton. Lacy wasn't worried about the fact that the pictures of her and the three other women in golden dresses stuck in a golden cage had disappeared. It was obviously a good thing. But while they were still posted, the pictures had helped her find the dark web path to other women she believed were connected to the underground sex trafficking trade. Maybe even to the same one that had held her and her captivity "sisters."

US Marshal Jonas Petry liked to tease Lacy about *going to the dark side* in his favorite Darth Vader voice when she was cyberstalking. It was reassuring that they could joke lightly about something that had caused so much pain for a short period of her life. It was only because she was using her pain to find answers and planned to empower kidnapped women.

Lacy had fallen in love with Jonas. Not that she'd acted on it. She would be an idiot to declare her feelings now. The minute she did that, the marshals would deem this situation inappropriate and reassign him. Lacy didn't know what she'd do without Jonas. He had been there through the whole process of acclimatization to her new norm. It had been his job to be there.

Jonas had been nothing but a gentleman. She had no reason to suspect that he felt the same way about her, but she knew he did. She could feel his eyes on her from across the room. She noticed the way he stood just an inch closer than he needed to when they were in a room together. And when they sat at the computer while Lacy explained the new dark web discovery she'd made, she couldn't miss the way his leg rested against hers while Jonas stared at her, his eyes deeply searching hers. It was enough for now to hope he felt the same way about her.

Despite his constant nearness, Lacy's focus was sharp and clear. Not only was Lacy helping find trails to the men who had kept her in captivity, she was developing a program to detox women who had been held against their will, empower them to overcome their fear, and introduce them back into society. That last piece—going back out in public—was still missing because neither Lacy nor the other rescued women had been let back out in the world. They would be in the relocation program until the authorities took their captors down.

"So, here's my idea," Lacy was explaining to Jonas. "If we identify where the missing women are from, and we see a pattern of several who are from the same area, can we conclude that's the hub?"

Word had gotten to them that Anthony Gerritt had agreed to inform on a much larger organization before someone had killed him. Lacy knew it meant the place they had held her and her friends wasn't the only location, nor were they the only women to be placed in a golden cage. But she also had a theory that there must be a local hub. A place from where all activity originated.

Jonas was shaking his head. "Sex traffickers transport women all over the world. It would be hard to track."

"Hey!" US Marshal Mike Bacon interrupted. He was watching TV with his feet up on the coffee table in front of him. "Can we not say *sex-trafficking* around the ladies?"

Jonas blushed.

Lacy's eyes fell on the women who had been held with her. They sat on the floor, legs crisscrossed as they played cards. Of the three of them, Lauren seemed to be struggling the most with the relocation. They had confirmed that Lauren's daughter was alive and well and living with her grandmother. Instead of calming Lauren, this news seemed to hurt her. Lacy wondered what it would be like to know she was free but not able to see her child.

"Also, are you sure she should be investigating? Is this healthy? I feel like Sikes would have our heads." Mike crossed his arms and glared at them.

"Actually, what I'm doing is most likely illegal, and if Jonas clicked around in the dark web, your boss might have his badge. I need to be the one to do this. To help find who did this to us and prevent this from happening to anyone else," Lacy's voice was strong and held a stubborn edge.

Mike grumbled his reluctant acceptance and looked back at the TV.

"It's a gray area," Jonas further defended Lacy's activity.

"You see, someday I plan to help more than just these three." Lacy tilted her head toward the women she'd been instrumental in helping rescue. Without Lacy's escape, no one would have known where they were.

All eyes fell on Isa, Lauren, and Emma. They huddled closely together on the ground, cards forgotten, talking quietly amongst themselves. Lost in their own world. A world few would understand. *Final Girls,* Lacy called them. They were still so afraid. Lacy knew this because she still had her moments as well. But fear was a bondage worse than any physical captivity. It was an emotion that trapped them in their own minds.

Lacy sighed. Someday, they would get back into society. But for now, she knew the women had been together in the earth prison so long that this behavior was their norm. They could never go back to who they had been before, but Lacy knew they could thrive in new lives, which had to be better than this.

That had to be true... right? Otherwise, what else was she fighting for?

4

MAK

"Tell me again why we're driving six hours away for a playdate?" John grumbled to Mak. They'd already been driving for three.

"We're taking a little vacation from the *real world*," Mak answered. Her conscious pricked her. She was lying. Well, she wasn't telling the whole truth and John knew it. He always knew when she was hiding something from him.

"The *real world* being your physical therapy?" John asked rhetorically. "You know you can't really be gone that long."

"I know. It's just a few days. It's not a big deal." Mak tried to wave off his concerns.

"Makayla, tell me the truth." John glanced at her, then back to the road. John was the only person, other than her dad, who Mak trusted to drive her anywhere. Not to mention, she wasn't really released to drive this far yet.

"Fine," Mak lowered her voice and looked in the back seat. Lately, her daughter had a very bad habit of repeating things she wasn't supposed to when the wrong people were around to hear it. Luckily, Harper had dropped off to sleep. "I have an assignment."

"From work?" John's voice went a few octaves lower. "You're on leave. No way did Sikes—"

"Shh! You'll wake Harper. It's not a case. Sikes asked me to check on Wilton," Mak admitted. Embarrassment flooded through her. Was she really that desperate for a break from her boring routine of going from home to physical therapy that she'd decided to do this?

"Hmm," John said.

"I don't have to justify myself to you," Mak whispered guiltily, knowing if John and Harper were coming with her, she had no right to keep it from him.

"Okay," John responded.

"I know it's not *okay*. I didn't even want to do it!" Mak continued.

"I see." John nodded.

"Are you messing with me right now?" Mak peered hard at John's face.

John's eyes flicked to her, and he smirked a little. "I don't have to. It seems your guilt is getting the best of you."

"It's not like I'm spying!" Mak argued. Ever since her injury, she noticed she was a little more on edge. Quicker to snap. If John noticed, he didn't say anything. "Sikes is worried about him. He hasn't been answering his calls or texts."

"So, not spying. What would you call it?" John finally engaged.

"Getting out of the house for a little family vacay," Mak defended.

"Our family plus Wilton's family?" John asked.

"Fine," Mak said. "If you must know, I turned Sikes down. I told him no. Then I got curious."

"Curious?" John raised an eyebrow.

"Yeah, I mean… What if Wilton really isn't okay?" Mak wondered.

"You couldn't just call or text him and ask?" John inquired.

"I tried. I couldn't really tell. Then he invited me to come for this weekend while he had Anna. It seemed like a good chance to check on him in person. I was a little worried." *And bored,* Mak kept that thought to herself.

"Well, then. We'll go check on your partner. Now that I know the purpose of our visit, I'm all on board. Honestly, Makayla, you need to trust me with your intentions. Wilton isn't just your partner, he's your friend. Nothing wrong with making sure he's okay." John reached over and grabbed her hand. He pulled it up to his mouth and kissed it. "It's okay to care about other people. You planning to report your opinion back to Sikes?"

Mak shrugged. "I don't know. I really don't feel comfortable with that. I mean, they are really watching him closely right now. I don't want to accidentally say the wrong thing. It's just not my place."

John nodded. "Makes sense."

"Are we there?" Harper's little sweet, sleepy voice sounded from the backseat.

Mak laughed. "Only about three more hours, Harpy."

Harper groaned. "That's so long!"

"Hang in there. It'll be worth it when you meet a new friend," Mak promised.

Mak just hoped her own friend was okay. Because if Mak had to admit the truth, she'd say at some point during the last case, Wilton had crossed the line from partner to friend.

5

WILTON

Stephen sat comfortably in his parents' kitchen watching Harper and Anna through the window as they took turns bouncing each other on the large outdoor trampoline his parents had just bought. Stephen had teased his parents that they'd bought the thing to entice Anna to come visit more often.

One hundred percent correct, Linda had agreed and smiled shamelessly at Stephen.

Now, as Stephen sat watching his five-year-old, Anna, and Mak's three-and-a-half-year-old, Harper, he knew this big investment had been worth it.

"Best friends in the making," Stephen grinned at Mak and John who were also watching the girls play.

"You know it," John said, smiling back.

"Of course, everyone is Harper's friend," Mak mused.

"True," John agreed.

"How's PT going?" Stephen asked. He'd noticed how gingerly Mak was moving. "I think I could probably keep up with you now."

"Low blow, Wilton!" Mak gasped. "Kicking a fellow marshal while she's down?"

Stephen chuckled. He'd taken up running and speed walking just to keep up with his partner after their first case. "No, but seriously. What's your status?"

"Well, PT is definitely not fun, and I'm ready to be done. Not to mention, I didn't hit my goal—"

"Which was completely unattainable to begin with," John cut in.

"Still, I had planned to be back to work by now," Mak complained. "And I'm not."

"Patience," Stephen said, momentarily distracted by what looked like a challenge happening on the trampoline. Anna stood over Harper with her hands on her hips. It only lasted a minute before they switched positions and Harper mimicked Anna's stance. He shouldn't have worried. His parents were outside on the back porch watching the girls.

"I suppose I could say the same thing about you, you know," Mak said.

"What?" Stephen focused back on her and John.

"Patience," Mak said. "Bet this leave is killing you."

"You have no idea." A storm of anger crossed Stephen's face. "What am I supposed to do? Take up knitting?"

"Indeed," John said. "Mak is the same way when she's on leave. She's only tolerable this time around because it takes her hours to walk across the house, which makes her days that much busier."

"Hey!" Mak protested.

Stephen laughed with John.

The front door burst open and closed quickly. Stephen noticed Mak's eyebrows rise in surprise. Before he could explain, Beth burst into the room, clearly a ball of nervous, excited energy.

"Hi, hon. Sorry I'm so late!" Beth rushed to Stephen, put

her arms around him, and gave him a quick kiss. "Work meeting ran late. I've only got forty-five minutes before I need to head back."

"No problem," Stephen said kindly. He settled an arm around Beth's waist and turned to Mak and John.

"Beth, this is my partner, Mak, and her husband, John," Stephen introduced. "Guys, this is my girlfriend, Beth Donovan."

Mak's mouth dropped open. John comically put his hand under Mak's chin and gently tipped it up to close her mouth before he reached out to shake Beth's hand.

Mak recovered quickly and reached out to do the same. "Sorry, Stephen didn't mention he was seeing anyone."

"Yeah…" Beth's voice trailed off as if she didn't really process what Mak had said. Her eyes strayed to the girls on the trampoline. "Which one is Anna?"

"The one who looks like me," Stephen teased her, tickling her side. There was no missing Anna's blond, unruly curls.

"Right," Beth was clearly flustered. She turned to John and Mak. "I've never met Anna. I'm so nervous. What if she doesn't like me?"

"What? She's gonna love you!" Stephen encouraged.

"Should we go out there?" Beth asked.

"Nah, let's wait until they come in for lunch," Stephen answered.

"So, Beth, what do you do?" Mak asked.

Beth tore her eyes away from the children. "I'm an accountant. Super boring, I'm a numbers nerd."

Mak smiled and nodded.

Stephen knew Mak would never say so, but he was sure she agreed with Beth. "Mak isn't much of a details person," Stephen explained.

Before Beth could answer, the back door flew open, and two bundles of energy came barreling through the door.

"I'm hungry!" Anna announced, her cheeks pink and her blue eyes wide with excitement. Her blond hair was wild and curly with a few frizzy strands from the static electricity the trampoline had generated.

"Me too!" Harper agreed loudly. She could not look more different from Anna with her straight auburn hair and green eyes. Harper's clothes matched where Anna's did not. But despite their year age difference, they were about the same height and seemed to get along well.

Linda and Bruce, Stephen's parents, came in next. After a round of introductions, Linda pulled out finger sandwiches, chips, and cheese and crackers. Stephen spied a cookie platter just out of reach of the girls. Stephen kept the introduction between Anna and Beth short and simple. Beth looked relieved when it was over.

"Wow, mom. This is quite a spread." Stephen layered a piece of cheese on a cracker and popped it in his mouth.

"It's nothing. Not every day I get to hang out with all the important people in my son's life," Linda smiled with contentment.

They grabbed plates and looked up. The girls sat at the table. The adults moved to the open living room, where they continued talking. Stephen watched as the girls crammed food in their mouths. When the girls were done, they stood up, looking reenergized.

"Can we go back out on the trampoline?" Anna asked.

"You need to wait until someone can be with you," Stephen stated.

"Ohhhh," Anna whined in a sing-song voice.

"Here, I'm all done," Linda stated, picking up her plate and taking it to the dishwasher.

"Me too," Bruce agreed, giving his wife a look of adoration before getting up to follow her.

"Are you sure?" Stephen asked. "Anna can wait."

"No, no, it's fine," Linda dismissed his concern.

The grandparents and two kids shuffled back out of the room.

"I need to get back to work," Beth said, jumping up from the couch. She put her plate in the kitchen, then came back, leaned over to where Stephen was sitting, and kissed him a little longer than might have been comfortable in the company of others. Then she straightened, seeming to remember herself. She turned to Mak and John. "It was nice to meet you."

"You too," Mak gave a small wave.

Beth disappeared out the door.

"Well, that's new," Mak said, watching through the window as Beth jumped in a bright red compact Mini Cooper. Stephen knew Mak wanted to say more.

"Beth is Lacy Donovan's sister," Stephen reminded Mak. "I told you about her when we were on the last case. I went to high school with her. Remember?"

Mak's eyes got wide. "*That* Beth?" Mak's eyes flitted to John, then back to Stephen. "Does Beth know about *you know who?*"

Stephen knew she was talking in code to protect Lacy's identity. Lacy Donovan had been kidnapped during their last case. Because Lacy could identify her kidnappers, who they had discovered were involved in trafficking, the US Marshals had placed her in protective custody until the criminals were behind bars. No one, not even her sister, Beth, could know Lacy was still alive.

"Of course not," Stephen answered quickly.

"How can you keep something so big from someone you're seeing?" Mak challenged.

"Just like this," Stephen quipped. "By not telling her."

"This doesn't sound like a good idea, Stephen," Mak

chided. "Remember when you admitted you sometimes mixed personal with business?"

Stephen frowned. "Yes."

"Well, have you thought this through?" Mak asked.

"Makayla, Stephen is a grown man. I'm sure he's capable of deciding who he would like to date," John interjected.

"Thanks, John," Stephen lifted his water bottle as if to toast John.

"What about Alyah?" Mak lowered her voice.

"What about her?" Stephen answered, his voice taking on a hard edge. He felt his heart rate triple and pain seep into his chest at the mention of her name. He didn't admit how much her leaving had hurt him. Not even to himself.

"Are you giving up?" Mak pushed.

"Alyah told me to move on. I can respect that she did it in person. I can't fix her fear, and I don't plan to get a new career anytime soon. I don't see much reason to wait around anymore. That's a closed door."

Before Mak could respond, there was a knock at the front door.

"Expecting someone else?" John asked.

"No," Stephen got up with a frown that quickly turned to a smile when he opened the front door. "Hey!"

"Hi, Stephen," Captain Roger Higgins greeted.

"Come on in. Meet my friends," Stephen opened the door wider.

Higgins took a step in, looking uncomfortable.

"This is Mak Cunningham, my partner and fellow US Marshal, and this is John, her husband," Stephen introduced them. "Roger Higgins here was my lieutenant when I was a detective in Little Rock. He's a captain now."

"Nice to meet you." Mak stood carefully.

John stood beside her.

They all shook hands.

"What brings you here?" Stephen asked.

Higgins didn't smile. "I'm not exactly here for a social call, Stephen. Maybe we can talk outside."

"We're among friends," Stephen protested. "Go ahead."

Higgins hesitated for a long moment as if considering then spoke. "Trevan Collins... you remember him?"

"Of course," Stephen nodded. He turned to Mak. "He's the guy who gave me the envelope with the picture of my brother."

Recognition lit in Mak's eyes. She nodded and turned to John. "Tell you later."

Stephen supposed it would be awkward to explain that his brother, Greg, was murdered, and up until Trevan Collins handed him an envelope with a picture of the real murderer's face, Stephen thought the murderer had already served his time.

"Trevan Collins is dead. Murdered," Higgins announced.

The silence in the room was thick. For a minute, no one spoke. No one moved, either.

"Ah hell, this is awkward, Stephen. I need you to come down to the station and answer some questions," Higgins said, his hand resting on his gun belt.

Stephen stared at him, understanding coming slowly. "Because you think I had something to do with this?"

"We got your fingerprints on Trevan's doorknob, and we found that envelope you showed me in Trevan's duplex. It also has your fingerprints on it," Higgins stated.

"Where in his duplex?" Stephen asked, trying to process the last place he'd looked at that fateful envelope. He always kept it under his passenger seat. He would have sworn it was there now.

"It was on Trevan's living room floor," Higgins answered. "Don't make me cuff you, Wilton. Will you come peacefully and have a conversation?"

Stephen nodded slowly and turned to Mak and John.

Mak's eyes were large, and John was looking at Stephen with concern.

"I'll get this cleared up," Stephen said dismissively. "In the meantime, can you do me a favor?"

Mak nodded wordlessly.

"When Anna was kidnapped, it was from here. My parents' house. Will you please stay here with the kids until I get back?"

Mak nodded again.

John stood stoic at her side.

"Let's get this over with," Stephen said as he walked out the door with Higgins.

He already had one murder hanging over his head. He really didn't need a second investigation happening at the same time. A thought occurred to Stephen. *Maybe, just maybe, it's time for me to call a lawyer.*

6

MAK

Mak paced around the living room and into the kitchen where she could see her daughter and paused to watch out the window. There was something calming about two young girls playing carefree and living in the moment. As if there was nothing wrong in the world. Mak would work hard to make sure Harper stayed that way for as long as possible.

How had everything turned so upside down? Mak was sure Wilton hadn't killed Anthony Gerritt. He had been at her house for crying out loud. She was his alibi. Now, given this turn of events, doubt crept in. What if she was wrong?

She was so deep in thought, the sudden hands on her shoulders made Mak jump.

"Let's have it," John said, his voice low and close to her ear.

Despite the ominous direction of her thoughts, Mak shivered over his nearness. She sighed. John knew her so well. "What if—"

John squeezed her shoulders as if to encourage her to say what she was thinking.

Mak dropped her voice to a whisper. "What if he had something to do with this?"

"Talk it through," John said. "What evidence do you have?"

"He's on leave for questionable behavior," Mak dared not say more. This was the part of her job that was so hard. So much of what she did was classified. Her brain made a connection. This wasn't unlike the way Wilton had to withhold information from Beth.

"You know I can hear you talking when I leave the room, Makayla. I know more than you think I do," John admitted.

"I hate the part of my job where I have to keep secrets from you," Mak admitted, still facing the window where she could see the girls. It looked like they were now playing some variation of Simon Says.

"Trust me, I don't want to know any more than I have to about your job," John said. "But who you partner up with is vital to your safety. Do you trust him?"

"Yes," Mak answered without hesitation.

"Okay, then I do too. Any chance he snapped under the pressure of everything while you were in the hospital?" John asked.

"Wilton doesn't lose control," Mak said immediately.

"But he has before," John challenged.

"He admitted it though," Mak answered. "Who does that? The guy's practically a Boy Scout."

"No one's perfect." John turned her around to look her in the eye. "What does your gut tell you?"

"He didn't do it." Mak didn't even hesitate.

"Didn't do the thing he's being accused of at work? Or this murder?" John clarified.

"Any of it," Mak said.

"Okay, then what are you going to do about it?" John asked. He knew her so well.

Mak was quiet for a minute. She knew the answer, but she'd decided she was going to slow down and think through outcomes before she came to a conclusion. On one hand, she could mind her own business, go back home, and continue physical therapy far away from her partner, a person who was in the spotlight for some questionable behavior. She wasn't a detective. In her experience, local law enforcement didn't look too kindly on amateur sleuths playing detectives.

If she found herself on the wrong side of the law, it would put Mak in danger. Which might put her family in danger. She was in no position to defend herself right now. Not to mention, if she stayed here too long, she would need to look into getting another physical therapist.

On the other hand, Wilton had become her friend. Friends helped friends out. *What if I found myself in this situation?* she considered. She would want someone to help her. Besides, Mak reasoned, she might be able to get into places undetected, whereas Wilton might be under watch. That is, if he got lucky and didn't end up in jail.

"I'm gonna help clear him of it." Mak nodded her head decisively.

John pulled her into his arms and hugged her. "That's my girl."

Mak pulled back and looked at John, feeling puzzled. "What? You support this?"

"I support you. Always. But one of the things I love most about you is your willingness to help others. Second only to your sense of fairness."

"Trust but verify," Mak mumbled automatically, thinking of the motto she adopted in college.

John nodded. "Besides, Wilton would do it for you."

"Let's hope he never has to," Mak said. The smell of smoke filled her nostrils and suddenly, her heart beat quicker in her chest. "Do you smell that?"

John sniffed and looked around.

Mak sat down hard at the kitchen table. Her mind transported to a time when the smell of acrid fire had filled the air. It was right after the deafening boom that occurred when she'd stepped foot onto the property where they suspected Anthony Garrett was holding three women as hostages.

That night, Stephen had put his hand on Mak's shoulder to halt her movement.

Wait, Stephen had said, his voice holding a tone of urgency.

There's no time to wait, Mak had replied, shaking off his hand. *Let's go.* She'd taken three quick steps onto the property when everything had ignited. A sound like the boom from a cannon echoed through the forest. Then the bright flash of light momentarily blinded her. She could feel heat lick up her body, flames so close she wondered if she was on fire.

Then she was flying through the air, stopping abruptly when her body slammed into a tree with a sickening smack—a noise she sometimes still heard in her sleep. She didn't register the pain until after she hit the ground. The searing agony in her back, the instant headache in her skull, and the quick shallow breaths she took over and over that made her chest hurt.

She'd passed out. But in her state of unconsciousness, she still heard the way Wilton took care of her. She heard it as if it was a voice at the end of a tunnel. The 911 call had been on speaker, so she heard the sound of panic in Wilton's voice as he followed the dispatcher's instructions to stop the bleeding under her head. Later, there was a moment in the ambulance when she was sure she could hear Wilton's voice yelling at her to *Wake the hell up* and *Don't just lay there and do nothing* because Mak was a fighter.

Mak had listened to those words. Clung to them as she was airlifted to a different hospital. She repeated them like a mantra as she went straight into back surgery. She did fight. Wilton had done all of that for her. He had helped her then. And she would help him now.

"Mak!"

Mak felt her shoulder shake. Startled, she found John in front of her, peering closely into her eyes with concern in his.

"Hey, you in there?" John asked as she focused on him and registered his voice. John wrapped Mak in a hug. "Where did you go?"

Mak shook her head. For a moment, she really thought she had been walking into the fire again. She sniffed the air. The thick, humid air lingered overhead. "Did something burn?"

John pointed to the stovetop. "Linda left some sandwiches in the oven."

Mak took in the charred pieces of bread and her stomach rolled. She barely made it to the restroom in time to throw up in the toilet. She rinsed her mouth and noted with a sinking feeling that PTSD was not an easy problem to fix.

7

———————

WILTON

Stephen sat uncomfortably at the cold steel table in the empty room with a two-way mirror and no windows. Not that he was uncomfortable in interrogation rooms, but he typically found himself on the other side of the table. The seat where Higgins now sat, grilling him for yet another murder he did not commit.

"Let's go over it again," Captain Higgins commanded.

"We've been over this three times, Higgins. My answers aren't changing. I don't know how that envelope ended up on Trevan's floor. As far as I know, the envelope I have is still shoved under my passenger side seat. If it's gone, I have no idea how or when it disappeared. How do you know the envelope you found isn't a fake—a duplicate of mine?"

"Your fingerprints are on it." Higgins crossed his feet at the ankles and leaned back in his chair. He stared at the wall behind Stephen's head. "We need to talk about the finger-prints on Trevan's doorknob."

"Yeah, that's a mystery to me, too. It's been four months since I went over to confront him. Unless..." Stephen paused, thinking aloud. "Did Trevan park in a garage?"

Higgins opened his file and thumbed through crime scene photos and the report. "It does say a black sedan was parked in a garage. Why would that matter?"

"Well, if Trevan didn't use the front door and didn't have much company, my fingerprint could still be there—on a metal surface—it would remain there until Trevan cleaned the doorknob or another person smudged it or put their prints over mine. If the killer wore gloves, well, that would explain why the fingerprint is still there."

"It feels like a stretch, but at least you have a possible explanation. That just leaves the envelope." Higgins appeared to be contemplating. "You'll give me permission to search your car?"

Stephen thought about it for a minute. He had nothing to hide. Often, total compliance with an investigation made the person look more innocent. Resistance made a person look guilty. Stephen didn't want to resist. He was generally a compliant person, especially when it came to the law. Stephen knew why Higgins wanted to look. If someone had stolen the envelope from Stephen's car, there was a chance there would be fingerprints on the door handle of Stephen's vehicle or somewhere else inside.

He sympathized with Higgins' position right now. But to say Stephen didn't know what he would do if he had to interrogate someone close to him would be untrue. He did know. At least, he knew what it was like to arrest someone who was close to him. It wasn't easy.

But Stephen had to consider what would happen if they could prove beyond reasonable doubt that the envelope they found on Trevan's floor turned out to be his envelope. Unless they found other fingerprints in his car, there would be no way to prove he was being framed, which was what his gut was telling him. His prints were on the envelope, and there was a good chance it was indeed his. He considered his other charge looming back in Kansas City. If Stephen said the wrong thing here, he could end up in jail—or worse. With that, Stephen made his decision.

Stephen folded his hands over his chest. "I would like to call my lawyer."

Higgins raised his eyebrows and let out a surprised exhale. Stephen had experienced the same disappointment more times than he could count hearing those words as a law enforcement agent. The minute someone asked for a lawyer, any further conversation was inadmissible in court. This was often a huge source of frustration for officers.

For a minute, Higgins regarded Stephen with the kind of disappointment only a mentor could show. Stephen knew he was letting Higgins down. More importantly, Stephen knew he was finally doing what was right for himself.

"You know we can get a warrant to search your car, Wilton," Higgins tried.

"I would like to make my phone call," Stephen re-stated firmly.

Higgins pursed his lips, got up, and escorted Stephen to a phone.

8
____

WILTON

Sandra Stockman sat across from Stephen regarding him coldly. She was polished and professional in her expensive-looking white suit jacket and matching pencil skirt. She wore a silky red blouse and tall black high heels with a red sole to match. Her coal black hair was pulled back into a low ponytail and her earrings were simple gold hoops.

It was no secret that Stephen wasn't Sandra's favorite person. After all, it was Stephen who had arrested Paige for murder years ago and Sandra Stockman who had to defend Paige and clear her of the charge. But Sandra was the best criminal attorney in the area.

Sandra's agreement to meet with Stephen had been reluctant because her loyalty was to Paige. Stephen knew that even after he assured Sandra that this case had no conflict of interest with Paige, that Sandra had done her due diligence and double checked. This most likely alerted Paige that Stephen was in trouble. A fact that Stephen would rather Anna's mother not know, but he didn't see any way around it right now.

The tap of Sandra's long, burgundy polished nails

against the cold table echoed and sounded like a tap-dancer. She had requested a private room with no two-way mirror and double-checked that all recording devices were turned off.

In front of her was a file with paperwork detailing the potential charges against Stephen. She scanned and rescanned, hesitating here and there, and flipped papers back and forth. Finally, she looked up.

"Stephen, did you kill Trevan Collins?" Sandra gave him a look that dared him to lie to her.

"No," Stephen looked right back at her with the confidence of an innocent man.

"Your fingerprints are on the doorknob at Trevan's duplex and on an envelope that was lying beside him on the floor by his deceased body. Why is that?" Sandra asked.

"Let me start at the beginning," Stephen thought back. "About five months ago, Trevan Collins approached me at a funeral. He handed me an envelope. I was reluctant to take it."

"Why?" Sandra asked.

"It seemed like he was trying to serve me at a funeral, which I thought was tacky and unprofessional." Stephen shook his head at the memory.

"Clearly, you took it," Sandra surmised. "What was in the envelope?"

"A photo of my brother's murderer. My brother, Greg, was killed when I was in high school. A teenager named Davey Stinnert, who was Greg's best friend, confessed to the murder. He served his time and got out early for good behavior. The picture shows a man who was not Davey with a gun to my brother's forehead minutes before he was killed. There's a timestamp on the picture. Which means it's evidence of who really killed Greg." Stephen took a drink of the water bottle Sandra had given him.

"Did you question why Trevan had this information?" Sandra's tone was clipped.

"Not at the time. He walked away too quickly, and I sort of threw the envelope in the back seat and forgot about it. After I opened it, I showed up at his duplex to question him. I did not get answers. I'm surprised my fingerprints are still on the door, but it is possible if Trevan didn't use the front door and didn't have company," Stephen explained.

"Not to mention, most visitors would wait for Trevan to open the door as opposed to grabbing the doorknob to let themselves in," Sandra mused, staring off for a moment, seeming to ponder. "Does Trevan have a porch or an over-hang that protects that door from weather elements?"

Stephen thought back to that day again, replaying it in his mind. Then he nodded. "Yes."

"I see. And when did this happen?" Sandra poised her pencil to write on a notepad.

Stephen remembered the timeframe well. "Little over four months ago."

"And why didn't you get any answers?" she wondered.

"Trevan ran out the back door the minute I showed up. I ran after him. He jumped his back fence. I followed him. Then, he jumped *me*, and we fought. He told me never to come there again. He acted scared, like I was exposing him by showing up there. It seemed like he was being watched."

"Interesting," Sandra stated. "Did you tell a police officer this information?"

"Captain Higgins, who was interviewing me before I called you, does know that Trevan and I fought. I mentioned it in passing the day after it happened. I didn't go into much detail though..."

"I think I can work with this, Stephen," Sandra said crisply. "Let me see if I can get you out of here." She paused and smirked. "Don't go anywhere."

Stephen was surprised by Sandra's joke. He wasn't aware she possessed the ability to laugh.

Sandra returned quickly. "You are not being charged with anything at this time. You are free. For now," she prefaced with a look of warning on her face.

Stephen stared at Sandra blinking. "How did you do that so fast?"

"I simply reminded Captain Roger Higgins that you told him about your altercation with Trevan Collins when it happened months ago. He had prior knowledge that you were at Collins' residence along with the reason why you were there. Further, I told the captain that if we go to trial, I would likely put him on the stand as the key witness to explain why your prints are on the door. Between you and me, what we can't explain is how the envelope with your prints got in Trevan's duplex. So, while you are not under arrest, you cannot leave the area," Sandra explained.

"About that..." Stephen began. "I might have another issue. Related to a different murder."

Sandra crossed her arms over her chest and raised an eyebrow. She tapped her stiletto on the floor.

"I'm on leave from the US Marshals pending an investigation into the murder of a criminal whom they had just granted immunity. They allowed me to leave the state, but if they call me back for another hearing, I will need to leave Arkansas," Stephen told her.

"Did you kill that criminal?" Sandra asked.

"No."

"Why do they think you did?"

"Because I handled him too roughly when I was arresting him. They're calling it *abuse of power*." Stephen kept it simple.

"So, in both cases, physical altercations have pushed you to the top of the list of suspects."

"Apparently," Stephen agreed.

"You don't strike me as an overly violent man, Stephen." Sandra looked him up and down.

Stephen snorted. "Some would say the nature of a law enforcement job is to be violent."

"Perhaps. Do you think these two incidents are connected?" Sandra asked.

"I don't see how they could be." Now Stephen crossed his arms across his chest, mirroring her stance. What was she getting at?

"Well, I'm not an investigator, Stephen. That's your job. But, if I were you, I would ask myself if someone is framing me for murder. Think about it. Your fingerprints are on the outside of the envelope as well as on the photo inside. Who has access to your car and the ability to take that envelope out? Do you leave your car unlocked?"

"No." Stephen stared at her, denial crowding his brain. There wasn't a connection between Trevan Collins and Anthony Gerritt, right? Before Stephen could dismiss the idea, a snatch of conversation he'd had with Anthony Gerritt came back to him.

You kill me and your only lead on your brother dies with me, Gerritt had said.

Stephen had paused, his fist pulled back, ready to strike again. *What?*

Your brother. I know more about your brother than you do, Gerritt had smiled.

"I suggest you figure out what's going on, Stephen. Before they find more evidence against you," Sandra stated directly. "Next time, it might not be so easy to stay out of jail."

9

____

LACY

On a fifty-acre property, in a basic ranch-style house that likely hadn't been updated since the late 1980s, Lacy Donovan sat *sukhasana* on her bed and waited impatiently. There were two times of day Lacy treasured the most. Times that she would never again take for granted, given the trauma of being held captive underground. When the sun rose over the mountains in the morning, and when the sun set in the evening. During those moments, Lacy found her stillness and sought time to herself.

She had positioned her bed facing her wide picture windows so all she had to do was sit on top of her blue, flowered comforter with her curtains open and watch the beauty of nature unfold in front of her.

Her breath caught in her chest as rays of yellow, orange, and purple cast colors over the sky where it would stay until the inevitable darkness set in. This was what Lacy feared the most when she was held captive—never seeing another sunset. The freedom to view it reminded Lacy she was alive, and she would never take that for granted again. She would never waste another minute taking life's beauty for granted.

She took a deep, cleansing breath in and blew it out audibly. She watched as vivid colors took their time painting the sky. Time was an illusion. Lacy had plenty of it to spare these days. She watched in stillness. She found her breath and made peace with her emotions.

Today, despite her gratitude for the scenery, she felt discontentment. It wasn't a new emotion, but it felt out of place. How could she be in this beautiful place, safe with the people she loved, and still feel discontentment? Lacy waited until the colorful sky was all that was left as the sun sank lower and she closed her eyes. She placed her palms up and open on her knees in a gesture that meant she was ready to work through her emotions and receive meaning.

To Lacy's surprise, a memory surfaced. She felt her mouth turn downward. Her body tensed. She felt afraid.

It's okay, Lacy, you're safe. Let it play out, she encouraged herself. Like she was watching a movie from the safety of a theatre, Lacy let the images come.

Her sister, Beth, and her dad entered the room, like they were nothing more than actors on a screen. Lacy viewed the drama that unfolded. She knew this memory. She was six—or almost six. She remembered she had a birthday coming up. In fact, that was what they were arguing about.

Where do you think you're going, young lady? It was the gruff, masculine voice of their dad. At the time of this memory, her dad's hair was black. He sported a thick mustache. His eyes were blue, the same color as Beth's.

Beth jumped and whirled, her long black hair whipping around with her. Clearly, he had busted her doing something wrong.

I'm going out, Beth had snapped. *There's no crime against that. I'm twenty-one. It's what we do.*

Her dad had closed the gap between them quickly with

fury on his face, causing Beth to take a step back. Fear replaced the defiance in Beth's eyes.

She needs you! he hissed, pointing down the hallway toward Lacy's bedroom. *When are you going to grow up and make better choices?*

No! She needs you and mom. You took that choice from me a long time ago. You don't just get to pick and choose when it's my turn. Beth's fists clenched and unclenched at her sides. Then her voice softened, her face fell, and for a minute, she looked like she might cry. *Besides, we both know I'm no good. Everything I touch turns to shit.*

Don't talk like that! her dad shouted. *Grow up!*

Beth smiled sadly. When she spoke, her voice was robotic. Emotionless. Her tone was icy. *I did. I grew up six years ago. I learned that the people you let into your life will take the most precious thing from you when you least expect it and force you to live a life that is not your own.*

Her dad backhanded Beth, and Beth flew sideways, hitting the ground with a hard thump.

Lacy cried out.

Both her dad and Beth looked up at Lacy, shock etched on their faces, telling Lacy they both were thinking the same thing. Lacy wasn't meant to hear that conversation.

How dare you! Lacy screamed at her dad. *You had no right—*

Lacy's dad bared his teeth in a growl that sounded inhuman. Uttering no intelligible words, he stalked from the room, went down the hallway, and slammed a door.

Lacy ran to Beth, dropped to the floor, and folded her into a hug. They clung to each other as they both cried. Lacy brushed Beth's hair out of her face and could see an angry red mark across her cheek.

As Lacy sat on her bed, she remembered well the feeling of anger and fear in that moment. She'd never seen her dad be violent. But she would never look at him the same way.

That one incident changed her relationship with the man forever. Lacy acknowledged her feelings and let the memory continue.

I have to go, Lacy. Beth had sat up and brushed her tears away.

Don't go, Lacy had cried. *Stay. We'll watch movies. Whatever you want. Even those dumb, girly ones you like.*

Beth laughed, but put a hand to her cheek, wincing in obvious pain.

Wait here, Lacy said as she ran to the refrigerator to get an ice pack.

When she returned, Beth was on her feet, and she was smiling a smile that didn't quite look right. Fake. Lacy stared at her sister. If Lacy didn't know Beth better, she would have believed Beth was just fine, back to normal, like nothing had happened. Only Lacy knew Beth wasn't okay. She wondered how many times Beth had pretended to be okay when she wasn't.

Come on. Lacy grabbed Beth's hand and led her to the sofa.

Beth sat down and cuddled Lacy close as she reached for the remote. Beth had a mischievous look in her eyes.

Wanna watch a real movie?

Yeah, Lacy agreed, but didn't know what she was deciding. As far as Lacy knew, all movies were real. That night, they'd watched *Dirty Dancing.* Lacy didn't understand half of it at that age and still teased Beth to this day about her terrible influence when they were younger.

Lacy sighed, feeling overcome with sadness and sentimental feelings toward her sister as she fully came back to the present. Not all memories were good ones, she knew, but that one was bittersweet.

She would be lying if she said she didn't miss her sister. It would also be dishonest of her to say Beth wasn't a big factor in why Lacy had left home without a forwarding address when she turned nineteen. Beth had become like a second mother to Lacy. A mother who hovered and controlled her, even after Beth had moved into her own duplex. One mom had been enough. But two had been downright overwhelming.

That's when the truth hit Lacy. She gasped. Her eyes flew open. Her stomach heaved. Her head seemed to pulse with the truth of that memory. At six, she had been too young to process what had happened, and her brain might have blocked it out. She'd always wondered why Beth was so much older than she was.

Lacy also knew the universe revealed truths when she was ready to receive them. But the sudden, overwhelming emotions made her feel dizzy and sick to her stomach. Because Lacy understood with stunning clarity. The reason she always felt like she'd had two moms was because she did.

She had a biological, birth mom who had been reluctant and too young to raise her. And she had the woman she knew as her mother, who had taken responsibility for Lacy her entire life, allowing Beth to live a normal teenage life into adulthood. Then there was the man who lived in the home resenting them all for it, taking on a guardianship he didn't want because he wasn't Lacy's father after all.

Lacy had never felt more alone than she did right now.

10

MAK

At the home of Wilton's parents, Mak drummed her fingers on the kitchen table and watched as her partner walked through the door of his childhood house looking extremely stressed. It was well after ten and the sun had long since descended into the night.

From the front door, Wilton could clearly see Mak when he walked into the room. His eyes roamed around the quiet home, then connected on Mak's, a weary expression in his eyes.

"Where is everybody?" Wilton asked. He walked into the room and tossed his keys on the kitchen counter. Mak pictured him doing that as a teenager. It seemed habitual.

"Your parents went to bed an hour ago. John took Harper to an Airbnb we rented. And Paige came and picked up Anna," Mak ran through the list.

Wilton went to the refrigerator, opened it, and peered in. "That leaves you."

Mak tilted a glass beer bottle at him. "Your mom offered me this before she went to bed. There's more in there if you're interested."

Wilton shrugged and rooted around. "I'm more interested in this." He pulled out the platter of leftover sandwiches and placed it on the table.

"There's pizza in there too. Ordered it for dinner," Mak told him.

Wilton's eyes lit up and he went back for it. He grabbed a beer while he was rooting around. "Something tells me I might need this."

Mak shrugged a shoulder.

"Why did you stick around, Mak?" Wilton asked.

"For answers," she replied amiably.

"What does everyone think?" Wilton sat down and took a big bite of the little sandwich.

"That you had to go down to the station," Mak told him.

"They don't know why I had to go to the station?" Wilton took a gulp of the cold beer and made a face. Beer clearly wasn't his alcohol of choice.

"Just John and I do. Your parents assumed it was work related. Paige, though... she's a smart one. She knew something was up. She didn't say a word and she did a great job of telling Anna that daddy had to go to work, but..." Mak tapped the side of her head with a look of admiration.

"It's because I chose to get a lawyer. Her old lawyer, to be specific. Paige isn't her client anymore, but I'm sure Sandra Stockman had to check in with Paige to get her blessing to take me as a client." Wilton polished off the sandwich.

"I see," Mak said, though she really didn't. "Why did you get a lawyer? Did you kill that man?"

"No, I did not kill Trevan Collins," Wilton replied.

"Why do they think you did?" Mak asked.

"They found that exact envelope Trevan gave me with the picture and my prints all over it on the floor next to Trevan's body. And my fingerprints were also on the doorknob of his house."

"Why were your prints there?" Mak took a drink of her beer.

"Remember when I went back to Arkansas for the weekend and came back with a bruised and busted up face? I'd found Trevan, went to his place, and confronted him. I wanted answers. He didn't want to give me any. Instead, we fought. I left with more questions than answers. But that's why my prints are there," Wilton explained.

"That was months ago! Would your prints really last that long?" Mak's voice held no challenge, just curiosity.

"Best I can figure, it's because Trevan parks in a garage. The doorknob is metal. Provided he doesn't get many—or any—visitors, my fingerprints would have remained."

"And if the killer wore gloves—"

"Right," Wilton answered her train of thought.

"Are you in real trouble here, Wilton?" Mak wanted to know.

Wilton paused mid-chew and regarded Mak. His eyes held a defensive edge as he searched Mak's face. Then he dropped his guard. He swallowed as if it took great difficulty. "Well, the correct answer would be, no, not at the moment. My lawyer was able to get me out of there without jail time. But when she asked me not to leave town, I had to admit what was going on with the investigation at work. She made an interesting observation."

"Which was?" Mak leaned forward.

"She thought it was suspicious that I was under two different investigations for murder and asked me if I thought I was being framed," Wilton answered.

"Framed? I fail to see the connection between—"

"Mak," Wilton stopped her from finishing her sentence. "There's a connection."

Mak's eyebrows shot up. "Do tell."

"Well, I never would have put it together either. I almost

missed it myself. But after Anthony Gerritt set my house on fire, the night I... well, you know—"

"Beat him up," Mak supplied.

"Yes. When I was in the process, he told me I needed to stop hitting him because I would want to know what he had to say."

"Which was?"

"He said he had information about my brother. I asked him point blank. *Do you mean you know who killed him?* He said *yes.* But he said he wouldn't tell me until I got him to the station. Authorities picked him up and, as you know, I never talked to Gerritt again." Wilton grabbed a slice of pizza and took a big bite.

"Is it common knowledge that they incarcerated the wrong guy for your brother's murder?" Mak interrogated. "Have they reopened an investigation?"

"No." Wilton shook his head. "I barely just found out myself. My parents don't know, and I would like to keep it that way."

"Who else knew about that envelope?" Mak was thinking aloud.

"Captain Higgins," Wilton thought for a minute. "And Alyah."

"That's it?" Mak watched Wilton's face. *Is Wilton being honest?* Something wasn't adding up.

"Yep," Wilton shoveled in more pizza.

"What about Beth?" Mak asked directly.

"What about her?" Wilton's voice took on a defensive tone.

"You're going to tell me there was no chance for her to find that envelope or at least have knowledge of it the entire time you've been together?"

"Beth has nothing to do with this. She's a victim. Her

sister was taken. Nothing more." Wilton slashed a hand sideways.

Mak thought about the brief, quick moment she met Beth earlier and dismissed her suspicions. Beth didn't seem like the type to entrap someone. "Although…"

"Although what?" Wilton's eyes held that hard look that matched his tone.

"Beth's sister was taken by Gerritt. Gerritt told you he knew who killed your brother. The common denominator here? Beth." Mak brainstormed out loud.

"No," Wilton said strongly. "You leave Beth out of it. She's innocent in all this. She's been through enough. With Lacy's disappearance and now this—"

"This only works if you tell me the whole truth, Wilton," Mak warned.

"What only works, Mak? What is *this*?" Wilton shot back.

"I want to help you get free of all of this, but I need to know everything. No surprises." Mak leveled him with a stare.

Wilton stared back, chewing quietly for half a minute as if contemplating her words. "You've guessed correctly that I will be investigating this, but you aren't. I don't accept your help. You know I can't guarantee *no surprises,* especially when we can't use our badges. I can tell you from experience that Higgins does not appreciate civilians nosing around in investigations."

"You trust him?" Mak asked.

"Higgins? With my life," Wilton replied with conviction.

"But he and Alyah are the only two people who knew about that envelope?" Mak pushed.

Wilton nodded once.

Mak shrugged. "I guess that just leaves the picture in the envelope. Tell me everything."

"The perp was male, Caucasian, prematurely gray, looked

to be in his mid- to late-forties. He was holding a gun to my brother's head. There was a timestamp in the corner. I recognized the box in the corner. It was bodycam technology. The kind we used at the station—"

"That doesn't mean—"

"It's a cop, I know, Higgins said the same thing. Still, the box tells the date, the time, and the make and model of the tech. It was seconds before my brother's time of death. I've run it through facial recognition and there's nothing. No hits whatsoever." Wilton put his hands palms-up on the table to indicate that was all he knew.

"And the background?" Mak probed.

"Blurry. The camera is zoomed up close on Greg and his murderer. It does look like there are a few people standing around but it's too blurred to make them out. You know what happens when you try to blow up something pixelated?" Wilton challenged.

"Yeah, it's gets fuzzier." Mak nodded, puzzling over the information. "I wonder why this is all coming out now?"

"Trevan said how it all ended never sat right with him. That's all I could get him to say." Wilton shoved pizza crust in his mouth and brushed the crumbs from his hands.

"All right," Mak picked at a piece of pizza. "I believe you. I'm in."

Stephen paused a little longer than normal. "Mak, you're injured. Your healing needs to be top priority. I can't put you in a position where you're hurt worse because of me."

Mak waved a hand side to side. "I've already started to search for a new physical therapist here in Little Rock. Not to mention, I noticed an alternative healing clinic a few miles away."

"Like a witch doctor?" Wilton smirked.

"Wilton! I'm surprised at you. You seem like a guy who lives in this century. Noooo, it's a clinic that does acupuncture, biofeedback, and yoga." Mak rolled her hand like she was impatiently saying *et cetera*. She was very interested in biofeedback. Maybe it would fix the way her brain seemed to be skipping around.

"You need to find a physical therapist as well as a woo-woo clinic," Wilton bossed as he got up and started cleaning off the table.

Mak stood too. "Yeah, yeah. If I agree, will you let me help you investigate?"

Wilton looked surprised. "I wasn't aware I had a choice. I would rather have you *in* my car than following behind it. Though, there will be no running after criminals or physical activity of any kind for you."

"Yes, dad," Mak stuck out her tongue.

"Mak." Wilton's eyes were serious.

Mak looked him in the eyes in a short stare-down.

"You'll have to be the brains on this and let me be the muscle," Stephen stated. "I would never forgive myself if anything else happened to you. Especially when it's not official marshal business. This is personal for me."

"Fine," Mak reached out a hand and shook Wilton's. Her left hand stayed behind her back.

"Don't think I don't know you're crossing your fingers behind your back there." Wilton knew better than to grab her arm to prove it, especially in her weakened state.

"Fine." Mak ground her teeth. "Just don't put me in a position where I need to rescue you."

Wilton sighed. "This might be a terrible idea."

Mak smiled with excitement. "You'll thank me some day, Wilton. I'm very good at getting to the truth." Mak tipped an imaginary hat at Wilton. "The truth will set you free."

11

———

WILTON

Stephen had lied to Mak, but he wasn't sure why. As he tossed and turned that night analyzing the day's events, the thing his mind kept coming back to wasn't his trip to the police station. It wasn't the fact that he'd caved and called a lawyer. It wasn't even that someone out there could be framing him. It was the lie. There was another person who knew about that envelope. Someone he wanted to protect.

Beth.

Stephen thought back to the day he and Trevan had gotten into that fight. He'd gone straight over to Beth's house afterward with his face bruised and swelling. He admitted he'd fought with Trevan. Beth had taken care of him. Stephen smiled in the darkness remembering Beth's initial reaction. She had wanted to go over and give Trevan a piece of her mind. Her sister had been kidnapped and Beth had been worried about Stephen.

Beth had rushed to his defense with very little information available. It had endeared her to him. It made him want to protect her now—even if that meant lying so she didn't come under scrutiny.

Stephen had told Beth about the envelope but had never shown it to her. Nor did he tell her where he kept it. And Stephen knew she had nothing to do with Trevan. She was innocent in all of this.

What he couldn't figure out was why he felt the need to hide that truth from Mak. Then it hit him. Mak was like a dog with a bone. He could tell when Mak met Beth that she had reservations. Most likely, Mak just needed to get to know Beth better. Mak would learn that Beth was the most selfless person Stephen knew.

Stephen's phone rang. Surprised by the way it jolted him out of his reflection, he grabbed it. Thinking it was Beth, he answered without looking at the incoming call.

"Hello?" Stephen squinted at the clock. It was late.

"Stephen? It's Paige."

Stephen sighed and laid back down flat on the bed. "Is Anna okay?"

"Yes, she is," Paige answered. Her voice was like velvet, and it took Stephen back to a time when he would have done anything for her. Even when it looked like she had done horrific things.

"Well, then what's up?" Stephen hated how abrupt his voice came out.

"Are you okay, Stephen?" Paige asked.

"Of course. Why do you ask?" Stephen didn't want to fill in the blanks. Things were looking bad for him right now. He didn't feel like admitting that to an ex.

"Sandra Stockman called me to make sure there wasn't a conflict of interest to represent you. Why do you need a lawyer, Stephen?" Paige's voice took on a concerned tone.

"Paige, it's not something I can talk about—"

"Can't or won't?" Paige interrupted.

Stephen stayed silent. He knew this side of her. "Sounds like you've already made up your mind about that."

"Still the same old Stephen, huh?" Paige said softly, bypassing the sting of his tone.

Stephen sat up in bed, irritation flooding into him. "What's that supposed to mean?"

"When things get hard, you shut everyone out like you're carrying the weight of the world on your shoulders, and you have to do it alone. You won't trust anyone with your secrets because you're afraid. It makes you seem dishonest."

"Dishonest!" Stephen's voice rose in indignation.

"Yes. What are you afraid of, Stephen?" Paige pushed.

I'm afraid I won't get my job back. I'm afraid I'll go down for a murder or two that I didn't commit. I'm afraid Beth will suffer because of all of this, and I'll lose her. Stephen's thoughts tumbled around in his brain.

"I'm not afraid," Stephen denied while rubbing the bridge of his nose. "At least, not anymore. I got a good lawyer, and it's all going to work out."

Now Paige was quiet for half a second. "Fine, Stephen. I understand why you don't want to talk to me. But I hope you talk to someone. That partner of yours, for instance. Keeping secrets when you're in trouble in your line of work can get someone killed."

"That's a bit dramatic," Stephen tried to laugh off her words.

"It's true and you know it," Paige insisted. "Do everyone around you a favor and just tell the truth. But it starts with you being honest with yourself. Face your fears, and then go clean up this mess."

"Thanks for the unsolicited advice," Stephen knew his tone was testy. Of course he would tell Mak everything. Eventually. Everything Mak needed to know and not one thing more.

As he hung up the phone, Stephen felt his conscience

poke at him. His mind returned to his lie about Beth. Then, he strengthened his resolve. After all, there was nothing to tell. Beth had been loyal to him. He would do the same for her.

12

MAK

When Mak slipped into the Airbnb that night, John was up waiting for her, watching TV. She gazed at him, lying shirtless on the couch, his chiseled abs standing out in the darkness. His eyes connected with hers and Mak let out a sigh of contentment.

"You're back," John said unnecessarily. His eyes were heavy as if he'd been about to drop off to sleep.

Mak toed off her shoes, walked to the couch, and snuggled herself into her husband. She stared at the TV a few seconds without really seeing it. The flickering lights were hypnotic, and she thought she might be sleepy as well.

"Well, do you believe him? I assume he told you he's innocent." John put an arm around Mak and settled her closer against him.

"Yeah, I think I do," Mak answered after a slight pause.

"You think?" John raised his head in question.

"Yes, I do. I think he was honest with me."

"But…?"

"But I do feel like there's something he's holding back. I

can't put my finger on it. I don't think he killed anyone, and I do think he needs my help," Mak summed up.

"Does he *want* your help?" John asked knowingly.

"Of course." Mak frowned. "Who wouldn't want my help? I'm very useful."

"Indeed." John kissed Mak's neck. "It's just that—"

"What?" the word came out with a knowing singsong tone.

"Are you sure you aren't just looking for a project?" John never shied away from the truth.

"No. Stephen is my partner, not a project. If I were in his situation, he would come to my rescue," Mak explained neatly.

"You do know you still need to get better, right? Isn't it enough to prioritize your healing and take time for yourself? What happens if you get in a situation where your physical limitations hold you back?" John asked.

Mak sucked in a breath. There it was. She sat up abruptly. She hadn't expected John to be the one to throw that in her face.

"Hey." John gently grabbed her wrist. "I want to know that you are looking out for yourself above all else. That if you figure out Wilton is guilty or he's so much as lied to you, you'll bow out. And yes, maybe I am worried about you. You're both on leave. You don't have badges and guns to hide behind—"

"I have my off-duty weapon," Mak corrected him.

"Okay, but what will this look like without support from the office? Are you two going to play junior detectives?" John asked. He looked more awake now as he sat up next to Mak.

"I suppose so. I'm sure Wilton's contact over at the police station will help if we need—"

"The one who arrested him today?" John interrupted. "He didn't look very helpful."

Mak took a deep breath in. "Okay, we don't have a plan yet. We'll figure it out as we go."

"Makayla." John pulled her toward him.

Mak reluctantly moved closer. But she kept her arms crossed tightly over her chest.

"You haven't been released from physical therapy. If you aren't ready for the field, you're setting yourself up to get hurt again. Not just once. Over and over again. I need to know that you have a therapist set up before you go playing cops and robbers with Stephen."

"Relax," Mak assured him. "I found a clinic. I'll call them tomorrow and make sure they take my insurance."

"And are taking new patients," John added.

"Right. It's the alternative healing place. I'm pretty excited about it." Mak nodded convincingly. "They have the therapy I need to get better."

"That does sound promising," John agreed slowly.

"I'm going to do everything I can to get better. But I don't want to live in fear. I can't sit around all day doing nothing because I'm afraid I'll get hurt again." Mak looked John in the eye with intensity. "And I don't want you to be afraid, either."

"I trust you, Makayla. I always have. But if there's one thing I know about you, it's that you get impatient when things take too long—including your own healing. Your body will heal when it heals. You cannot compromise that, skip over it, or push it forward. I would never try to stop you from doing what you want to do with work. But I strongly suggest you prioritize *you*."

"How long can we keep this place?" Mak asked abruptly, looking around the Airbnb with appreciation. "It's pretty nice."

John blinked a few times. "Umm… I think it was available for a few weeks at least."

"Good." Mak nodded her head like she had settled something. "Stay here with me. You can hold me accountable. We can extend our little mini-vacation while I help my partner clear his name."

"All the while—"

"Taking time to heal," Mak finished his sentence. "Now, where's the bedroom?"

"You're tired?" John asked as he led the way.

"Something like that." Mak grinned at him mischievously. She grabbed the waistband of John's sweatpants and pulled him into the bedroom.

13

LACY

Darkness had crept over the house at the foot of the hills surrounded by nothing but land. To say Lacy had been rattled by what her afternoon meditation had revealed would have been an understatement. Her mind kept coming back to the newly discovered truth. It gave Lacy an urgency to break the rules—to find a phone and call Beth. It was forbidden. It would put them all in danger. Still, the desire to talk to Beth was overwhelming.

Tonight, Lacy was sitting alone in the dark living room. Everyone else had gone to bed hours ago. She marveled that in four short months, Lacy had found more solace and safety surrounded by two US Marshals and three other Final Girls than she had her whole life. They were all survivors of a sex trafficking ring.

They had no idea why Isa, Lauren, and Emma had not been sold and had lived in those inhumane conditions as long as they did. But each of them had received a miracle. They felt relief and gratefulness. They chose to look for blessings in the midst of such a nightmare. Lacy had nothing but admiration for these women.

Lacy hadn't been in the earth prison as long as they had been. That was her own personal gratitude. Her mind had wavered after so few days there. She had no idea what would have happened if she'd stayed there as long as they had.

Now, Lacy stared out the window, viewing the outline of the mountains in the distance. But the longer she stared, the more she could only see the outline of her own face. Hers was a pleasant one. She was blond with curious blue eyes. Her nose was small, her face an oval shape. She had high cheekbones. She would have called herself pretty before all this. Taken it for granted, even. Now, she didn't care what anyone thought about the way she looked. She would rather people see kindness when they looked at her.

She glanced back at her laptop, the only light glowing in the corner of the otherwise dark and quiet house. Jonas teased her that she was becoming obsessed. She'd learned just enough to be dangerous in an online cybersecurity course. She'd learned all about the dark web and how to access it.

But now, she could argue that it was all paying off. Taking a snip from these sites didn't work. They were untraceable. The only thing that worked, she'd discovered, was taking pictures via a phone. But she didn't have one, so she needed the one that belonged to Jonas.

Lacy got up and stood outside Jonas' bedroom door. She hesitated. She knew he was sleeping just beyond. Should she attempt to wake him? Gone were the days when one marshal would stay up and take a shift to watch the house. They were all convinced no one would find them here. Not only were there state-of-the-art alarms and outside cameras, the house was miles from civilization. Not to mention the electric fence that surrounded their land.

But this could not wait for morning. Lacy tapped lightly on his door. She heard a mumbled reply and assumed Jonas had given her permission to come in. Lacy nudged the door open and entered the room. Jonas was sleeping soundly, a sheet twisted around his body and his arm slung over his face.

She stood a moment, feeling indecisive. Then she thought of the information she'd just found on her laptop and pushed forward. Her eyes fell on the cell phone on Jonas' nightstand. The thought crossed Lacy's mind that she could take his cell phone, take a picture of the computer screen, then make an untraceable call to Beth. She stretched a hand toward his cell but then pulled it back.

No, Lacy! her mind chastised her. *You'll compromise everyone. You'll get them all killed!* She sighed and turned back to the sleeping man before her.

"Jonas?" Lacy leaned down and whispered into his ear as she gently shook his shoulder.

Suddenly, Lacy felt a strong grip on her shoulders and her body did a semi-flip that landed her on her back in Jonas' bed. Jonas turned his body toward Lacy, slung an arm around her stomach, and threw a leg over her, cuddling her close.

Lacy was breathless. She had never been this close to him before. Her heart raced. She'd be lying if she said she'd never fantasized about this exact moment. But then she reminded herself that Jonas was sleeping and none of this was intentional. Further, this sort of activity would likely get him fired.

Lacy gently pushed his arms away and tried to roll out from under his grip.

"Jonas!" she whisper-yelled. "Wake up!"

"Go back to bed, Lace. It's still dark outside," Jonas mumbled, reaching for her again. He pulled her back in, this time spooning her tightly against him. Lacy felt her cheeks flush, hating how awkward this was going to be when he finally woke up.

"Right actions, wrong moment," Lacy cursed under her breath. At least he hadn't said some other woman's name. She elbowed him in the stomach.

"Oomph," Jonas let out a gasp of breath.

"Wake up!" Lacy growled, still trying to keep her voice low to not wake the whole house.

"Lacy?" Jonas dropped his grip and sat up quickly, leaving Lacy feeling cold. "What the—"

"Sorry, this is awkward, I know. I have something that won't wait until morning. I came in to wake you up and you sort of threw me in bed and cuddle-suffocated me." Lacy wiggled herself to the foot of his bed and stood up. She readjusted her t-shirt over her pajama pants.

"Jeez, Lacy. I'm sorry. I didn't realize what I was doing." Jonas shook his head and then rubbed his face a few times like he was trying to clear away his sleepiness. "What time is it?"

"It's past midnight," Lacy said as she turned toward the door. "Come on. I need to show you something. It can't wait. Grab your phone."

Jonas got up.

Lacy walked out to give him privacy. He would need to pull on a pair of pants. She only knew that because he hadn't been wearing any when he'd pulled her into bed. She gritted her teeth. They were in a difficult situation. Both of them were adults with feelings for each other, struggling with the impropriety of the fact that Lacy was Jonas' full-time job.

Jonas met her in the corner of the room where she had left her laptop. He chuckled a little when he stood beside her. "Super creepy, Lace, sitting here in a dark corner with the only light coming from your laptop screen."

"Yeah, well, it paid off." Lacy angled the screen at Jonas.

Jonas blinked three times at the screen. "Is that..."

"Yes. He's finally reposted another Golden Girl, which means he's been lulled into a false sense of security after four months of not getting caught." Lacy viewed the picture again. There was a thin, blond girl lying unconscious in a cage painted a golden color. She was wearing a tiny golden dress that barely covered her body. Lacy knew her abductors had called her and the other girls "Golden Girls" on the sale site because she'd found their pictures after they were rescued and before their kidnappers had time to take them down.

Lacy closed her eyes for a second as the flashbacks seemed to hit her like vivid flashes. In her head, it was her in the cage, waking up from a spell of unconsciousness where men had done who knew what to her while she had been blacked out. She could hear the men bidding loudly in the other room. They hadn't expected her to wake up early. But that had been what saved her. Lacy now knew something or someone bigger than herself had a hand in all the circumstances that had led to her escape. That's why she believed in God now. How could she not? God had saved Lacy, which, in turn, had saved the three other women.

"Hey, honey—I mean, Lacy—are you okay?" Jonas put a warm hand on her shoulder.

Lacy opened her eyes. "Yeah, sorry. Flashback."

"Maybe this isn't good for you. Maybe you should stop—"

"No! This makes it all worth it. He's live streaming this." Lacy didn't remind Jonas that she too must have been live streamed during her time in the cage.

"What do those numbers and letters up there at the top mean?" Jonas leaned in and Lacy could feel the heat radiating off his body.

"That's the most exciting part." Lacy sat up straighter and pointed to the numbers all mashed together. Date, time—see the hour, minutes, and seconds ticking?"

Jonas nodded.

"See these letters here—AR?" Lacy pointed. "That's what I'm most excited about."

"Why?" Jonas asked. "What do you think they mean?"

"I believe that's the state where this girl is currently located. Take a picture of this."

"Arkansas?" Jonas pulled out his phone. "I need to call Sikes."

"Right, that's why I woke you up. The sooner we can get people on this, the sooner we can get him," Lacy stated. "Provided Mickey Upton is actually there in the same location with this kidnapped woman. There's no real guarantee, you know."

"Oh, he's there. Gerritt was killed. Boyd Allister is in jail. Mickey Upton is the last man standing. I can't imagine why he wouldn't be there. Hey, what are those numbers?" Jonas pointed to the last string of numbers that were ticking up quickly and showed well over a hundred thousand dollars.

"The bid for her," Lacy said softly, emotion in her tone.

Jonas clenched his jaw and turned to look at her. His eyes were searching her face. His mouth was an inch from hers. He was close enough to kiss her, so he pulled back abruptly. "I'm sorry you went through this, Lace."

Lacy felt disappointment flutter in her heart but shook it off. *You can't kiss him!* she chastised herself. She nodded wordlessly.

Jonas dialed Sikes' number. "Go to bed, Lacy. You've earned it. I'll take it from here."

Lacy stood. Jonas broke their unspoken agreement to keep distance and pulled Lacy to him, folding her into his arms. Her face rested on his bare chest and for half a second, Lacy melted into him. Then she heard the gravelly voice of Deputy Director Sikes answer the phone, reminding her she needed to behave and be mindful of where she was.

As she pulled back abruptly, Lacy realized if she wanted

Jonas in her life, she needed to maintain her space for now. Crossing that line could mean a reassignment for Jonas. Lacy would rather have him here with her untouchable than have him removed from her life permanently. Especially when there was so little Lacy could control in her life as it was.

14

MAK

Mak's phone started ringing as she pulled up to the small alternate healing and wellness clinic. For a minute, she just sat in her car, ignoring her ringing phone. She'd driven by this place when she and John first drove into town. The name on the sign said *The Healing Hospital.* Healing was a big claim, and it was what Mak needed. Mak hoped they could deliver on that promise.

The office looked small and homey on the outside. It was painted dark green with a cobblestone entrance. Two sturdy trees stood on either side of the clinic. There was a garden feature in front with a small waterfall flowing into what Mak bet was a Koi fishpond.

Before the phone could go to voicemail, Mak answered.

"Hey, Mak!" Sikes' voice filled the car that had been quiet seconds before.

"Hey, Sikes. How's it going?" Mak answered, her eyes still on the sign. She had an appointment she did not plan to miss.

"Good. Hey, did you make contact with Wilton?" Sikes

asked, cutting right to the point. Mak always appreciated that about Sikes.

She was silent for half a second. "I was serious about what I said, sir. I don't plan to play spy games with my partner."

"Mak, I'm not asking for insider information. There's a reason I want to know the answer to that," Sikes answered.

"I'm listening. But I do have to be in a therapy appointment in about three minutes," Mak responded, her eyes flicking to the clock on her dashboard. She knew she should use the word *therapy* loosely. But Sikes didn't need to know she wasn't exactly going to a traditional physical therapist.

"We have reason to suspect there's another Golden Girl being auctioned off in Arkansas, which leads us to believe—"

"Golden Girl?" Mak interrupted. She racked her brain for why that seemed familiar but couldn't come up with the answer. She sighed to herself. Once again, her mind felt altered.

"We discovered that's the name Lacy and her friends were given when they were in captivity, and it's the name this trafficking ring calls the girls they sell," Sikes explained.

"Oh, okay," Mak wondered how they knew that. Was it a well-known fact in the case?

"This leads us to believe that Mickey Upton, the last criminal still free, might be in Arkansas as well. We need a person in the area to be on lookout." Sikes rattled the words off quickly.

"Arkansas is a big state," Mak said, processing aloud. "Can your mysterious source narrow it down any more than that?"

"She sent us all she has—"

"She?" Mak repeated.

Sikes chuckled. "Lacy Donovan, our kidnapped victim, is quite the girl. She's been learning how to access the black web. She found another girl up for sale in a golden cage, wearing a similar golden dress to the one she and the other women, wore. She's convinced the missing woman's location is somewhere in Arkansas."

"Okay, I think you mean *dark* web and I assume there's an APB out for Upton?" Mak asked. Her head was spinning in surprise that Sikes would allow Lacy, a kidnap survivor, to do illegal searches to find her own captor. Mak knew Wilton would have so many questions right now.

"Of course," Sikes answered.

"Okay, then you should know I *am* in Arkansas and *yes*, I have been in contact with Wilton. I'm still not going to answer any questions about him. I'll try to encourage him to answer your calls. I can, however, touch base with Captain Higgins from the Police Station of Little Rock and let him know about the lead."

"That would be a good start," Sikes agreed.

Then Mak got an idea. "What if—" she tried to think through the logistics of how she could lead on this. "What if we bid on and won the Golden Girl?"

"What?" Sikes barked.

"Yeah." Mak was warming to the idea. "We could partner with the police station, get a team together, and pick her up after winning the bid."

"There's just one problem with that, Mak," Sikes protested.

"Which is?" Mak asked.

"You have to pay for the girl first. I believe you pay in untraceable bitcoin. I don't know if we have the resources to scrape that together—"

"Well, could you look into it on your end? Once we get this guy, we could recoup our losses by freezing his assets, right?" Mak was feeling eager.

"It doesn't work like that, Mak," Sikes warned. "Besides,

if we're caught bidding on a girl, I don't have to tell you how difficult that would be to explain to the authorities why we shouldn't go to jail."

"Well, just throwing out ideas. I'm here to help however I can. But right now, I need to go get some healing." Mak turned off her car, got out, and walked toward the front door.

"Okay, touch base with me after you talk to the captain," Sikes requested.

"Will do," Mak said. She hung up the phone and walked inside. After she checked in, she turned to settle on a large, overstuffed couch in the sage green and white lobby, but she barely had time to sit down before they called her name.

A kind woman wearing scrubs with a name tag that read *Caryl* was waiting for her. She held a clipboard in her hands. "Come on back, Ms. Cunningham—"

"Mak. I go by Mak," Mak corrected her.

"Okay, welcome, Mak. I'm Caryl." She led Mak into a nice sized intake room. "Let's get some quick stats."

As she worked, Caryl put a clipboard in Mak's hands. "You'll have time to fill this out as Dr. Mott is running a smidge behind this morning. But the notes from your phone call said you broke your back recently?"

Mak nodded as a blood pressure cuff squeezed her arm. "I've been in physical therapy for the last four months. It has only helped a tiny bit, but I need to get released to go back to work. I need to be at one hundred percent, not seventy-five."

"I see. Well, you'll find that we believe in healing from the inside out here—"

"What does that mean?" Mak interrupted. It sounded like that would take a lot more time than physical therapy.

The woman smiled. "It means with a broken back, we assume that some trauma happened to your mind as well as your body, and healing begins by working through that trauma. So, we won't just prescribe you physical therapy, you will likely see a counselor who will help you create a habit of meditation, journaling, and talking through that trauma. You can go to specialized yoga sessions, acupuncture, massages, and hot and cold therapy. Dr. Mott will check your back alignment regularly to make sure it's healing correctly. And yes, you will have to do some physical therapy-type exercises. It's a lot of hard work. But you'll be stronger in the end."

"What about biofeedback?" Mak asked. "I read on your website you offer that. I also had some mild brain trauma. Sometimes I worry I'm forgetting things."

"Are you having headaches or migraines?" Caryl's eyebrows drew together in concentration.

Mak shook her head.

"Anxiety?" Caryl persisted.

Mak shrugged. "Well, I had this reaction yesterday where it felt like I was transported to the scene of the accident, and I swore I was reliving it. It was vivid. Afterwards, I got nauseated and threw up."

"I'll write down PTSD on your chart for Doc to look into," Caryl nodded knowingly. "She might have you do EMDR."

"What's that?" Mak asked.

"It stands for eye movement desensitization and reprocessing. It's a therapy used when trauma gets stuck in places it shouldn't, and you can't seem to move forward. Doc can explain it better than me," Caryl stated.

"Would that affect memories I have—or don't have—before and after the event?" Mak wondered.

"It might, but you'll need to ask Doc about that. This is all a part of that healing from the inside out program we'll place you on."

"Then sign me up." Mak smiled winningly. "I need to get better."

"So, you've said," Caryl removed the blood pressure cuff. "Blood pressure is good. What do you do for a living?"

"I'm a US Marshal," Mak said casually.

Caryl's eyes widened. "You are the first woman US Marshal I've ever met. Impressive."

Mak shrugged. "It will be impressive when I get back to work."

Caryl stopped entering information into a computer and leveled Mak with a look. "You are impressive, and whether you are at work or on leave, you are enough. Just sitting there, you are enough. Don't ever forget that."

Unexpected tears sprang to Mak's eyes. Where was this emotion coming from? Was this another side-effect of brain trauma?

"Okay, take your time filling out your forms. Doc will be in soon," Caryl said cheerfully as she left the room.

Either it had been Caryl's goal to evoke uncomfortable emotions from Mak or she hadn't seen Mak's tears. Either way, Caryl was gone, leaving Mak alone with her unexpected emotional state. A thought popped into Mak's brain that wasn't as easy to wipe away as her tears. *Did I ever cry over the explosion or breaking my back?*

No, because crying is weak, the critical side of her brain answered. The loving side of her brain argued, *What if it's not weak? What if it's strength?*

Mak shook her head. She'd been in this clinic for less than an hour and already she was arguing with herself. She hoped her time here proved to be more productive than that.

15

WILTON

Stephen left his parents' house that morning with a quick cup of coffee and *goodbye*. Then he drove to Beth's house, surprised to find her still at home. She typically went to work early in the morning. Since he'd moved back to Arkansas, Stephen had only accumulated a small drawer of clothes, a new watch, and some toiletries.

It still amazed him how little he missed the belongings that had burned up in his house fire. It had been too easy to replenish the few things he'd needed. He was still waiting on a check from the insurance company, which he would use for a down payment on a new house. But he wondered if his new house would be as empty and meaningless as the last one.

He jumped out of his car and used the key Beth had made for him to open the front door. He froze when he heard a shuffling noise coming from the bedroom. Alarmed, he called out. "Beth?"

The shuffling noise stopped.

Stephen entered the bedroom to see all his belongings dumped on the floor. Beth's hand was in the pocket of a pair of his jeans. She stared at him with guilt on her reddening face. Stephen stood in the doorway and stared at her wordlessly.

Beth stared and lifted her chin with defiance. Her hair was up in a messy bun. She still wore pajama pants and a t-shirt. She looked very undone, which was not typical for Beth.

"Stephen, do you have something to tell me?" Beth stood up as tall as her height would allow. She crossed her hands over her chest. Her cheeks were flushed. Over being caught riffling through his belongings or indignation, Stephen did not know.

"Are you going through my things?" Stephen asked without answering her question. He took another step into the room and slowly took off his jacket. He draped it over a chair. His mind was racing. How would Beth have heard about his trip to the police station?

Beth avoided his question. "Do you know where I spent the afternoon yesterday, Stephen?"

Stephen resisted the urge to repeat his question about her invading his privacy because his curiosity got the best of him. "No. Where?"

"The police station," Beth gritted out. "Do you know why I was there?"

Stephen slowly nodded his head. "I was going to tell you about that."

"Well, you didn't. I know Trevan Collins was murdered, but I had to hear it from the police captain. Apparently, I'm your alibi for that night? That seems like an important bit of information to give your girlfriend a heads up on, wouldn't you agree?" Beth seethed.

"Yes. Absolutely." Stephen held up his hands like he was surrendering. "In my defense, I didn't know they would call you in for questioning."

"That's the reason you think you should have told me?" Beth blew a piece of stray bangs out of her eyes. "No other reason than *that* to tell me you were a suspect in Trevan's murder?"

Stephen sighed. "I'm not that good at transparency, Beth. I'm used to having to keep things secret in my job. So much of what I do is confidential. Surely, you can understand how unflattering it would be to confess I'd been pulled in for questioning."

"Unflattering? How about dangerous? You put me in danger!" Beth shouted. Her eyes were wild. "What happened?"

"I can't comment on an ongoing investigation—"

"I already know Trevan was murdered!" Beth interrupted. She started fanning her face. Tears lined her eyes.

"I thought you and Trevan weren't close." Confusion seeped into his brain. Why was Beth so rattled over someone she knew back in high school? He wondered if she felt embarrassed over her trip to the station. Stephen took a few steps closer to comfort her.

Beth took two steps back with a look of terror on her face. "Don't come any closer!" she hissed.

Stephen froze and stepped back. "Beth, what are you—"

"Did you do it?" Beth's voice was barely over a whisper. Then it rose a decibel. "Now is not the time to play innocent. You got into that awful fight with Trevan a few months ago. I remember. Now he's dead, and I want you to look me in the eye and tell me if you did it." Tears streamed down her face. Panic made her eyes wide. Her body was stiff.

"No! I was with you that night—"

"Well, I had to fall asleep sometime! Who's to say you didn't sneak out after that?" Beth's voice was getting louder and her tone was getting angrier.

"I didn't. I didn't sneak back out, and I didn't kill Trevan." Stephen clenched his hands. Now, adrenaline and anger coursed through his veins. "I'm getting a little tired of people accusing me of things I didn't do. Did you vouch for me or not?"

"That's what you're worried about right now? Your fingerprints are on Trevan's door. That picture was found in his living room—"

"They told you all that?" Stephen felt confused. No way would Higgins have given her that much information. He knew his old commanding officer and knew Higgins would only give enough information to get the answers to his questions. Something wasn't adding up. Beth seemed to know answers that she should not know. Not to mention, they had been together for four months. Beth should know him better than that by now.

Beth's eyes flicked to the left so quickly, Stephen almost missed it. They landed back on his. "Yeah."

Stephen felt like he'd been punched in the gut. She was lying to him. "What are you not telling me?"

"What are *you* not telling *me*?" Beth returned hotly.

Stephen felt the air whoosh out of him. It was a fair point. He knew he had way more secrets from her than she held from him.

"I want you to go," Beth said, her voice now quiet with resignation.

"Go?" Stephen asked, unsure what she meant. "Beth, I'm sorry."

"Take your things and go, Stephen. We're done." Beth turned from her place by his drawer and tried to brush past him.

Stephen reached out and put a hand lightly on her arm to detain her. "Beth, wait. I can explain."

Indecision wavered in Beth's eyes for a second, then they hardened. "It's too late. You had your chance to explain. I don't trust you anymore."

"Beth, come on. I'm not very good at relationships and

transparency. I can do better." He felt hopeful when Beth turned back around. But the look in her eyes told him everything he needed to know.

"Take your things and leave your key. We're through." Her eyes held fear for an instant. Then, they hardened and she pointed toward the front door.

Stephen packed everything he owned, noting how it all fit inside one gym duffle bag. His heart was heavy as he looked one more time around the room for anything he left behind. He'd spent four months making great memories with someone he could see a real future with. But now, that was over. Only, he wasn't exactly sure why. He couldn't shake the feeling that there was something more to this.

Beth was nowhere to be found as he took out his key and left it on the credenza by the door. He let himself out. As he started his car and drove back to his parents' house, he wanted to feel furious about whatever lie she had told, whatever piece of information she was keeping to herself. Instead, he felt concerned and confused. He'd had many breakups. But of all of them, this was the one that made the least amount of sense to him. When things were good in a relationship, it was possible to work through the misunderstandings. He couldn't understand why Beth was so quick to throw what they had out. Unless what they had hadn't gone both ways.

16

WILTON

Stephen focused on the road in front of him. He'd only driven to Davey Stinnert's place one other time, but he had memorized the route that day. His mind went back to the day he'd tried to go visit Davey unannounced, but it had seemed the man hadn't been home.

Mak cleared her throat and Stephen glanced over at her with a sheepish look. He'd almost forgotten she was in the car with him. The burns on the side of her face from the last case had almost healed up, but the scar over her eyebrow would be there forever. She was holding the handle above her head, looking mildly uncomfortable. Stephen rolled his eyes. Mak was seriously overreacting to riding passenger in his car.

"How was therapy?" Stephen asked.

"It was great, actually," Mak responded.

"You sound surprised by that." Stephen grinned.

"Yeah, I guess I am. The doctor was nice. They have this interesting philosophy on healing. They believe in whole body healing. Like that podcast I was listening to. Do you remember it?" Mak asked.

"Not the *Mind, Body, and Soul Guy*," Stephen groaned.

"Laugh all you want, Wilton," Mak smiled. "But I think they're on to something. They created a new routine for me and they want me to make it a habit. It's daily yoga and meditation. They'll administer acupuncture, I'll do hot and cold therapy, massage, EMDR, with some biofeedback—"

"Whoa, I don't even know what some of that is," Stephen admitted with a laugh.

"It all adds up to my body healing naturally. Almost in a way that gives me some control," Mak mused.

"It sounds like spa treatments," Stephen admitted.

"Yeah, maybe so." Mak nodded and switched the topic. "Now, explain to me again why we are going to see Davey Stinnert. You said you've gone out here before, and he didn't answer the door. What makes you think he will this time? This is a guy who willingly went to jail for your brother's murder. Falsely. If he still has something to hide, he sure won't want to see you."

"You're right. But I have to try. I don't have any other leads." Stephen slowed his car as the road turned into rough gravel.

"Stephen," Mak hissed. "What if he killed Trevan? Did you even think of that?"

Doubt flickered in Stephen's eyes as he glanced at Mak. He had not. "Doesn't make sense," he stated, snapping into detective mode. "Think about it. The only bit of evidence they found with Trevan's dead body is that picture—the very same one that had been in my car, which Trevan had given to me."

"You are absolutely sure that envelope was the one Trevan gave you?" Mak asked. "There might be other pictures out there."

"I checked when I left the police station, and the envelope under my seat was gone. Not to mention my fingerprints were on it," Stephen stated.

"Did you dust for prints inside your vehicle?" Mak let go of the handle over her head and lifted her hands as if she could be smudging evidence.

"Yes, I did, actually. I didn't lift one. Which means the thief was wearing gloves. Just like I think he was when he killed Trevan."

"What if he took your envelope and went straight to Trevan's place?" Mak cringed at the thought.

"It's possible. I didn't see any forced entry into my car either. No broken locks, but you and I both know how to open a locked car. I bet the thief can too." Stephen drove slow on the gravel drive.

"So, back to Davey," Mak routed the conversation.

"That picture proves that the man who killed my brother was not Davey. Davey just got out of prison. Why kill someone who possessed evidence of his innocence?"

"Hmm…" Mak appeared to be trying to follow Stephen's logic. "Trevan gives you the photographic evidence. When he's found dead, that exact photographic evidence is lying beside Trevan. Like the killer is sending a message."

"Message to who?" Stephen wondered. "And what kind of message?"

"I don't know who. Maybe it's something like, *This is what happens when someone betrays me*," Mak surmised.

"Not sure. When I went to see Trevan for answers, he beat me up and told me I shouldn't have come. He seemed panicky about getting me out of his house. Like he didn't want anyone to see me there. I wonder if he thought he was being watched?"

"Good possibility since whoever killed him had your photo. If the killer was watching Trevan, he would have seen you that day and might have heard you asking about it. Have you thought about that, Wilton? This creeper found out that envelope was in your car. Which brings us full circle to this point. Higgins didn't find a print in your car, either?"

"No, I didn't let him get that far. I asked for a lawyer and told him he needed a warrant to search my car." Stephen clenched his jaw.

"What are you afraid of, Wilton?" Mak's words were direct.

"I keep going down over the absence of evidence—" Stephen began.

"Explain."

"They can't prove who killed Gerritt, so I'm under suspicion. Higgins knows I had the picture and that Trevan is the one who gave it to me. If he searched my car on that day and the photo was gone, it would have implicated me because it would prove that it was the same envelope and not a duplicate copy." Stephen let out a frustrated sigh.

"Just because the photo is missing does not mean you're guilty."

Stephen didn't respond as they pulled up to a dingy white double-wide trailer. A beat-up pick-up truck with rust in multiple spots sat just outside the door.

"He's home." Stephen threw the door open.

Mak opened her door as well.

Stephen put out a hand to detain Mak. "I don't know this guy's state of mind. Can you just be backup for me while I talk to him?"

Mak's jaw dropped and she looked offended. Before she had time to form a response, the loud crack of a shotgun rang out. Where the shot hit, they didn't know. Stephen immediately dropped behind his open car door. Mak dropped back into the passenger seat, keeping her body down in the floorboard.

Another shot rang out, echoing throughout the cavernous

valley, telling them Davey Stinnert was home, but he was not happy to see them.

17

———————

MAK

The sound of a shotgun echoing through the woods still rang in Mak's ears as she frantically dug through her wallet, feeling thankful she hadn't left home without her US Marshal badge. She bravely stuck the badge up over the car door she'd left open when she hid on the floorboard.

"US Marshals. We come in peace. You're gonna want to stop shooting at us, Mr. Stinnert," Mak yelled.

"I know who you are!" Davey yelled back. "I see you, Stephen Wilton. You get off my property or the next bullet will be for you. I missed on purpose."

"I just want to talk!" Wilton yelled back. He was still crouched behind the door, but he had pulled his gun.

Mak caught Wilton's eye and shook her head at him. The gun Wilton held was not department issued. Using it on Davey would be highly illegal in this situation. Mak, on the other hand, still had her badge and weapon. But she knew better than to use it here in an unofficial capacity.

"I got nothing to say to you, you hear me, Wilton?" Davey yelled. Anger was evident in his voice. "I done my duty. Leave me be."

"What do you mean *your duty*?" Wilton shouted back.

"I did what I needed to do to keep my family safe. Now, if you want to keep *your* family safe, you get off my property!" Davey yelled, his voice sounding more panicked now.

Mak held a finger up to Wilton as he started to respond. "Davey, I'm US Marshal Mak Cunningham. We're just here to talk. If I stand up, are you gonna shoot me?"

There was silence on the other end. Mak peeked from her place on the floorboard. Davey was staring in her direction with his shotgun angled down at the ground. His straight, blond hair was messy and on the long side. He was tall, gangly, and thin—perhaps too thin—as his t-shirt and jeans seemed to hang on him. His wild eyes looked dark, brown maybe, but with the way his pupils were dilated, Mak couldn't be sure.

Encouraged, Mak rose up with both hands pointed in the air. Her gun was sitting on the seat where she could see it and reach it if need be. "I put down my gun, please put yours down and we can have a civilized conversation."

"Civilized!" Davey shouted. "Civilized! Do you know what I came home to—after I was released from prison?"

"I don't." Mak shook her head.

"They're dead." A strangled sob caught in Davey's throat. "My mom and my sister. Both dead. After all I did for them. They promised—"

"Who promised what, Davey?" Mak stayed behind the door, using it as a possible shield.

"It's not Davey no more! That name died in prison with my childhood!" Davey wiped tears that now fell down his cheeks. "It's David. I go by David now."

Wilton stood with hands raised and David immediately picked up his gun and pointed it in Wilton's direction.

"Don't worry about him, David. Put your gun down or I'll have no choice but to arrest you," Mak was bluffing. She had no grounds to arrest David. They were on his property uninvited.

David lowered the gun and glowered at Wilton.

"Why don't we ask Wilton to sit in the car while you and I talk? Will that work?" Mak asked sweetly.

"Over my dead bod—" Wilton started.

"Shut up, Wilton, and get in the car!" Mak hissed.

Wilton gave Mak a dirty look but obeyed.

David lowered his gun to the ground.

"Good," Mak said with relief. "Now, we know you didn't kill Greg Wilton."

"What?" David's eyes bulged as he took a step toward Mak. Though she could take him, Mak had learned not to underestimate a desperate man with a gun within arms distance.

Mak held up a hand. "That's close enough. We have photographic evidence that puts a different man at the scene of the crime with a gun to Greg's face minutes before Greg died. Can you tell us who that man is? Who really killed Greg?"

David was silent. Then he began frantically scanning the trees. "You get off my property. Right now! You hear me!" Before he dropped to grab his gun, Mak saw fear in his eyes.

"What are you afraid of, David?" Mak asked.

David turned and took two steps closer to Mak. He pointed a finger. His eyes were hard. "You have no idea what you're getting yourself into."

"Why don't you tell us?" Mak requested. "It sounds like you know everything and we don't. You know who killed Greg and you took the fall for him for some reason. If you have information about that, we can protect you."

"No, no, no! You can't protect anyone from them!" David waved a hand wildly, gesturing toward the forest.

"Protect you from who?" Mak pressed.

"You get out of here. I've done my time. Now let me live my life in peace." David stalked back to the door of his trailer.

"Wait!" Mak commanded. "I'm reaching into my wallet to grab a card. The card has my number on it. If you decide you want to talk, please call me. If you come forward with information that leads to an arrest, we can protect you."

"Get out of here." David picked up the gun, pointed it in their direction, and looked around his property again. "While you still can."

18

———————

WILTON

Stephen reluctantly drove away from David Stinnert's house. He shook his head a little.

"Is that how you imagined that playing out?" Mak tilted her head toward the trailer as it disappeared behind them.

"No." Red crept up the back of Stephen's neck. "I've called him Davey my whole life and now I'm just supposed to know him as David now?"

"That's your takeaway from all that?" Mak said sarcastically, waving her hand in the air.

"Of course not," Stephen sat up taller in the driver's seat. "He definitely knows who killed Greg."

"But he was never going to tell us. He's scared. Present tense. Which tells us the killer is alive. And David acted like that man was hiding out in his woods," Mak commented.

"He could just be very paranoid. He's been to prison, remember?" Stephen objected.

"Juvenile Hall," Mak corrected.

"Well, he might have started in juvie, but they sure transferred him to prison after he aged out... Hey, what was with you promising him protection?" Stephen asked. "Neither of us is in a position to grant that. Not to mention, we aren't on an official case. This is more like a cold case—"

"With a very warm lead," Mak interrupted. "Surely, you realize Trevan's death is connected to your brother's murder, specifically to that picture. That envelope has brought you nothing but trouble... David can tell us who he took the fall for."

"Well, yes, that's all true. What I didn't tell you is I went to see Davey—David—after my altercation with Trevan months ago. Trevan told me David knows the truth. And he does! You saw it." Stephen tapped his brakes like he might turn around.

"Whoa, there. David isn't going to tell us the truth right now. But if he decides to come forward, we and the police can protect him just like any other citizen. You know if he becomes an informant, we can put him in witness relocation," Mak explained her logic. "Besides, he had one hand on a gun. I said what came to mind at the time."

"But pulling him into protection would mean we'd have to get Sikes involved," Stephen pulled out onto the highway, feeling better to be heading back toward civilization.

"Would that really be so bad?" Mak asked.

"Are you kidding me?" Stephen's head whipped around to her. "Sikes thinks I killed Anthony Gerritt."

"You don't know that. He's just following protocol," Mak defended their boss.

"Oh, I know. I saw the way he looked at me. If they can't solve Gerritt's murder, I won't be going back to work," Stephen said. He pulled into a parking spot at a local coffee shop. He turned off the car and faced Mak.

"Did you kill Anthony Gerritt?" Mak looked Stephen straight in the eyes.

Stephen was offended for half a second. His heart sank. He couldn't take his partner questioning him, too.

"Just look me in the eye and answer the question, Wilton. Did you kill Anthony Gerritt?" Mak asked again.

"No," Stephen answered her without blinking.

"There. See, was that so hard? If you didn't kill him, there's not going to be any evidence to suggest that you did. Did you beat the crap out of him because you were sick of him stalking you, messing up your entire life, and burning down your house? Yeah, you did! And for that, I wanna give you a high five!" Mak held up a hand.

Stephen left her hanging.

Mak shrugged, lowered her hand, and looked around. "Hey, why are we here?"

"Donuts and coffee sound really good to me right now. Not to mention, there's a small, soundproof conference room in the back with a closed door. We just lost the only lead we had, and my case is about to stall out unless we come up with a new one." Stephen got out of the car.

"What did you do if you lost your lead when you were a detective?" Mak asked, following Stephen inside.

"We need to go back to the beginning."

Mak followed him inside the coffee shop and stood in line with him. "Is that a reference to *Princess Bride*? *We go back the beginning*. It's a very man-in-black thing to say."

Stephen smirked. "Only if I get to be the man-in-black."

"Wait! What would that make me? Andre the Giant?" Mak protested.

Stephen clicked his tongue. "His name is Fezzick."

Mak opened her mouth to reply but the barista called out "Next!" and they stepped up to order coffee and pastries—a donut for Stephen and a blueberry muffin for Mak.

"Is your conference room open?" Stephen leaned forward to ask.

"Yep! Sure is. Want me to pencil you guys in for an hour?" The barista was a thin blond woman with pink tips in her hair. She grabbed an old-fashioned scheduling book and flung it open.

"Yes, please," Stephen replied with a charming smile.

The barista smiled back and winked. A small blush crept over her cheeks. "Name?"

"Put down Mak," Mak stepped in quickly.

"Oh," the barista looked disappointed and a little surprised. "Okay, gotcha down, Mak."

"Thanks," Mak said and turned to wait for her coffee.

"What was that?" Stephen asked as the barista turned to start their coffee.

"People around here know you. You're under a lot of... pressure right now. Maybe you should be a little more incognito."

"Oh." Stephen shrugged, glancing back at the woman. "Okay."

"Aren't you in a relationship right now, Stephen? Surely, you aren't checking her out," Mak grumbled.

"I'm not checking her out. But, if you must know, Beth and I broke up," Stephen admitted.

"What? When?" Mak demanded, her full attention on Stephen now.

"This morning," Stephen answered.

Mak closed her mouth. She looked like she wanted to say more. When she didn't, Stephen wondered if she was waiting for him to speak. *That's new,* he thought. Still, he didn't exactly want to talk about it.

They took their coffees and pastries and settled into the conference room.

"Okay," Mak said once the door closed. "Take me to the beginning. The day Trevan gave you the envelope."

Stephen shook his head. "Further back. To my brother, Greg. See, after he died, there seemed to be this consensus with everyone that Greg was a bully. Davey—I mean, David, got on the stand and testified that he had finally had it with Greg's bullying, and he'd just snapped. But I always thought David was Greg's best friend. And I swear to you, I never thought of Greg as a bully. I would know! I lived with him. It wasn't just older brother worship, either. I have really good memories of Greg. I also have some of the normal, older brother torment stories. Nothing over the top, though."

"Of course," Mak mumbled with her mouth full of muffin.

"I always thought I must have just not known that side of him. But when I met up with Beth, we talked about it a little. She said she didn't remember Greg that way either. She basically said he'd always been good to her. David Stinnert is the key to all of this. I know it!" Stephen smacked the table.

"Okay. Well, he's not going to talk to us right now. But yes, he must know the real killer well enough that he offered himself up." Mak tapped the table.

"Maybe that means the real killer had something on David?" Stephen speculated.

"What if—" Mak started, paused, then started again. "What if David was afraid he would be next. Maybe Greg knew something that got him killed. David might have known the same thing and chose to put himself behind bars rather than face the killer."

"He thought he'd be safer in prison?" Stephen gave Mak a doubtful smile.

"We're brainstorming here. There are no wrong answers in brainstorming."

"Ugh!" Stephen growled. "I wish I still had that photo. I really need to see it again."

"Why? You put the picture through facial recognition, right?" Mak asked.

Stephen nodded. "But there's more to the photo."

"Oh?"

"The background is blurred. But it almost looks like there's a circle of people standing around—"

"What? There are more witnesses out there?" Mak interrupted.

"Don't get too excited," Stephen warned. "When I say blurry, I mean the kind where if I blew the picture up, it would be one pixelated blob."

"Sure, if *you* did it. But did you ever work with anyone on the force that had special photography skills? What if they could clean up the background and shrink it down so it's not pixelated?" Mak asked.

Stephen stared at Mak for a good second. "Yes, actually, I did work with someone. That's brilliant!"

"Thank you." Mak beamed triumphantly.

"Only one problem... That picture is locked up in evidence." Stephen gulped the last bit of his coffee.

"Oh yes, that is a problem," Mak agreed.

"Unless—"

"What?"

Stephen eyed Mak, wondering if he dared to suggest it. "I think I could get the picture out and back in without anyone realizing it's gone."

Mak gave him a suspicious look. "What are you—"

"The less you know the better. We just need to take a trip to the police station, and you'll need to distract Higgins," Stephen began.

"No way am I doing anything illegal, Wilton!" Mak protested.

"You aren't. Like I said, the less you know, the better. Now we just need a way to get in front of Higgins."

"Well, I do need to connect with him over Mickey Upton, the third man in our trafficking ring—"

"Right, the criminal who got away," Stephen interrupted Mak impatiently. "What about him?"

"We have it on good authority that Mickey Upton is here in Arkansas. There's an APB out for him. I promised Sikes I would connect with Higgins to collaborate." Mak grinned sheepishly.

"What?" Stephen exploded. "You didn't think to tell me that?!"

"I kinda forgot." Mak held up her hands. "In my defense, we've had a lot going on. Not to mention, you haven't been reinstated yet. Nor have you answered or returned Sikes' phone calls lately."

Stephen waved his hand back and forth dismissively. "I need to know if a criminal is in the area. Especially that one. Do we know where the intel came from?"

Mak stood and nodded. "Yep. Are you ready for this?"

Stephen stood as well and tossed his coffee cup. "Yes."

"Lacy Donovan." Mak pulled open the door.

"What the—"

"Come on, I'll explain on the way to the police station."

19

LACY

In the dawn of the early morning, while it was still dark outside, Lacy Donovan woke before her alarm went off and before anyone else in the house even stirred. The house was still with the silence and occasional snores of sleeping people who had been through a lot in their lives.

Lacy Donovan was one of them. Only, she didn't sleep as long as her roommates did. She quickly threw her covers off and jumped up with excitement and energy. She did twenty jumping jacks the minute her feet hit the floor. She was up before dawn crept over the picturesque mountain range off in the distance. Just like every other morning, she made her bed and went to make coffee. This was the best part of her day.

Once her coffee was doctored, she turned off the home alarm and let herself out on the back deck. Most mornings, she opened her blinds and settled back on her bed to watch the sunrise in the stillness of her own room. But it was warm now, and Lacy longed to watch the view and then meditate outdoors today.

As her bare feet hit the cool, wooden deck, she took in a deep breath of fresh, chilly morning air, snuggled into her thick sweatshirt, and put her hands in the pockets of her sweatpants. No matter how warm it got outside during the day, mornings here were always cooler.

Still, the fresh air did something for her heart. It made her feel alive. She sat in a deck chair and pulled her feet up into lotus position. She took a long, gratifying drink of hot coffee just as the first rays of the sun illuminated the sky.

An unexpected hand closed on her shoulder, startling her out of her peaceful moment. Lacy jumped and dribbled her coffee on her sweatshirt as she quickly whipped her head around to see who had touched her.

Jonas stood over her, a smirk evident on his handsome face.

Anger and adrenaline downloaded into Lacy's system when she realized the threat had been nothing. She had over-reacted.

"Cheese and rice, Jonas! You cannot sneak up on me like that!" Lacy pointed a warning finger firmly at him, then toward the house, and lowered her voice. "That goes for them, too. You had me in full on fight or flight with that one action!"

The smirk fell from Jonas' face. "Lace, I'm sorry!"

Lacy's gaze swiveled back to the sunrise. "And now I'm missing it. You ruined my sunrise!"

"Would you like me to go back inside?" Jonas asked sincerely.

Lacy instantly felt bad for yelling at him. She shook her head. "But you need to sit quietly and give me a chance to find my inner peace again until the sun is fully in the sky."

Jonas nodded, his face a mixture of regret and apology. He wordlessly sat in the deck chair next to Lacy. Together, they silently watched the rest of the sunrise. True to his word, Jonas waited until the sun hung overhead. The sky streaked a myriad of colors, the most prominent a deep purple.

When the sun had fully risen and the sky had settled on a lovely clear blue, Lacy gave Jonas her attention.

"Lacy, you can't turn the alarm off to the house and come outside without giving me a heads up the night before," Jonas stated directly. "What you felt when I put a hand on your shoulder is what I felt when I was notified that the alarm had been disengaged. How do you even know the code?"

"I didn't think about that," Lacy admitted. She took another drink of coffee. "You aren't exactly secretive with the code. I'm not being held here against my will as a prisoner, right?"

"No." Jonas shook his head. "You aren't. I just need full communication to keep you safe."

"Okay, that's fair," Lacy agreed. "Can I tell you something *I* need?"

"Of course," Jonas leaned closer.

"I need paint—acrylics preferably—canvases, and four easels. Then I need breakable glass, which I have every intention of breaking, empty cardboard boxes, trash—big and small pieces, and a baseball bat—make that four baseball bats," Lacy delivered her list.

Jonas gaped at her. "What are you up to, Lace?"

Lacy ticked her head toward the house. "The girls are stuck. They aren't healing, and I think it might be time to give them a few outlets to help them along. I was doing some research about repressed emotions. Everyone deals with anger and sadness differently. Some people find painting to be a nice outlet to express feelings. Others do well when they can break and hit things. We can turn the garage into a—"

"Rage room," Jonas finished her sentence and was nodding before she finished her words. "You really want to help them, don't you?"

"I want to do more than that. I want to build a program

that helps Final Girls heal from the trauma, go back out in the world, and live normal lives, whatever that looks like. Not just for them, but for others who are rescued next," Lacy admitted.

"Wow, Lacy, that's beautiful." Jonas' eyes were wide. "And big."

Lacy put up a hand. "It will be. Someday. But I don't want to think about that yet. I just want to develop a program that works and seems duplicatable. If I can help them, I can help others."

"But you're not a counselor," Jonas reminded her.

"Right, but the other day when I asked you if we could bring one in, you vetoed my suggestion. I understand it would compromise us, but I still believe in patient confidentiality," Lacy argued. Seeing that her meditation time would not happen this morning after all, she untangled her legs and swung them to the ground.

"I know, and I heard you. I've been doing my own research, and I found a grief group. It's anonymous, international, and phone based. I believe all four of you could attend with an untraceable number. You would just need to agree not to share explicit details of your case—"

Before Jonas could finish his sentence, Lacy was out of her chair, hugging Jonas, her arms wrapped tightly around his neck. She moved her head and was suddenly aware of how snugged up to him her body was. Her eyes locked on his. They froze, painfully aware of how easy it would be to steal just one kiss.

Lacy jumped back at the same time Jonas said her name with warning in his voice.

"I'm sorry!" To her horror, tears filled Lacy's eyes.

"Lace, don't," Jonas leaned over and gently swiped her eyes. "I feel it too, okay? But I think what we have is bigger than a stolen moment here and there. I believe in you. I see

—" his voice broke, and he cleared his throat. "I see your vision, and it's powerful and important. I support it. I support your dream. But we can't mess that up right now. You and I—we have to be careful and smart with our feelings. Okay?"

Lacy's heart burst with hope and excitement. He felt the same, and he believed in her. "Yes."

Jonas dropped his hand to Lacy's wrist, and he rubbed a couple of soft circles. "Good. It's going to be hard, but for now, I need to stay in this job. We can work on this together. I could help you build this. I even think you could get government funding for a project like this."

"Really?" The thought hadn't occurred to Lacy.

"Really," Jonas confirmed. "But our priority right now is to put these criminals away first. You and the girls are the most important pieces of that puzzle. Step one, put the ring-leaders in prison. Step two, come up with a process to help the women. Step three, research. Step four, apply for grants. Step five, turn a ranch into a Final Girls' detox and healing center."

"This ranch?" Lacy breathed, her chest tight with emotion as she glanced around, visualizing the plan.

"Or one like it. This one is the property of the government. I'm not sure. I'm just dreaming out loud and making it up as I go. What do you think?" Jonas asked.

"I love it!" Lacy said. But as she looked into his eyes, Lacy thought she might love Jonas as much as this new plan.

20

———————

WILTON

As Stephen and Mak walked through the door of Stephen's old police precinct in Little Rock, memories flooded back to him. Some good, some not good. He and Mak were uncharacteristically silent until they pushed the door open. He was quiet because he was lost in memories. He couldn't begin to know why Mak was quiet. It happened so rarely.

"Show time," Stephen said quietly under his breath.

Mak nodded almost imperceptibly.

"Well, Stephen Wilton!" A receptionist sat just inside the double doors. Her voice held the smallest twang of an accent. She fluffed her platinum bob. "Is that really you? How in the world are you?"

"Hi, I'm great, Constance! How are you?" Stephen greeted the pretty middle-aged woman.

"Wonderful!" Constance looked at Mak with questioning eyes.

"Oh, this is my partner, Mak Cunningham." Stephen grinned his most charming smile. "She's going up to talk to Captain Higgins."

Constance nodded at Mak. "Captain is up on the second floor. There's the elevator."

Mak smiled kindly, walked to the elevator, and pushed the up button. The doors opened immediately. She walked inside, and the doors slid shut effectively cutting her from view.

"So, you heard about Higgins becoming a Captain, huh?" Constance smiled. "'Bout time, I say!"

"Me, too!" Stephen agreed.

"And how's life treating *you*? You big-shot US Marshal?" Constance winked.

"Great! Things are great." Stephen smiled a convincing smile.

"Got yourself a pretty little girlfriend?" She wagged her eyebrows.

"Yes," Stephen lied.

"Do tell!" Constance leaned forward to catch all the details.

Before Stephen could answer her question, the phone on Constance's desk rang. Stephen listened to the one-sided conversation and knew that Mak had requested a file that Higgins would not have on his desk—the one on Davey Stinnert. Stephen knew that file would only be in the archives. He also knew Mak was planning to admit she was working with Stephen to help him solve who had killed his brother. Further, the filing room was a locked space to the left of the desk where Constance sat. The first step in their plan was working.

"Sure thing, Captain. I'll grab that right now and bring it up." Constance put the phone down. Her eyes flicked up to Stephen. She paused like she was considering whether to say something but changed her mind. "Don't go anywhere. I want to hear all about your girlfriend. But first, I gotta run something to the Captain." Constance got up and unlocked the file room.

Stephen watched Constance walk into the file room. He waited patiently for her to come back out. He positioned himself right where she would open the door and step out in case he needed to catch the door.

"Oh, Stephen!" Constance exclaimed as she rushed out of the room and walked straight into him. She put a hand to her chest. "You startled me. Sorry about that. I'm in a bit of a hurry. Gotta take this up to Captain. Are you okay?"

"Of course," Stephen pretended sheepishness and pointed to a door just down the hall to explain where he was going. "Bathroom."

"Okay, I won't be long," Constance promised and shuffled into the elevator. Not only had Constance not re-locked the door, she hadn't clicked it shut all the way, either. That would make things easy.

Stephen waited until he heard the elevator door shut, then he pushed the door open and rushed inside. He guesstimated he had three to five minutes—tops. He walked in and quickly found the evidence locker. The keys to the locker dangled in the lock.

"They really need better security," he said as he threw the door open.

It took Stephen less than a minute to find the envelope he needed and pull it from the evidence locker. He shoved it under his shirt and exited the room. He let the door fall shut behind him. He'd worry about getting the envelope back in on a different day. He walked through the double doors, out to the parking lot, and straight to his car. Once there, Stephen safely stowed the photo where he'd kept it before— under his passenger seat.

He searched through his contacts and found the one for Bernie Miltner. Bernie had been a photographic evidence expert Stephen had used many times when he'd been on the force. This next part of the plan was going to be tricky. He knew Bernie would help him. He just didn't know if Bernie would keep it quiet from Higgins. Stephen had a plan that involved a hefty payment on the front end and another when the job was done. He hoped Bernie would agree to it.

Not only did he want Bernie to clean up the photo to identify the other witnesses, he needed a few convincing copies of the picture to keep for himself. One that would go right back into the manilla envelope he'd slip back into the evidence locker. Sooner, rather than later, he hoped.

Stephen listened to the phone ring several times before voicemail picked up.

It's Bernie. You can leave a message, but text would be better…

Stephen switched to text message and sent Bernie a quick request to meet up. Stephen walked back inside to find Constance at her desk. He jiggled his phone at her.

"Had to take a phone call," Stephen said. "Now where were we?"

Constance sighed. "I'd love to sit around and chat all day, but Captain gave me some work to do. And he requested you come on up. *No need to loiter in the lobby,* he said."

"Oh!" Stephen felt surprised. He was sure Higgins didn't want to see him after Stephen silently left here the other day with his lawyer. Stephen hesitated and weighed his options. He supposed it would look odd to leave now. Suspicious, even. He sighed and walked to the elevator with a small wave.

When he got off the elevator, he immediately heard his name.

"Wilton!" Detective Brandt shouted.

"That's US Marshal Wilton to you." Stephen grinned at his old friend.

"Oh, big man. What brings you down here to your lowly little police roots?" Brandt gave Stephen knuckles.

"Just in town visiting the folks—"

"With your partner?" Brandt pointed to Mak who was talking in Higgins' office. They could see her through the clear glass.

"Oh, you met Mak?"

"Yeah, I did. Shook the hand that didn't have the wedding ring on it," Brandt smirked.

"Aren't you married?" Stephen asked, feeling his face storm over, trying to put Brandt back in his place. Mak didn't like being hit on or treated differently due to her gender.

"Separated. Earlier this year," Brandt admitted.

"Sorry to hear that," Stephen said with surprise and genuine feeling.

Brandt shrugged. "You of all people know how it is. This profession is hard on relationships. Still single yourself?"

"Plead the fifth." Stephen put his hands up. "Hey, don't you have some investigating to do?"

"Yeah," Brandt lowered his voice and peered at Stephen. "Trevan Collins' case. Got a murderer to catch."

"The sooner the better—"

"Yeah, for you!" Brandt quipped.

Stephen felt his face turn hot. Before he could respond, Mak and Higgins stepped out of Higgins' office.

"I'll keep you posted on my end," Higgins was saying.

"Same on mine." Mak smiled easily as they walked toward Stephen. Mak held Davey's file, or a copy of it, in her hand.

Higgins stopped in front of Stephen with his hands on his hips. He stared at him for half a second, then acknowledged him. "Wilton."

"Higgins."

"Alright, my work here is done," Mak said quickly. Stephen knew Mak was jumping in to rescue them from the undisguised irritation between the two of them.

"I guess we'll get going then," Stephen said. He turned to Higgins. "Unless you needed something from me?"

"No, I would just rather you come on up than distract Constance from getting her work done." Higgins rocked on his heels with a knowing look on his face.

"Well, you know where to find me if you need me," Stephen said over his shoulder as he turned toward the elevator.

They stepped on the elevator, off at the lobby, and out the front door with a quick wave to Constance on their way out.

As they sat down in the car and buckled seatbelts, Mak asked. "How did your covert operation go?"

"Feel below the seat to answer your question," Stephen answered.

"Umm... I'd rather not," Mak quirked an eyebrow at him. "I'll just take your word for it. The bigger question is, did you pull it off?"

Stephen shrugged. "For now."

21

WILTON

Stephen loitered just on the outskirts of town. The sun was setting, casting long shadows on the abandoned school yard. As he waited, he watched the thick plastic swings sway in the cool, gentle breeze. The color of the plastic seat bottom had long since faded from red to pink. He studied the rust rimmed metal with white paint flecking off the frame. The other playground equipment was equally run down.

He remembered playing here with his brother, Greg, when he was a kid.

"Hey!" A voice sounded low and urgent behind Stephen.

Startled, Stephen whirled quickly, his hand on his weapon. "Geez, Bernie! You almost got yourself shot. Don't you know better than to sneak up on an officer?"

Bernie smirked. "Hear you're not an officer anymore."

"Okay, yeah... US Marshal," Stephen corrected.

"So, this is official business?" Bernie asked.

"No," Stephen said quickly. "But I have cash. I'll pay half upfront and half when you complete the job. Just like I promised. But if you can't clean up the photo, deal's off. If you break confidentiality, deal's off."

Bernie considered Stephen's words. "Well, let's see what you have. I'll tell you if I think I can work a miracle. That's what you need, isn't it, Wilton? A miracle?"

"Yeah." Stephen stared at the man. Bernie looked trustworthy enough. He was the same height as Stephen, though thinner. He had straight brown hair that hit his ears, black wire-rim glasses, and piercing dark brown eyes. He wore jeans, boat shoes, and a long-sleeved t-shirt. He supposed it was a bit on the cool side this evening. Stephen reminded himself that Bernie had always been loyal and kept his work confidential at the station back in the day.

"Well?" Bernie pushed his glasses up on his nose. "Have you decided if you can trust me?"

Stephen sighed. "I'll be honest with you, so you'll be honest with me. I'm in hot water. This is deeply personal. It's not police or marshal business, but I can pay you well. My life depends on this staying quiet... from other authorities."

"Dramatic." Bernie rolled his eyes and held out his hand. "Honesty is overrated. I believe in confidentiality. Do you think I was ever honest about who all my clients were with my other clients? If I started reading the roster of who I've worked with, I'd be out of business."

Stephen took the envelope he'd been holding against his chest out from under his jacket. "I really want to ask you more about what you just said."

Bernie wagged a gloved finger at him. Of course, Bernie would think to wear gloves to avoid finger smudges. "Would you want me to tell them about you?"

Stephen didn't answer. Instead, he gritted his teeth and handed Bernie the photo. "I need two identical copies of this back by tomorrow morning. I need the background cleaned up so I can see who the witnesses are in the picture. How about I pay you a quarter today, a quarter tomorrow, and half when I get the cleared-up photo back?"

Bernie slid the photo out and studied it. He squinted his eyes and held it up to the sun that was rapidly disappearing on this already overcast day. He pulled out his phone and turned on his flashlight. He inched his face closer, muttering to himself.

"Can't blow it up. It'll just create blobs. In fact, that's probably how they got so pixelated in the first place." Having concluded his train of thought, Bernie looked up at Stephen. "It's not the original. This has already been blown up from the original."

"Any chance it's been doctored, too? Did someone put a different face on the man with the gun? Or orchestrate the entire picture?" Stephen asked.

Bernie looked back down at the photo. His eyes got big and he seemed surprised as he studied the picture in front of him. "Hmm, it would have to be a good artist. My gut is telling me *no*. I'll know more when I start working on it. In order to try—and I mean *try*—to get a shot of who's who in the background, I'll need to shrink the picture back down. I really want the original—"

"If I had the original or any clue where to look for it, do you think I'd be here?" Stephen heard his words come out sharper than he intended. He felt instantly contrite. "Sorry, I'm under a lot of pressure."

"I'll say," Bernie agreed. "That's your brother, isn't it?"

"What?" Stephen felt his blood turn to ice. "You knew him?"

"Yes, I knew of him. Come on, man, Greg was a legend. You know, the big, bad, untouchable senior. I was a year younger than him in school. Even if I hadn't gone to school with you guys, I would have heard about what happened to him. Murder didn't happen much in our area."

"Bernie, I'm sorry. I guess I didn't know you in high school. Did we ever meet?" Stephen wondered aloud.

Bernie shrugged. "Nah, I kept to myself. Listen—" Bernie stopped himself.

"What?" Stephen asked. He was suddenly desperate to hear what Bernie had to say.

"I know what people said after... but... I never thought Greg was a bad guy. Popular, sure. Untouchable, absolutely. Open to making new friends, no way. But he was always kind to people, you know?" Bernie scratched his chin stubble.

Stephen nodded. "I do know. And you're not the first one to tell me that. It's become a theme. So, you can see how sensitive this situation is and why I appreciate that you keep things confidential. Clearly, that man in the photo is not the man who went down for Greg's murder. But the truth is, I'm at a dead end. If I can find these witnesses, I can get some answers."

"Unless they're dead too, now." Bernie carefully put the photo back in its envelope.

Stephen's heart dropped. He hadn't even considered that. "Do you think it's possible to clear it up enough to get their identities?"

Bernie shifted his weight from foot to foot. "I won't know until I try."

"Can you meet me here tomorrow at ten in the morning with two convincing duplicates?" Stephen pulled out a smaller envelope with cash inside.

Bernie eyed the envelope greedily. He licked his lips in anticipation. "Can we say eleven?"

Stephen nodded. He always trusted his gut. Not with women, of course. That had always been one fail after another. But as a law officer, Stephen had been dead-on much of the time. He looked Bernie in the eye and knew he could trust him. Not only had Bernie always been trustworthy when Stephen was on the force, Stephen could tell that

Bernie needed the money. The sooner he finished this project, the sooner Bernie would get paid more.

"I'll meet you here tomorrow at eleven," Stephen agreed. "And Bernie?"

Bernie had turned to walk away but looked back over his shoulder.

"Thanks," Stephen said. "For what you said about Greg."

Bernie nodded. "I hope I can help you get answers."

22

———

MAK

Mak was lying face up in corpse pose on a yoga mat. She had just completed her first yoga session since she broke her back. She had to admit to herself that down dog had been a struggle. Had the instructor made them hold it much longer, Mak would have had to collapse into child's pose.

As she lay there and thought through the experience, she knew she had to be honest with herself. She'd never thought of yoga as a real workout. It was humbling, even in her state of brokenness, to shake so badly when trying to hold a pose that would have been easy for her on a different day—in a different season.

She tried to quash the feelings of inadequacy and frustration over her slow healing. She'd come back this morning to what looked like a rigorous schedule that she knew was meant to expedite the process. Mak had liked the sound of that. Until she started day one. Today, she did acupuncture, which had also been a first. She was no fan of needles and had ground her teeth at the thought.

Then she had challenged herself. *Suck it up, buttercup. You're never going to get better if you don't do the work.* She would meet with a therapist tomorrow and she knew better than to admit how hard she was on herself. Afterwards, Mak would do a round of red-light therapy, which would help heal her wound, decrease her muscle pain, and reduce her inflammation.

But now came the icing, as Dr. Mott had called it—an hour-long deep tissue massage. Most people loved massages. At least, that's what Mak had always heard. To Mak, having to lie still in one place for so long, not to mention a stranger rubbing her back, sounded like torture.

Still, if it was in the name of quick healing, Mak was in. When she was ready to get off the floor, Mak got up and rolled her mat with a sigh. She threw it in the locker she was using, then she checked in at the front desk. When they instructed her to have a seat, she pulled out her phone and called John.

She'd made a deal with John that if this was what she chose to do in place of physical therapy, that she would put her whole heart into it. John wasn't convinced that physical therapy hadn't been working. He had a theory that Mak was resisting and not doing her exercises. It had been a source of contention between them. Of course, Mak was doing what her physical therapist instructed. She just wasn't a typical patient and needed someone who would challenge her a little more.

John answered the phone sounding a little breathless. "Hey!"

"Hey, babe. Just checking in. You okay?" Mak asked.

"Yep! All good. Making breakfast. Couldn't find my phone for a minute, but it's all good. Want me to save you some bacon and eggs?" John asked.

"No, I'm about to go in for a massage," Mak said glumly.

John laughed. "Only you would have issues with that, Makayla. What have you done so far this morning?"

"Acupuncture," Mak answered.

"How was that?" John asked curiously.

"Weird, but I felt great afterward. Then immediately after, I went into a yoga session." Mak sat back on the couch where she was waiting.

John snickered. "I'd love to see that!"

"Glad you find this amusing," Mak sighed. "Everything I've done today has been a first for me. I'm good with a challenge. But three in a row..." Mak let her sentence trail.

"It's almost like you asked them to help you get better faster," John teased.

"Ha, ha," Mak responded dryly. She heard someone call her name. "Gotta go. My luxurious massage awaits."

"See you later," John made a kiss noise.

One hour later, Mak understood the appeal of a massage. Once she instructed the therapist on the right amount of pressure, Mak practically fell asleep and felt sure she'd drooled on the table. If she would have known massages were like this, she would have gotten one years ago.

When? her brain argued. *You never had time to stop for massages.*

Well, maybe she would make time after she got back to work. After all, there was only one of her. She had to take good care of herself to be the best mom, wife, and marshal.

When Mak left the clinic, her whole body felt like one soft puddle of muscles and tissues. She was relaxed as she slid behind the wheel of her car and pulled out onto the main road to go back to the Airbnb.

That's why she almost missed the car that zoomed by her. There was something familiar about that car. It was small and red. Mak was sure she'd seen it somewhere before.

Mak and the driver of the little red car came to a stop side by side at a red light. Mak had accelerated to catch up, and the driver of the red car had to slam on her brakes to stop in time. Mak casually looked over at the other driver.

It was Beth. Something in Mak made her decide she didn't want to be spotted. She turned her head and pretended to look for something in her passenger seat. When the light turned green, Beth took off and Mak let her car fall behind.

Mak pulled behind Beth and even let a car get between them. Not that Beth had been paying attention to her surroundings at all. She looked pretty focused on wherever she needed to go.

Mak's eyes flicked to her dashboard. It was almost eleven. She knew Beth worked a corporate job. Was Beth on a lunch break? Mak shrugged. Maybe Beth was late for a doctor's appointment.

But as Mak tailed her, she realized Beth was not going to the doctor. She was heading out of town. When Beth pulled into what looked like an abandoned playground, Mak kept driving, but quickly circled back to find a place out of view to watch Beth.

That's how she spotted Stephen talking to a tall, wiry man in a t-shirt and jeans. And Beth was staring right at them. Was Beth meeting Stephen here? For a moment, Mak felt like a jerk for being suspicious. Then Mak noticed the angle of Beth's car. She was parked just off the lot in such a way that Stephen would not spot her.

Mak drummed her fingers on the steering wheel. Beth made no move to get out of the car. Mak watched as Beth picked up her phone, pointed it toward Stephen and the man he was talking to, and touched her phone several times.

Was Beth spying and taking pictures?

"Surely not," Mak scoffed to herself. Didn't Stephen say Beth had broken up with him? If that was the case, why would she be stalking Stephen?

After another five minutes of Beth sitting in the car and staring, Beth pulled out of the parking lot and drove away.

Mak kept her distance and followed. Beth went through a fast-food drive-thru, then drove herself back to work.

Mak kept driving, this time back to the Airbnb. She made a note to ask Stephen about the strange behavior. Mak touched the side of her forehead and wondered, *Was Beth always like that?* What did Mak know about Beth? She racked her brain and came up empty. She couldn't remember anything about Beth prior to meeting her at Stephen's get together the other day.

Maybe Stephen had invited Beth to meet him, but when he took so long, Beth gave up and drove away. Because if that wasn't the case, how had Beth known where she could find Stephen and that he'd be in what looked like a top-secret meeting on the edge of town?

Mak knew Stephen was meeting up with the photographer, but Stephen had not even told Mak where the meetup was taking place. And he had been secretive about his source. Which begged the question.

How had Beth known where to find Stephen?

23

MAK

Wilton had called to let Mak know he had his duplicate fake photos, and they were a spectacular likeness. Now, he just needed a way to sneak one of them back into evidence. Mak had invited him over. As she waited, she paced the front room, knowing how difficult it was going to be to deliver the news she had for him.

The knock at the door halted Mak's pacing. "Come on in, Wilton," Mak called from where she stood.

"Hey, man! We were just about to have Monte Cristos," John greeted jovially as Wilton walked in. "Can I make you one?"

"Monte Cristos?" Wilton wandered to the stove to inspect John's handiwork.

"Yeah, it's basically grilled cheese with some deli meat in the middle with homemade jam I found at a farmer's market on top."

"Wow!" Wilton exclaimed. "Yes please!"

Mak cleared her throat.

Wilton turned his focus to Mak. "I met up with Bernie

and got some very convincing photos back from him, if I do say so myself." Wilton proudly produced the pictures.

"That's good," Mak said, relaxing her stance to appear nonchalant. "Did you plan to meet anyone else there?"

"No. Just Bernie and me. We met at this old, abandoned playground where my brother and I used to sneak off and hang out by ourselves. Even back then it was run down, and my parents never wanted us to be there because it's just on the outskirts of town." Wilton grinned like a kid. "I thought it was a poetic place to meet considering what we are trying to figure out."

Mak nodded. "Does Bernie think he can clear up the photo and determine who else was there?"

Wilton shrugged. "He doesn't know and won't know until he tries."

"And you think you can trust him not to go blabbing your business?" Mak asked.

"Well, he was always trustworthy when I used him at the police department. My gut says he's still trustworthy, but I guess we'll see. In the meantime, we need a way to get this photo back into evidence."

"What's the plan this time, Wilton? You gonna seduce Constance?" Mak grinned unashamedly at her joke.

Wilton rolled his eyes. "That's why I'm here, actually. Pretty sure I'm gonna need your help again."

"Ugh!" Mak exclaimed. "I don't love all this shadiness. I looked up evidence tampering, and you can get anywhere from a five thousand dollar fine to seven years in prison."

John looked up at Mak in surprise, then watched Wilton's reaction.

"I know," Wilton admitted. "*If* they can prove that my intent is to interfere with an investigation or obstruct justice. We all know it's not. My intent is to solve this thing. Regardless, I'm too far in it now. Gotta finish this off and get a photo back in evidence before they realize it's missing. If you want to bail out at any point, you can."

"Okay, we can talk about a plan… But first, how well do you actually know Beth?"

Wilton's eyebrows rose, and he looked surprised at the subject change. "Well, like I've said before, I didn't know her very well in high school. I just knew of her from hanging out with my brother. But I've gotten to know her better for the last four months."

"Right, but how well do you actually *know* her. Did you guys talk about your hopes and dreams? And future? Or were you just hanging out?" Mak was tiptoeing into what she really wanted to ask.

Wilton regarded Mak with suspicion as John put a plate in front of him. Wilton mindlessly took it as he sat at the small dining room table. "I'm starting to think you have a reason for asking me that, Mak." Wilton's tone had adopted a steel edge.

John called Harper into the room to eat and set a plate down at the chair beside Wilton. He gave Mak and Wilton a warning glance as Harper came scampering into the room.

"Yeah, I do, and you're not gonna like it. I'm glad you're sitting down. I saw Beth driving a little fast and erratically as I was leaving therapy today. I recognized her car, and I followed it. I confirmed it was her at a stop sign. So, I kept following her."

"You followed my ex-girlfriend because she was driving bad?" Wilton took a bite of the Monte Cristo and made a noise of appreciation.

Mak ignored Wilton's snarky tone. "She ended up at the exact location where you were talking to Bernie. She watched you from the parking lot for quite a while. I even think she might have taken a picture. Do you have any idea why she would do that?"

Wilton's mouth gaped open. "No! How would she even have known where to find me?"

Mak took a deep breath and let it out slowly. "Well, if we separate out the *why* and just answer that question, we know that it's possible to put tracking devices on cell phones and cars."

"But that doesn't make sense!" Wilton shook his head.

"You're talking with your mouth full," Harper giggled, wagging a finger at Wilton.

"Sorry, Harper," Wilton said automatically, but his mind was considering the possibilities. "Tracking device on my phone?"

"Do you think Beth has the capability and know-how to do that?" Mak asked. "How about a tracking app on your phone. Could she have connected you to her phone that way? Maybe when you were sleeping?"

Wilton took out his phone and stared at it. "Sure, that's possible."

"Open your app store and check what apps are downloaded. She could have hidden it from your desktop," Mak suggested.

"Right, okay." Wilton opened his phone and started scrolling. He mindlessly ate his hot sandwich. Then he looked up. "Life 360?"

"Yeah, I've heard of that one," Mak said.

Wilton clicked on the app and his eyes got big. "We are, indeed, connected on Life 360."

"There's your how," Mak concluded.

"Now about the *why*," Wilton mumbled, looking perplexed. He stood up like he planned to go ask Beth right now.

"Sit down, Wilton. Finish your food. Why don't you tell me your plan for sneaking evidence back in? I'll let you know if I decide to help this time around."

"Okay, But then I need to find Beth."

24

MAK

Mak was enjoying the warm day while watching Harper slide, run around to the back, and repeat. Mak remembered those days in her childhood. The good ones where she got stuck in a loop of energy, happiness, and repeating an activity over and over again until she swore she was sick of it. Then she would do it again the next day.

Her finger tapped quickly against the thigh of her jeans, a sure sign that she had been sitting still too long. Mak hated sitting still. John, who sat beside her, placed his hand on top of hers.

"Relax," he said in a hushed, calm voice.

"I'm sorry. I just feel like something is happening out there—without me," Mak admitted with a sigh.

"Something *is* happening." John tilted his head toward Harper, who was now whooping loudly as she slid on her bottom.

"I remember when I would be right there with her sliding," Mak admitted, taking out her phone to capture yet another picture.

"What, a few months ago?" John's eyes twinkled with laughter.

"Yeah... so, what?" Mak asked.

"So, you wish you could be out there now," John answered.

"Of course I do," Mak agreed.

"You're getting stronger, Makayla. It's only a matter of time before you can do all the things you did before—"

"The explosion," her tone came out bitter.

Mak's phone rang, cutting off John's response. She checked the screen and showed it to John.

It was Sikes.

"Take a walk around the track," John suggested, his finger making a circle.

Mak nodded and stood, walking toward a nice, paved track that looped around the playground. She answered the phone. "Mak here."

"Mak, it's Sikes. How are you?" Sikes sounded a little breathless.

"I'm good. Getting stronger every day." Mak chose to use John's words.

"Truly?" Sikes' voice held some doubt.

"Yes," Mak smiled. "I've found a clinic that focuses on healing. They have me on a good program."

"That's good to hear because I might have a job for you. We are willing to reinstate you for light duty with limited tasks. This job is low key, but I'll only assign it if you think you're ready to do a little work?" Sikes asked.

"Of course. Whatcha got?" Mak asked.

"You still in Arkansas?"

"I am," Mak confirmed.

"We got a hit on Mickey Upton. A civilian called in a complaint that their new neighbors down the road are moving dirt with heavy equipment at all hours of the night.

They wanted local PD to give them a citation for breaking a noise ordinance. But when PD ran the address through the system, they found a new corporate permit. They thought it was odd that corporate builders would work all night long. Found a name on a signed document. It was—"

"Mickey Upton," Mak finished for Sikes. "You know, I remember when I thought those two goons with Anthony Gerritt were just bodyguards. I thought Gerritt was the brains of the operation and Upton and Allister were just henchmen. What were the chances that they were all equal partners?"

"Pretty good considering the new night building project with Upton's name on it, which might connect back to the Golden Girl lead Lacy found," Sikes concluded. "I'm having the team look for any other building permits he might have signed to a get a full picture of his reach."

"Well, do we know what he's building?" Remembering the underground Earth prison where Gerritt, Upton, and Allister had kept Lacy Donovan and three other women, Mak could take a good guess.

"I don't want to make any assumptions. I want eyes on them. You up for some recon? By recon, I mean a stakeout with binoculars a very far distance away from the property," Sikes clarified.

"Light duty," Mak considered the assignment. She shuddered, thinking about the last property that she had stepped foot on that Gerritt had owned. That explosion haunted Mak. Then an even more horrific thought occurred. "You don't think he's building—"

"A compound to keep women? Anything is possible." It wasn't hard for Sikes to read her mind. "And I think we should assume the worst. That's why we need eyes on the property. He could be building an office, making another prison, or prepping a graveyard. Right now is the best time to see anything. Before they start pouring concrete."

"Geez, Sikes, that got dark really fast," Mak breathed out. That's when she noticed she had made at least three loops around the park without feeling winded. She felt amazing. She had no pain. She wondered how long before she would start taking that for granted like she had every day she'd woken up without pain in the past—before the explosion.

"Well, we need to be prepared for anything. But I can't have you react and go in guns blazing. You aren't cleared for that. This is purely recon," Sikes commanded.

"If I can't, maybe I could take someone along who could. Because you know if I see women held hostage, or bodies, nothing will hold me back," Mak warned.

Sikes chuckled. "I know. That's what makes you one of the best. Keep me informed of any plans."

"What about Wilton? Will you be reinstating him, too?" Mak asked. Mak felt a pinch of guilt. If only Sikes knew what Wilton was busy doing these days.

"Wilton would do well to answer the phone when I reach out. You know I can't comment on that until I speak to him." Sikes cleared his throat in annoyance.

Mak tried to change the subject. "Is Allister talking yet? He's been in jail for quite a while." Surely, he tried to make a deal by now.

Sikes sighed. "If only… Although, when a criminal makes a deal, it's not a win-win. We saw that with Gerritt. He deserved to go down for his crimes. But he started talking and got his freedom. I sure don't want Allister back out there."

"Only, Gerritt didn't end up free, he ended up dead." Mak waved at Harper from across the track when her daughter paused at the top of slide, looking around for her mother.

"True," Sikes agreed.

"Any news on that? You really can't tell me when you're bringing Wilton back?" Mak pressed.

"Can't talk about that either. But if I could, I would tell you that the bullet that killed Anthony Gerritt does not belong to any guns registered to Wilton. You didn't hear that from me. But maybe it will help you encourage Wilton to take my call."

"That's great news, sir." Mak smiled, feeling relief. "I'll see what I can do. In the meantime, send me the location of this compound and we'll go check it out."

"Will do." Sikes hung up the phone.

Mak rerouted and walked back to her family.

"Just in time to get some burgers," John announced.

"Isn't it a little early for dinner?" Mak asked, checking the time on her phone.

"No way, I'm hungry!" Harper protested.

"Burgers though?" Mak asked. "How about a nice, healthy salad?"

"Ew!" Harper squealed. She plugged her nose and crossed her eyes. "Salads are gross!"

"You're gross!" Mak leaned down to tickle her daughter, noticing the absence of pain. Her back didn't grab in a bad way.

"You are!" Harper shrieked between giggles.

"You both are!" John had the final word as he dug in his pocket for his keys.

"Fine, one hamburger. Then mommy has to go to work," Mak announced. She shared a meaningful look with John.

They got in the car blissfully unaware of how dangerous Mak's job was about to get.

25

WILTON

Stephen followed Beth's car from a distance and watched as she pulled into a bank where she did not work. He assumed she would pull into the drive thru, but she didn't. Instead, she parked her car and sat staring straight ahead. He watched as she picked up a to-go coffee and put it to her lips. Why was she just sitting there? Stephen almost felt bad for lurking. But he had to know what she was up to.

He got out of his Tahoe and walked swiftly to Beth's car, taking a chance that the door would not be locked. It wasn't. He quickly opened the door and sat down in the passenger seat.

Beth jumped, still holding her coffee cup, spewing coffee drops on the dash. "Stephen, you scared me!"

"Why did I scare you, Beth?" Stephen asked with intensity as he sat beside her. He checked his watch. Though it was only four in the afternoon, he was surprised by how empty the parking lot was. Maybe the bank was about to close.

Beth's laugh spilled out of her, that light, airy tone that Stephen had grown so accustomed to. He used to love her laugh, but now as he studied her with a different perspective, he had to wonder if it was fake. Perhaps it was, along with their whole relationship.

"You came out of nowhere, Stephen. I wasn't expecting you. How did you find me?" Beth didn't seem as light now. In fact, if Stephen hadn't been watching her closely, he would have missed the annoyance that flickered in her eyes before she schooled her expression into one of curiosity.

"Funny you should ask me that." Stephen slowly and deliberately took out his phone and unlocked the screen. He opened an app with his finger. He showed her the screen and jiggled the phone at her. "I found this app on my phone. Handy little thing. It's called Life 360. We're connected on it. You can see me. But I can also see you. But then you already know that because you installed it—"

"Stephen, I didn't—"

"Don't, Beth. Don't try to deny it. The puzzling part of this is, it requires permission. See, I know I didn't give you permission to connect on this app. So, I asked myself, how in the world did it come to be on my phone, connected to yours?" Stephen drawled, tilting his head to the side.

"You have some nerve coming here like this, Stephen!" Beth's voice was now an angry hiss. She put her coffee cup down in her cup holder, her movements quick and jerky.

"We're both adults here. Can we just own up to our actions?" Stephen insisted, keeping his voice low and calm.

Beth crossed her arms over her chest. "Okay. You first."

Stephen was truly at a loss. He shook his head slowly in confusion.

"I know why you've been put on leave, Stephen," Beth broke his momentary silence with the force of her words.

"Oh?" Stephen had told Beth the basic story, but he had a feeling this went further than the glossed-over version he had given her.

"They're investigating you for a murder—a different one than Trevan's. You forgot to tell me that, didn't you?" Her eyes searched his face for the truth.

"Whose murder?" Stephen played dumb, but his mind was racing. How could Beth possibly know this?

"Anthony Gerritt," Beth announced.

"Beth, I don't know what you heard—"

"Don't lie to me!" Beth put a finger in Stephen's face.

Stephen shut his mouth.

"I know more than you think I know," Beth snapped.

"Clearly," Stephen answered. "But how do you know any of it?"

Now Beth was silent. She seemed to be searching her own mind for an answer. One that Stephen was sure she was in the process of making up. He thought he knew her so well, but he did not. Beth looked cornered, like a trapped rat.

"You talk in your sleep." Beth's eyes shot to the left, a tell. She was lying.

Stephen's heart sank and he nodded. "I see. But you still haven't explained why you installed a tracking app or why you followed me to the playground."

"I did no such thing—"

"Beth, I can see your movements, too," Stephen lied, not willing to out Mak. He wiggled his phone at her.

Beth shut her mouth and clenched her jaw.

"Who were you were talking to?" Beth asked.

Stephen wagged his finger. "Uh-uh, you first. Why did you follow me?"

Beth sighed. "Sometimes I miss you. I thought I would see if I caught you alone. Like you caught me today." Beth smiled weakly but her eyes darted left again.

Stephen cursed silently. The Beth he knew didn't lie. But now he was questioning how well he knew Beth in the first place. "What are you up to? How do you know those things about me?"

"So, you don't deny it?" Beth's look turned knowing. "You *are* being investigated for two murders."

Stephen looked around to ensure no one was within listening distance or watching them. "Keep your voice down. The less you know, the better. That was always my plan—to keep this quiet. Not to mention, I'm bound to keep these things confidential. If you knew half of what I knew, it would—"

"Put me in danger?" Beth asked.

Stephen's mind went to Alyah. "Yes."

"Don't you think me *not knowing* could put me in more danger? If I don't know what's going on, I won't know how to defend myself," Beth whispered.

"That wouldn't have been a problem. I always would have protected you." Stephen clenched his fist.

"There are some things you can't protect me from." Beth grabbed her keys abruptly, gathered her purse, and put her hand on her door. She threw it open and got out.

Stephen got out of the car too and stood to face her on the other side. He slammed the door shut.

"I have to make this deposit before they close. This conversation is over. We are over. Don't ever approach me in public like this again, Stephen." Beth turned and walked toward the bank, but not before hitting her auto clicker.

"Sure. Let me just uninstall this app so you aren't tempted to follow me again," Stephen called after her retreating back.

Before Stephen's thumb could hit uninstall, his phone rang. It was Mak. He answered the phone while he watched Beth disappear inside the corporate structure. He turned back to his car and headed to meet Mak.

A heavy, ominous feeling settled into his gut. Beth was lying. He just wished he knew why.

26

———————

MAK

Mak walked into the Police Station of Little Rock with Wilton right in step with her. Wilton had caught up with Mak over her quick family dinner of hamburgers. Mak had explained her conversation with Sikes. Then she'd pulled out her phone and handed it to Wilton.

"Call him," Mak encouraged. "I don't want to go back to work without you."

Surprisingly, Wilton took her advice. Sikes had apologized that they had suspected Wilton of murder. Sikes reinstated Wilton but put him on probation. It was the best that Sikes could do since Wilton's actions had warranted the disciplinary action. Wilton had accepted the olive branch.

But now, Wilton had to return the duplicated picture he'd stolen back to the police station. Despite Wilton being reinstated, Mak was feeling edgy about it. She wanted no part of Wilton's plan. Her gut told her to stay away from that, and she made it perfectly clear when Wilton tried to tell her his plan.

It was close to six in the evening when they pulled into the police station to meet Captain Higgins.

"It's kinda nice, you know..." Wilton hedged as he walked beside Mak.

"What?" Mak demanded, her mind on what Wilton was about to do next.

"That I can keep up with you now." Wilton shot Mak a smile that Mak was sure some young—or old—woman would melt for.

"Don't get used to it. I'm getting stronger every day. And save that smile for Constance. It's wasted on me." Mak's hand waved over Wilton's face.

"You're the one who didn't want to know anything about my plan." Wilton shrugged.

"I still don't. I told you before. This is one hundred percent—"

"My plan. Yeah, I know. You know nothing about it. I've got this, Mak. Trust me." Wilton shot her another grin.

That was the thing. Since Mak had come here to Arkansas, she had begun trusting Wilton a whole lot less. But she did have an appointment with Captain Higgins because she now had a job to do. They both did. She just would feel better if Wilton stopped towing the line of gray.

"Hi, Mak!" Constance greeted brightly when they walked through the door.

"Hello!" Mak responded.

"And hello to you, Stephen!" Constance batted her eyes.

"Hey, aren't you about done for the day?" Stephen grinned.

Constance nodded at him.

Mak pointed toward the elevator.

"Go on up, he's expecting you." Constance smiled at Mak.

Mak turned her back to them and pushed the elevator button to go up.

"Hey," Wilton said as he bent over in front of Constance's

desk. "This envelope was on the floor. Did you drop something?" Wilton's voice sounded behind Mak.

The elevator door dinged and flew open, drowning out the reply Constance gave him. As Mak got on the elevator, she saw Wilton hand the envelope with the picture in it to Constance. As the door closed behind her, Mak shook her head. That was it? Wilton's plan had been to pretend the evidence had been dropped on the floor and simply hand it back? Either Constance was gullible, or Wilton was that charming, because there was no way Mak would have been able to pull that off.

Mak got off the elevator on the second floor and found her way to Captain Roger Higgins' office. He waved her in before she could knock. Of all the law enforcement officers, Higgins was by far one of the easier ones Mak had worked with. So far.

"Afternoon, Mak," Higgins greeted. "Coffee?"

Mak shook her head. "All coffeed out for the day."

"Right, well come on in and sit down. I have a hunch this is going to be a longer conversation," Higgins said as he settled down into his high-backed chair.

Mak observed his office as she sat. It looked like a nuclear bomb had gone off. Papers were piled in a non-discernable way with messy stacks all over the top of his desk. There was a bookcase that lined half the wall, but Mak could see the books were dusty as if they hadn't been read in a century. At least she could see the floor. There was a walkway from the door to where she now sat down.

Mak supposed she shouldn't judge. She didn't really have an office back at the marshal building because she was always out in the field. Office work didn't suit her, and she refused to claim a space just to put her name on it.

"What did I miss?" Wilton asked as he came strolling around the corner.

"We were sitting," Mak said.

"Oh, okay." Wilton took the chair next to Mak.

"Mak here was about to fill me in on the news. Some criminal movement in our area," Higgins informed Wilton.

"Ah." Wilton turned expectantly to Mak.

Mak cleared her throat. "Right. Well, it appears Mickey Upton has been very busy lately building a compound of sorts less than an hour from us. Only, he's not building in broad daylight. He has construction crews that have been running all night long."

"Wow," Wilton said.

Higgins nodded. "Upton is wanted in conjunction with those four missing women you all found months ago—the Lacy Donovan case—correct?"

"Yes," Mak affirmed.

"Great!" Wilton said, half-rising from his chair. "Let's go pick him up."

"We don't know if Upton himself is making appearances there. A neighbor called it in and complained about the noise from the overnight construction crew. Said she couldn't sleep. When they pulled the permit, Upton's signature was on it," Mak clarified.

"In a residential neighborhood?" Wilton asked.

"It's just outside the neighborhood and zoned commercial," Mak answered.

"So, all we know for sure is Mickey Upton is building something less than an hour from here that has all the legal permits, and he might not even be on site?" Wilton continued.

"Yes, but if you remember, Anthony Gerritt did something similar. He started construction on his property management building before he actually came to live in the area. These guys worked together. It stands to reason that Upton might be following the blueprint," Mak mused.

"Where is this building located?" Higgins wanted to know.

"Sikes texted the location to me." Mak pulled out her phone and showed it to Higgins. "Here."

Higgins pulled on a pair of readers and squinted at Mak's small phone screen. "Hmm." He found his mouse under an avalanche of papers and jiggled it around. He hunted and pecked on his keyboard. "That's Faulk County in Conroy, about forty minutes from here."

"Well, let's go," Wilton said again.

"Hold on there, son." Higgins held up his hand. He picked up the phone. "I need to touch base with the police department there to collaborate."

"We usually just show up in person and announce our presence. We use the element of surprise." Wilton grinned.

Mak shot him a look and shook her head like a disapproving parent. Reinstated or not, Wilton was on shaky footing with the captain, given the suspicion Higgins had over Wilton's involvement in Trevan's murder. Before Wilton could respond, Higgins' phone started ringing. He put it on speaker.

"Pottstaff," came the gruff, direct answer.

"Hey, there, Sheriff. This is Captain Higgins over here at the Police Station of Little Rock—"

"Higgins, how the heck are you?" Pottstaff greeted. "Captain now? You got a big fancy title since we last talked."

"Yeah, I did… Listen, I need to give you a heads up on a criminal that may have been spotted in your county. Me and a few marshals are coming over to check it out tonight," Higgins told him.

There was a silence. Then Pottstaff answered flatly. "I see."

"You've got a known criminal who signed off on a little building project," Higgins continued.

"What do you mean by that? I think I would know if I had some criminal building an evil empire. It's not the biggest town. Who's the criminal?" Pottstaff scoffed.

"Micky Upton. There's an APB out for him in connection with a sex trafficking ring. I've got a document with Upton's signature on it for a building loan. We have cause to arrest the man on sight. I'm not saying that's what's going to go down, but I am giving you the courtesy of a heads-up that me and two US Marshals are coming to your county to observe the build," Higgins told him.

Mak listened as a string of curses erupted from the sheriff's mouth on the other end of the phone. "You listen to me. Senator Upton is a good man. I don't know how he got dragged into all this. But you mark my words, the man is innocent."

Mak's mouth fell open. *Senator?* she mouthed to Wilton.

Wilton shrugged, his eyes wide with surprise.

Higgins' eyes flicked to Mak and back to the phone in his hands. Higgins went silent for a second. When he finally spoke, his tone was not friendly, and his words were slow. "We have eyewitnesses that place Upton in an active role as a kidnapper guilty of sex trafficking. I didn't call to debate if the man is guilty or innocent. If you don't want to do your job, then I suggest you step aside and allow us to come in. We'd be happy to do it for you."

The pause on the other end was heavy. Finally, Sheriff Pottstaff grunted his approval. "Fine. Let me know when this little recon mission is going down, and I'll be there."

"Mighty kind of you, Sheriff," Higgins said with sarcasm as he hung up the phone.

"He's going to be a problem," Mak stated the obvious.

Higgins nodded. He regarded Mak with thoughtful eyes. "You know, Faulk County is forty minutes away from here. It might not be a bad idea for you two to tail Sheriff

Pottstaff. I got a hunch he might be in the old senator's pocket."

Mak drummed her fingers on the desk. "Since when is he *Senator* Micky Upton?"

Higgins stroked his beard. "It's been a good seven years since he was cast out of Washington. He wasn't charged with anything, but rumor had it, Upton was dirty enough that he was asked not to come back. He somehow got a get-out-of-jail-free card."

"Why don't we have any record of this?" Mak palmed her cell, texting Sikes.

"That's just it." Higgins shook his head sadly. "When politicians are disgraced but not convicted, it's all just hearsay and rumor. Nothing permanent goes on their record."

"It's like a pattern. The same was true for Anthony Gerritt. The guy was dirty as sin, but he had nothing on his record to show for it." Mak sighed.

"Keep your eyes up and watch your back," Higgins advised.

"Any other cliches you want to throw at us, Captain?" Wilton smarted.

"Yeah," Higgins speared Wilton with a look that said he knew more than Wilton thought he did. "Keep your nose clean, Wilton."

27

———

MAK

It was a dark, moonless night. Much like the one that occurred in the not-so-distant past that had changed Mak's foreseeable future. That night, Mak had stepped into a minefield that had been rigged to blow. She'd gotten lucky that the blast threw her backward instead of burning her alive. Unconsciously, she traced the place on her face where her skin had been charred. Mak shuddered at the thought of how close she'd come to losing her life.

"Cold?" Wilton whispered.

Mak shook her head but didn't elaborate. She never thought she would consider breaking her back good luck.

True to his word, Captain Higgins had gotten in the car and marched Mak and Wilton right into Sheriff Pottstaff's office just as the sun had started setting over the horizon. Sheriff Pottstaff, much to his credit, looked humbled and seemed apologetic. He explained that he had made a few phone calls and got up to date on the APB for Mickey Upton. While he was sad to learn of Upton's illegal activities, Pottstaff promised to be nothing but professional. His job, after all, was to catch criminals.

Mak didn't trust Pottstaff, nor did she believe a word that came out of his mouth. Her instincts were telling her he was dirty. But she would play along while keeping her guard up.

Now, they were all dressed in black from head to toe, lying on the ground, surveilling the night build through binoculars from a safe distance. The neighbor who had called in the noise complaint had not been exaggerating. There was no way anyone could sleep through this racket.

Several back-hoe tractors scooped dirt from one end of the field and dumped it around what looked like a concrete compound. *What are they building?* Mak wondered. A basement had already been dug, and the foundation had been poured. There looked to be four rooms sectioned off.

Mak tried to find a connection between this build and the place where Anthony Gerritt, Mickey Upton, and Boyd Allister had held the women in their previous case. She tried to remember Lacy's description of the Earth prison where they had kept her. But the details were fuzzy.

Mak only knew the women had been held underground. To be dropped in a hole under the Earth with no way to climb back up and see daylight sounded like Mak's worst nightmare.

As her mind continued to wander, Mak wondered if her lack of focus was a symptom of her brain trauma, but then she decided she'd always been antsy when she needed to sit still for a long period of time. Her eyes focused on what was already built of the compound. There were four rooms being built into the basement. Anthony Garrett had held four women. But Mak knew she was reaching for answers she didn't have at this point.

Mak could hear soft grunts and groans as the men around her shifted positions to make this surveillance more bearable for them. She had to remember that Higgins and Pottstaff were in their late fifties. But if Mak were honest with herself, she could feel her own body tightening up as well. She would check with her therapist tomorrow morning to see what her limitations were on lying in one place for too long. Wilton was the only one who seemed unphased by the stakeout.

They watched for hours as two men operated two heavy machines. One moved large quantities of dirt from one side of the field, and the other moved gravel and rocks, dumping them around the foundation and packing them around the house. Occasionally, Mak took out her phone and snapped pictures. As Mak's eyes got heavy, she changed her mind. Maybe the sound of consistent machinery would eventually make a person feel sleepy.

When it seemed nothing else would happen, and Mak considered suggesting they call it for the night, a large truck showed up with a long flatbed trailer filled with bundles of lumber. The driver backed the truck to the front of the compound, stopped the truck, and jumped out.

The sudden silence created a pitchy echo in Mak's ears.

The men driving the backhoes put them in park, turned them off, and jumped down from the cabs. They met the man who brought the lumber. They huddled for a brief conversation. Mak zoomed her phone camera in as much as she could to take pictures of them.

Then, one man jumped up into the trailer while the other men waited expectantly on the ground. The men fell into a routine of picking up bundles and setting them on the ground, making swift work of it until all the wood was unloaded and sitting in a pile beside the truck.

Mak scanned each man's face for recognition, but none of these men were Mickey Upton. She felt disappointment settle in her, though she shouldn't have expected Upton to show up and get his hands dirty. He wouldn't do that until he had a new round of women imprisoned here. Mak was convinced that was Upton's ultimate plan—whether it happened here or somewhere else. Especially as she considered Lacy's evidence that Upton was holding women somewhere.

When they were finished, the men talked for a few more minutes. Laughter rang out in the night. Then the men broke apart and left. Two of the men got into one blue Chevy pickup truck and drove off.

The other man stayed back a minute, surveyed the work, then he got in the truck with the now-empty flatbed trailer and drove away. For minutes, none of the officers said a word. When they had waited long enough to be sure no one was coming back tonight—or was it this morning—they wordlessly shifted off the ground and stood peering into the darkness.

Each of them did a dance of swiping dirt off their clothing, stretching, and rolling wrists and ankles. Mak was sure she'd be sore tomorrow. But this had to be the beginning of Upton's plan and seeing it in motion had made the stakeout worth it.

She felt excitement as she thought about the jump they had on Mickey Upton this time. With a bit of luck and a lot of skill, Mak thought they could stop Upton's business before it even started.

They'd put a plan in place before they'd come here. After the stakeout, they would go to the police station to confer on their next steps. Mak, Wilton, and Higgins rode in one car. The sheriff rode in the other. They followed Sheriff Pottstaff back to his station.

"There were four rooms poured in the basement," Mak broke the silence as they drove through the dark, early morning hours.

"Four," Wilton said the word aloud like he was puzzling it through.

"We rescued four women total from them on the last

mission." Mak filled in the blank. "Maybe they like to work with four women at time."

"More manageable that way?" Wilton brainstormed with her.

"We need to make sure they never use those rooms." Mak clenched her jaw.

They parked their cars, and the four enforcement officers trooped into the Faulk County Police Station. This station reminded her of the other small-town police department where they'd worked their last case. It was small, but clean with a skeletal staff milling around. Mak could smell coffee and could hear it percolating from somewhere in the building.

Once they convened in Pottstaff's office, Mak pulled out her phone and studied the pictures she'd taken. They were far away but clear. She zoomed in on the three faces of them huddled together talking. She turned her phone to Sheriff Pottstaff.

"Do you recognize these men?" Mak asked.

Pottstaff nodded. "Yeah, they own a commercial building company."

"Are they known to build at night?" Wilton asked.

"No, I reckon I've never known of any they've done like this." Pottstaff scratched his head. "A commercial build in a residential neighborhood where they work past two in the morning?"

"Are they reputable?" Higgins asked.

"They're upstanding guys," Pottstaff stated. "But then, I told you the same thing about Upton just hours ago. There's a good chance they're just following orders and don't know what they're building or that the man they are building it for is a criminal."

Mak nodded at his acknowledgement.

Wilton looked at Mak. "Maybe we can go have a conversation with these gentlemen."

Mak nodded. "Sounds like a good idea."

"They have lunch at the same diner at the same time every day," Pottstaff wrote down the diner address on a sticky note.

"Thanks, Sheriff." Higgins shook Pottstaff's hand. "Appreciate your help today."

Mak, Wilton, and Higgins left. They were in the car before Mak spoke again.

"You trust Pottstaff?" Mak asked.

"Not as far as I can throw him," Higgins answered, confirming Mak's feeling.

28

WILTON

The clock on the dashboard read 3:48 a.m. It had been a long night and Stephen was feeling it by the time they got to the Police Station of Little Rock. Mak had been oddly quiet the whole ride back. Maybe they were just tired or lost in their own thoughts, but Stephen felt a tension in the air he could not explain.

His guilty conscience kicked into overdrive. He had to admit, there was something about being in this town, walking in and out of this police station—the one he used to work for—that made him feel like he was regressing. He'd gone too far with the stunt he'd pulled with the evidence. Mak was right. But there was a defiant part of Stephen that just didn't care right now. He had to get to the bottom of his brother's murder.

He would even wager that Higgins knew about Stephen's games. Stephen knew Higgins well enough to know when Higgins was angry at him. To be fair, this cold demeanor his former employer was putting off had started when Trevan Collins had been killed. But Stephen didn't think for a second that Higgins believed he had killed Trevan.

When Mak stopped the car, Higgins opened the car door. He hesitated before he got out.

"Wilton. A word?" Higgins grunted. He got out and slammed the door shut.

Stephen opened his own door.

Mak didn't try to hide the yawn. "You need me to hang back?"

Stephen shook his head and grabbed his keys out of his pocket. "No, this won't take long. Let's touch base tomorrow?"

"Night, guys." She got in her car and drove away.

Stephen followed Higgins out into the cool night air. They walked to Stephen's Tahoe, and Stephen leaned against it. Higgins crossed his arms over his chest.

"Cards on the table, son," Higgins drew out the words slowly like he was tired and disciplining a toddler.

"Why?" Stephen asked, the word lined with an undercurrent of suspicion.

"Because it looks like we are going to be working together, and I need you to stop sneaking around my station and tampering with evidence." Anger was evident in Higgins' tired eyes.

Stephen pushed off the Tahoe and stepped into Higgins' personal space. "Well, I'm a little tired of people I care about and respect treating me like a common criminal when I get anywhere near a crime scene."

"Just doin' my job. You and I both know that even the best law enforcement officers snap and go off the deep end. You're connected to Trevan Collins. The evidence was pointing to you." Higgins defended himself.

"What evidence? Fingerprints on an envelope that had been stolen from me and planted in Trevan's duplex? My prints on Trevan's doorknob? There was an explanation for those things. Do your job. I should never have needed to call a lawyer!" Stephen's fists were clenched at his sides.

Higgins took several deep breaths in and out, making an effort to calm himself. "Fine," he snapped, looking like he had made a decision. "I'm going to give you a key piece of evidence that you might not have thought to look for. But if I do, I need your word that you will stand down, stay out of the evidence room, and keep me posted as you continue that personal investigating you're doing."

"Who says I'm investigating?" Stephen's eyes narrowed as he remembered Beth following him around. Was she talking to Higgins about Stephen's whereabouts?

"Don't give me some bull about changing your ways. This is personal. You don't stop until you find the truth when there's a personal angle," Higgins stated.

"You would do the same thing. Don't even try to deny it," Stephen's voice was getting louder.

Higgins scrubbed a hand over his short beard. "Do you want to know the piece of evidence or not?"

"Of course," Stephen said as he felt his jaw clench tightly.

"Your fingerprints aren't the only ones on that envelope," Higgins studied Stephen's face.

Stephen was shocked speechless as he processed this bit of information. Why hadn't he run the prints on the envelope himself? Now that very evidence was in the hands of his photo guy, Bernie Miltner.

"Who else?" Stephen asked.

Higgins held up four fingers and ticked two of them down as he named the suspects. "Trevan Collins, you, your girl-friend, Beth—"

"We broke up," Stephen said immediately. But he felt the back of his neck burn and his heartbeat picked up. "We broke up because of this! Good grief, Higgins. What if she's the one who stole the envelope out of my car? I've been defending her this whole time! Wait, you had her prints on file?"

Higgins gave a curt nod. "You can look up her background, and I suggest you do. Arrested a few years back for a DWI."

"And you didn't think that was important information to tell me?!" Stephen shouted. "Were you planning to arrest her, too?"

"You were never under arrest. I just brought you in for questioning, which you decided you didn't want to do and called a lawyer." Higgins put his palms up.

"Semantics," Stephen grumbled. "You and I both know what direction that was headed."

"It gets worse, Stephen. I need to tell you the last name on the list of suspects." Higgins rocked back on his heels.

Stephen felt his mouth go dry as his brain flipped through the possibilities. "Okay."

"Mickey Upton."

29

———

MAK

Mak was home, but just barely. After her stakeout, she'd crashed for less than four hours, then gotten up and went to her therapy appointment. She was so keyed up from the night's events, not to mention wiped out from so little sleep, that she had a hard time concentrating on the session.

She'd gotten home in time to watch John slip on his tennis shoes to go for a run. She'd kissed him goodbye, envious of his ability to just get up and go run like she used to do. It was something she'd never again take for granted. She missed it.

Now, she sat on a comfortable couch, staring out the window at the view of the Arkansas hills. She enjoyed the peace and quiet, knowing Harper would be asleep for hours. Harper wasn't a morning person. Mak pulled her knees up to her chest, grabbed her cup of coffee, and took time to process her therapy session. While her body was feeling stronger than ever, Mak's mind was a contemplative mess.

Dr. Mott sat quietly observing Mak. Mak hated all silence, and it was never long before she broke it and started talking.

"So, I have this partner—"

"Romantic?" Dr. Mott asked.

"No! He's my partner with the marshals."

"Right. Sorry, go on." Dr. Mott's voice was quiet and smooth as silk.

"Well, I'm starting to feel uncomfortable with his style of investigation."

"How so?" Dr. Mott asked.

"I always thought he was a Boy Scout type—a real rule follower. But since we've been here in Arkansas, he's been really playing in the gray. I'm not the most straight and narrow person myself, but he's really starting to push my boundaries," Mak's words tumbled out with frustration.

"Bingo, Mak. You hit it. Good job. Boundaries are the key here," Dr. Mott praised. "What are yours like with him?"

Mak had to think about it. "I guess I always pride myself on being a good partner, and I would even go so far to admit I might cross a line into personal life, and even friendship, with the people I work with. It's hard not to. We spend a lot of time on the job together."

"Has this ever been a problem before?" Dr. Mott asked.

"No. If anything, I think it's been a strength. For instance, I've dealt with PTSD in this career, and when I noticed my partner having some similar symptoms, I walked him through it." Mak felt proud of that one.

"Why do you think it was your job to help him with his PTSD?" Dr. Mott asked.

Mak felt confused. "I guess I was trying to encourage him to get help."

"Did he?" Dr. Mott asked.

"Not that I recall. I just thought I helped him, and he was fine," Mak stated, her mind a whir.

"Do you think you're helping him now? As he dabbles in the lines of gray?" Dr. Mott asked.

"No. I'm really not. If anything, helping him could really cost me," Mak admitted.

"But you feel conflicted?" Dr. Mott asked.

"Yeah, I mean, he's my partner and my friend. I told him I would help him."

"You can change your mind. Or help him in a different way. One that doesn't cost you anything," Dr. Mott stated.

Mak was silent as she thought through this possibility. It made her feel guilty.

"Some people say the only people we can help is ourselves," Dr. Mott continued.

"Huh," Mak said. Her whole job revolved around helping other people. But this was on such a personal level.

"In fact, there's a term for it. Detaching with love. You are pulling back and giving that person the dignity of making their own choices whether you agree with them or not and loving them no matter what they choose." Dr. Mott paused and made some notes on the pad of paper in front of her. She looked up. "How do you feel about that concept?"

"I'm not sure. It's a new one."

The words were still playing on a loop when John returned from his early morning run. With how little sleep Mak got the previous night, she should have gone back to sleep but her mind was racing. Mak looked at her husband, feeling love surge in her heart. She felt so grateful for him and knew what they had was rare. She also knew her ability to be vulnerable with him only strengthened the bond they shared.

"John, have you ever heard of detachment?"

John used his shirt to wipe the perspiration from his face that dripped off his sweat-soaked hair. Mak took the moment to admire his six-pack.

"It's taking a step back from a person. Putting up a wall

and walking away, right?" John asked, still breathless from his run. He took a long drink from his Hydroflask.

Mak pursed her lips. "Not exactly. It's more like a boundary than a wall. It's showing a person love and dignity by allowing them to make their own decisions and loving them from a distance."

John froze, his eyes focused intensely on Mak's. "What are you saying, Makayla? Are we okay?"

Mak laughed and got up to put her arms around John and kiss him.

"Hey!" John protested. "I'm all sweaty!"

"Exactly," Mak smiled smugly. "I don't need boundaries from *you*. I'm talking about Wilton."

"Oh!" John sighed in relief. "That's good. What's he done?"

Mak shrugged. "I don't like this line of gray he's toeing."

"The evidence tampering?" John asked, referencing yesterday's conversation.

"Yes. You know, I always thought he was such a Boy Scout. Like he'd never bend the rules. But he did, knowingly. And I followed him. Like an idiot."

"Not an idiot. You trusted him. He's never given you a reason not to. Are you afraid of accessory?" John asked.

Mak nodded. "That and it just doesn't feel right."

"You aren't a detective, Makayla. You've always been a marshal. You get a case, and you go get the bad guy. As I recall, that's all you ever wanted to do. You weren't interested in the investigation into who did it. You just wanted to know who the bad guy was and to bring them to justice."

"True, but there's so much crossover in this job. If the Attorney General says *investigate*, we investigate. So, it's a weak defense to claim *I didn't know better*. We're like back-up to law enforcement when they're overloaded. It's my responsibility to know the laws so I can enforce them," Mak paused and sat back down, crisscross applesauce. "I just feel like I should have known the implications and bowed out. I should have realized that since we've been here, Wilton has been different."

"Different, how?" John asked.

"I dunno. Just... the bending rules—"

"Or outright breaking laws," John corrected.

"Okay, yeah. Let's go with that. It's almost like he wants to mess with his old boss. The man he claims was his mentor. Did you know Captain Higgins fired Wilton from the police force?" Mak admitted.

John's eyebrows rose. "I did not. Why?"

"Anna had been kidnapped. Higgins told Wilton to stand down. Wilton refused," Mak sighed.

"You would have, too."

"Exactly." Mak threw up her hands. "But I do think there's some sort of unhealthiness in their relationship, and I need to see myself out of that."

"Detachment?" John asked, using Mak's original word.

"Yes!" Mak snapped her fingers. "I can help Wilton, but not enable him or jump in when he does illegal things."

"Good girl," John agreed. "I'm going to shower. You joining?"

"Umm, yes!" Mak was already stripping off her shirt as she followed John into the bedroom, where there was a nice, big master bathroom. As he turned on the hot water, she closed the door behind them.

30

LACY

The sound in the garage-turned-rage-room was deafening. Jonas had come through. He'd brought dozens of mason jars and empty boxes, which Lacy lined up against one wall. He'd found old furniture, broken computer hardware, toys that had seen their last days, and a used mattress in decent condition, all of which he set up in the center of the garage. He'd found a good old-fashioned punching bag with boxing gloves. He hung that from the ceiling in the corner. It was sectioned off like an organized rage room.

The look on the women's faces had been comical when Lacy told them the plan.

"You want us to break glass?" Isa asked dubiously. "On purpose?"

Lacy nodded with excitement. "I want you to think of what makes you the angriest and throw it against that wall. The glass will break and fall into the box underneath. It'll be a great release to any pent-up anger."

"And you want us to hit this... junk?" Emma asked as she looked around at the chaotic mess laying in the center of the garage. Emma's finger trailed over the bat standing against the wall.

"Yes. Again, it's a great stress release," Lacy encouraged. Then she watched as Emma picked up the bat, put her hands over her head, closed her eyes for a second, then opened them and hit the mattress. In that moment, something seemed to unleash inside her. Emma screamed and hit the bat repeatedly into the mattress until she collapsed on the floor and cried. Tears streamed down her face.

Now, they were all breaking glass, hitting, kicking, and punching things. It was so loud, Lacy almost didn't hear Jonas walk up. He stood surveying the action quietly. Then he caught Lacy's eye and crooked his finger at her.

Lacy followed him up the stairs and into the house. He shut the door, leaving it cracked a little.

"Wow, it's really working, huh?" Jonas' eyes were shining with excitement.

Lacy nodded happily. "I finally think they're starting to tap into their feelings, thank God! It was really eerie around here. They're just so quiet!"

"Well, they aren't quiet now!" Jonas exclaimed. They could hear the loud sounds of crashing and yelling through the walls.

Lacy shrugged. "Maybe we can soundproof the walls?"

"Yeah," Jonas appeared to be thinking it through. "My uncle had a garage band once—"

"Literally?" Lacy smiled.

"Literally. They played in the garage, but his wife complained it was too loud. They hung egg cartons on the walls, and it muted the sound."

"Egg cartons?" Lacy asked. "You are full of creative solutions."

"Don't get too excited. That's a lot of egg cartons to find," Jonas pulled out his phone. "Oh, I almost forgot the reason I pulled you out of there. Your lead panned out. They were able to track down a new build in Arkansas with Mickey Upton's name on the loan."

"Did they find him? Is he behind bars?" Lacy grasped Jonas' forearm.

"No, not yet. But it's a good sign. They are watching for him now. They think he'll show up when the build is finished. I just wanted to tell you, good job on tracking him." Jonas took her hand off his forearm and held it a minute before placing it down by her side.

"Well, I am multi-talented." Lacy wiggled a happy dance.

Jonas' face turned pink. "You're killing me, Lace."

"Sorry." Now Lacy's face turned a shade of red.

They both spun when Bacon cleared his throat behind them in an obvious way. Bacon looked from Jonas to Lacy and back. Then he motioned for Jonas to follow him.

"Shit," Jonas whispered.

"Sorry," Lacy said, looking contrite. She watched him go for half a minute, pondering why all the good things in her life still seemed so far on the horizon. Then she turned back to the rage-room garage and joined the women who had found some loud heavy metal music to assist with their rampage. It was hard to feel bad when they were making such huge progress here.

Still, Lacy wondered how long she and Jonas were going to have to pretend that nothing was happening between them. Thinking about Bacon's reaction, perhaps it wouldn't be too much longer now.

31

___

WILTON

When Stephen woke, it was past noon. Somewhere around dawn, shortly after Stephen returned from the stakeout, Stephen had sent Beth a text:

Stephen: *We need to talk.*

Then he had buried his head under a pillow and willed himself to go to sleep. But the words Higgins had spoken were haunting Stephen. Beth was involved in this somehow. Why did she have to be involved? More importantly, why did Stephen keep choosing the wrong women?

Unless... Beth wasn't involved. Was there any logical explanation for why her fingerprints were on that envelope that would be innocent? Maybe she had been in Stephen's car and put her hand under the seat to grab something she dropped and had found the envelope instead. Maybe she never mentioned it because she was waiting for Stephen to bring it up.

If Stephen had learned anything in this past six months, it was just because someone looked guilty, it didn't mean they were. *Look at me,* he thought. *Though I had zero involvement, I've been accused of two murders with convincing theories on why I was supposedly involved, using just a few pieces of evidence here and there.*

Stephen sat up in bed. He remembered his lawyer's theory. She had said it looked like someone was trying awfully hard to set him up. But he refused to think who that might be. Someone who had been close to him. He lay back down with a long sigh. All roads were leading back to Beth.

Beth, whose sister had been kidnapped and held underground. Stephen still didn't have clearance to tell Beth that Lacy was alive and well. Beth was as much a victim in all this as Stephen was. Wasn't she?

Stephen felt around for his phone. It was on the nightstand where he'd left it on his charger. Beth had texted back.

Beth: *Not a good idea. I have nothing to say to you.*

Stephen sighed and typed out a longer text back. He thought about it, deleted it, and tried again.

Stephen: *Come on, Beth. I really don't want it to end this way. You mean a lot to me. Remember the coffee shop where we re-met? Call it closure… I just really need to talk to you.*

Stephen tried to ignore the way his conscience poked at him. He knew he was using their relationship to get back in front of Beth. But he had to know. He had to look her in the eyes and ask her about the connection to that envelope. Maybe even her connection to Mickey Upton. But most of all, Stephen wanted, no needed, to know if anything they'd had was real.

Beth: *Fine. I'll give you an hour. Meet me there after I'm off work tonight. 6p.*

Stephen: *See you then.*

Stephen sat up and swung his legs over the bed. It was unusual for him to sleep until noon. Especially with the bright sun streaming in the way it was. That stakeout must have really worn him out. Before Stephen could stand and head to the shower, his phone rang.

He glanced at his screen. It was Sikes. Stephen resisted the urge to ignore the call, because he didn't really have a reason to avoid Sikes anymore.

Stephen answered the call. "Wilton."

"Wilton, hey! Glad I caught you. Now a good time?" Sikes asked.

"It's fine." He stood up and looked out the window.

"Good, I know I went over this briefly on the phone yesterday afternoon, but I have more news."

"I'm listening," Stephen replied.

"Good. We're going to fully reinstate you."

"What about probation?" Stephen asked, not wanting to get his hopes up.

"No more leave, no more probation. We ran the ballistics on the bullet that killed Anthony Gerritt, and they don't match any gun that is registered to you. Unless you have an illegal weapon lying around," Sikes laughed rhetorically.

Stephen didn't find his joke humorous. "No, of course not. But it took you over five months to run ballistics and determine that?"

Sikes was silent. "This was an investigation, Wilton. We had to rule out every possibility before we put you back on duty. Are you ready to come back?"

Sikes had apologized on the last call for everything. Stephen had no reason to say *no*. But he knew he would have a hard time forgiving and forgetting. Despite that, he knew his answer. "Yes, I'm ready."

Sikes was quiet for another half second. "Great, we have some exciting movement in your area, and I need you to be part of the team. Let's talk more in depth later."

"Looking forward to it, sir." Stephen ended the call, walked into the bathroom and yanked back the shower curtain. He turned on the faucet to the hottest setting, letting it warm up while he brushed his teeth. His thoughts drifted. *I hope I can get over this false accusation sooner rather than later,* he thought. Because he still felt anger simmering just below the surface.

As he stepped in and let the hot spray hit the muscles in his body that were sore from lying prone in one position all night, Stephen realized what was holding him back. Did Stephen rejoining the marshals mean he'd have to clue Sikes in about his recent whereabouts and possibly admit to the other ongoing investigation?

Honesty didn't seem like the right route today.

32

—————

MAK

Mak and Wilton were sitting in the diner for lunch in Conroy. Wilton had called her here, claiming he needed her insight. It was a two-birds situation, as it helped them get eyes on the men from the construction company they had been watching last night. Now, as Mak perused the menu, she wondered why Wilton could possibly need her insight. These days she didn't think he liked her opinions much.

"What are you getting?" Mak asked, having trouble deciding.

"Double-decker burger," Wilton replied, sipping his coffee and looking distracted as he stared out the window.

"Hmm, looks good minus the onions and tomatoes," Mak murmured. She raised an eyebrow when she noticed Wilton had missed an opportunity to zing her because she didn't like some food he did.

By the time the server came to take their order, Mak had spotted the construction crew. She recognized some of the men from last night. Mak thanked the server and handed her menu back. She tried to think of the best way to handle them. On one hand, if she and Wilton started asking too many questions, it might spook them, and they might report it back to Mickey Upton.

She watched the server retreat to the kitchen. She scanned the diner again. It was a basic little hole-in-the-wall establishment. Mak had to double check the address when she pulled up because there was no discernible sign out front. It looked like a little white house. When she walked in, she noticed black booths with brown tabletops. A few tables lined the floor. Black cushion seats matched the booths. It was clean and it was busy. In fact, there was no way Mak would be able to hear the construction crew if she tried.

Mak had to lean forward to hear Wilton over the buzz of voices when she noticed his lips were moving. Was it that loud in here? Then she realized Wilton was just mumbling.

"What's going on with you?" Mak asked, looking Wilton in the eyes.

Wilton tore his gaze from the view of the parking lot and looked at Mak. "Higgins gave me some new information last night. I'm processing it."

"Does he know about the tampering—"

"Yes," Wilton told her curtly.

Mak's eyes bulged. "Are you in trouble?"

"I'm always in trouble with Higgins," Wilton snorted. "He's like my dad, and I'm a rebellious teenager. I swear I regress ten years when I return home."

"Huh," Mak acknowledged his comment. It was good to know Wilton was aware of his behavior. "So, Higgins is going to—"

"Look the other way," Wilton interrupted impatiently.

"Oh!" That surprised Mak. "So, what are we here to talk about then?"

"Beth," Wilton stated. He seemed nervous and agitated. Mak was curious but remained quiet.

"Her fingerprints are also on that envelope," Wilton admitted.

Mak slapped the tabletop. "I knew it!"

Wilton held up a hand. "Before you go celebrating your brilliance, there's more."

Mak made a motion like she was zipping her lips.

"Mickey Upton's fingerprints were on it as well." Wilton stared at Mak.

Mak opened and closed her mouth, utterly speechless for once. The food arrived and Mak dug into her Reuben. Wilton took a big bite of his burger.

"So, Beth and Upton are connected," Mak stated what she thought was obvious.

"No way!" Wilton said with his mouth full. He choked a little, took a drink of water, and swallowed his food. His eyes were watering.

"You okay?" Mak asked.

Wilton nodded.

"So," Mak was feeling more patient than usual. "What's your theory then?"

Wilton shrugged. "That envelope was under my passenger seat for a long time. Beth rode in my car. Maybe she leaned down and found it one day. But when she looked at the picture, she freaked out, didn't want me to know she'd seen it, and put it back without talking to me."

"Okay," Mak drew out the word. "How would it get from your car to Trevan's duplex? I'm pretty sure Upton didn't take it from your car. Beth has to be the missing link here. She's your transportation mule."

"I don't buy that for a second," Wilton argued. "I'm meeting up with her tonight."

"Are you just gonna waltz up and ask her?" Mak's mouth fell open. "Why would she tell you if she took the envelope?"

"Because of this." Wilton slammed a file on the table.

"Did you just pull that out of your back pocket?" Mak smirked as she pulled the hefty file to her. She opened it. Pictures of Mickey Upton in various stages of his life, from being sworn in as a US Senator, to meeting with a group of important-looking men, to dinner with a beautiful woman, were all stacked neatly inside. Underneath that was a court transcript of when Upton's integrity was called into question. Mak flipped through the pages, scanning and reading. She paused to look up at Wilton. "Where did you get this?"

"Sikes reinstated me—fully. I'm off probation now. I had him send this over." Wilton tapped the page in front of Mak.

"That's great news."

Wilton continued. "I wanted to have all the case files to help me get up to speed."

"You just ran down to your local UPS store and printed all of this out?" Mak asked, her eyes still skimming the court transcript.

Wilton rolled his eyes. "Don't get me started. I had to access the secure portal and connect wirelessly to my mom's printer. Meanwhile, a tech took over my computer to check for security breaches. It was a whole thing."

"So how does this file get Beth talking?" Mak asked.

"This woman," Wilton thumbed backward and pulled out the picture. "Is missing. Women who hang around with these guys tend to go missing."

Mak looked closer. "She's pretty. Tall, willowy, blond, just like the women they like to take."

Wilton nodded. "I figured Beth might like to know more about who he really is. Just in case they have met and there's a connection."

"So, you *do* think she's working with him!" Mak exploded. She got a couple surprised looks from the tables around them. "Sorry."

"If so, only incidentally. Her office is in a bank. Maybe

she made a connection. Like Mickey Upton is a client… I'm not sure. But she deserves the chance to explain how her fingerprints got on the envelope," Wilton said. He took another bite of his burger, then dipped his fries in ketchup.

"Why?" Mak hissed. "Beth is looking more guilty by the minute. If you don't see that, then you're in denial. If you aren't careful, you're about to spook her and let her get away!"

"What happened to innocent until proven guilty?" Wilton challenged. The back of his neck was getting red.

"That's in a court of law! What's your gut saying?" Mak argued.

"That she's an innocent victim in all of this—whatever *this* is," Wilton stood his ground. "She's had a rough year. Her sister was taken, and I'm still not at liberty to tell her that Lacy is fine."

Mak stilled, her mind suddenly racing.

"Mak, what now?" Wilton asked.

"This all started with Beth," Mak whispered, her eyes wide as her brain tried to make the connections. This was usually Wilton's area of expertise though, not hers.

"What?" Wilton snapped.

"Beth is the one who called you to tell you her sister was missing. Only, how would she have known Lacy was missing when Lacy never even told them where she lived? Beth could have called anyone, but she called you. Someone she hadn't talked to in over a decade. What if she was intentionally trying to pull you in to all this?" Mak was picking up speed and excitement as she spoke.

"That's ridiculous," Wilton scoffed. "She assisted in her own sister's kidnapping?"

"Wouldn't be the first time." Mak gave Wilton a knowing look.

"Then, what? Why would she need to involve me?" Wilton asked.

"To set you up. You were going to be the fall guy," Mak said, her eyes getting big. "Didn't your lawyer think you were being set up? What if Beth is the one who set you up?"

Wilton pulled out his wallet, grabbed some cash, and threw it on the table. "I wasn't aware we were playing make believe here." He rose angrily. "That's quite an imagination you've got there."

Mak pulled out her own cash, estimating the ticket with a tip since the server hadn't made it back with that. She stood next to Wilton. She sighed as she watched the construction crew all get up and leave the diner. "You need to consider that Beth could possibly be guilty before you make your next move. You have a track record with this stuff."

"What stuff?" Wilton's eyes narrowed.

"Let's just put it out there. You have terrible taste in women. It's like you gravitate to the worst possible female in the vicinity." Mak was following Wilton out of the diner now.

"Hey!" Wilton objected. "I'll have you know—"

"Hold on!" Mak held up a hand as they approached the door. Mak ticked her head to the side to direct Wilton's attention to the parking lot. Sheriff Pottstaff had pulled up and was now talking to the construction crew.

Wilton's eyes followed her direction.

Casually, Mak tore off a flyer attached to the glass door of the diner. She stared at the headline as she walked out the door. "Have you ever been to a rodeo before?"

"What?" Wilton looked at Mak like she'd lost her mind over her abrupt subject switch, then he glanced at the flyer.

Before Mak could answer him, they were outside.

Sheriff Pottstaff stood in the middle of the group of construction workers like he was showing them something on his phone. Before Mak could determine what he was showing them, the group of men started laughing.

"I take it he's not asking them official questions," Mak grumbled.

Pottstaff looked up and spotted them at that moment. His amusement faded and he cleared his throat. The guys standing around him looked up.

"Good to see you guys," Pottstaff said, clearly attempting to dismiss them. But Mak was having none of it. She walked right up to them.

"Afternoon, Pottstaff," Mak greeted. She turned to the crew. "I hear you fellas were up pretty late with that building project of yours."

The group fell silent, and a strained awkwardness fell.

"Oops! Where are my manners?" Mak made a show of patting down her pockets. She pulled a badge out and showed it to the men. "I'm US Marshal Mak Cunningham, and this is my partner, Stephen Wilton."

"US Marshal?" A man in the group spoke. Though he addressed Mak, his eyes fell on Pottstaff.

"You didn't tell him about the noise complaint from running those machines late into the night?" Mak asked jovially.

Brows furrowed and a few men crossed their arms. Another man spoke up. "Thought you said we were clear to build whenever we needed to, Sheriff."

Pottstaff's face turned a deep shade of red. He chuckled casually. "Did I really say *any* time?"

A few men nodded their heads.

"We'll figure out the details later." Mak waved her hand side to side like it didn't really matter. "Is there a reason your boss needs you to build at night?"

Now there was some visual shifting from foot to foot

happening. After the silence had gone on long enough, the same man who had spoken before answered.

"Look, ma'am, we don't know why he specified we build at night, and we didn't ask. He was just very specific about it, and we wanted to win the bid. So, we agreed to it."

Wilton stepped up. "What's your name?"

"Connor Dewie. I own this company," he pointed to the logo on his shirt that said Dewie Construction.

"Thank you for that information, Connor," Wilton said in a professional tone. "How often do you talk to Mickey Upton?"

"Not often. We spoke at length before the project started, and we've talked a few times since. Why? Is building at night going to be a problem?" Connor had no idea he'd just confirmed any lingering doubts that Upton was in charge of their project.

"Not sure yet," Wilton responded. "My questions might end up being for him. Do you know when he's due to arrive in town?"

Connor scratched his head. "He told me he'd be here for the rodeo, opening night. It's a pretty big event around here. We have some big name bull riders coming to town that night. That's all I know though."

"Do you plan to meet with Upton while he's in town?" Wilton asked.

"No, no plans to meet." Connor shook his head.

"Huh," Mak said with curiosity in her voice. "Seems like he'd make it a point to meet you all when he's in town."

Connor shrugged. "We just do the work we're commissioned for."

"Right." Mak agreed amiably. "Well, I hope you guys enjoy this warm weather we're having today."

The men nodded and shuffled off to their trucks.

When the construction crew had pulled out and the three of them were alone, they turned back to Pottstaff.

"You gave them permission to build at night?" Mak asked Pottstaff, not wanting to mince words.

Pottstaff shrugged. "I didn't realize it was going to be a problem."

It wasn't lost on Mak that Pottstaff had failed to mention his permission last night, but she filed the information away.

"Surprised you mentioned Upton." Pottstaff changed the subject. "Aren't you afraid you'll tip him off and make him run?"

"Should I be?" Mak asked coolly, her tone even.

Pottstaff wagged his head back and forth. "You're the one tracking a criminal. Who am I to question your ways?"

"Well, thanks again for your help last night," Wilton cut in abruptly. "Reach out if you hear anything else about Upton's whereabouts."

"Will do." Pottstaff turned his attention to the diner. "Going in for lunch. Care to join?"

"No, thanks, we just finished up," Mak declined.

"Alright, see you around." Pottstaff walked into the restaurant.

"What's going on in that head of yours, Mak?" Wilton asked as they walked to their cars.

"You heard Connor say Upton is planning to come to town. That's ballsy for someone who has a warrant out for his arrest," Mak hissed.

"Do you think Upton knows he's wanted?" Wilton asked.

"I would think so." Mak frowned. In her hand, she still held the flyer she'd ripped off the window. She uncurled it and read the title. "Tri-State Championship Rodeo."

"I've seen that look on your face before," Wilton said. "You're plotting something."

"I was just thinking. If Upton plans to show up..." Mak began.

"Let me guess," Wilton pointed to the flyer in Mak's hand. "You think we should go?"

Mak nodded once.

Wilton tipped his head to the side and studied Mak. "Proceed carefully. I'd be surprised if he's unaware that we're onto him. Him showing up to this event would make him either highly arrogant or stupid."

"But he told someone he'd be there," Mak stood her ground.

"Mak," Stephen stated. "I think it's a real long shot that Mickey Upton, a former senator and wanted criminal, will be hobnobbing at a rodeo."

"Hobnobbing?" Mak laughed.

"Hobnobbing," Wilton confirmed with a grin.

"Well, I have a good feeling about this," Mak insisted. "If Connor was telling the truth, and my hunch is he was, Upton will be at that rodeo."

"There goes that imagination of yours," Wilton tapped his head and opened his car door.

"Hey, Wilton?" Mak stood, looking uncomfortable.

"Yeah?" Wilton waited.

"You might want to consider telling Sikes about what's happening with Trevan's death and the possible lead on Beth Donovan."

"Not yet." Wilton exhaled loudly.

Mak held his gaze for half a second before she turned and walked to her car. Her gut was churning. Was there a reason Wilton didn't want Sikes involved?

Mak pulled out her phone and dialed her husband as she got in the car. "Hey, babe. Have you ever been to a rodeo?"

33

MAK

Mak had hidden herself away in the extra bedroom of the Airbnb they weren't using in an effort to concentrate on facts rather than using her imagination, as Wilton challenged. Harper was watching TV, and John had gone out to get some groceries. The house was quiet, so it was the perfect opportunity to get a clear picture of who was who in this case. But Mak felt frustrated. Her head was fuzzy as she tried to piece something—anything that made sense—together. She got the feeling she was missing an important fact that would bring it all together, but her brain wouldn't let her remember. Was this the new normal for her? Life after brain trauma?

Mak had reached out to her contact at the marshals' office and had him do a thorough background check on Beth Donovan. Which is why Mak was now looking at every run-in with the law that Beth ever had in her life.

The results were surprising. Beth had multiple infractions from age twelve to sixteen. Then there was nothing until a year ago when Beth got a DWI. It left Mak scratching her head.

"So, Beth was a troubled child. Got into trouble for four

years and then just stopped? Did she spend time in a child rehab facility?" Mak mumbled. To Mak's knowledge, troubled kids didn't just get better. "Maybe I should do checks on her parents…"

A knock at the door interrupted Mak's train of thought.

"Makayla? I'm back," John cracked the door.

"Okay," Mak said, still staring at the pieces of paper all over the bed.

"Whoa, what's all this?" John asked, peeking in.

"Just doing a little investigation of my own," Mak explained. She picked up a piece of paper. Beth had been caught shoplifting a cell phone. Mak wondered if this had been her first offense. She needed to organize these by date. Inwardly, she groaned. *Ugh! Wilton would be so much better at this than I am.*

"Looks… messy," John stated. He didn't try to come closer or read the information.

"Just like the situation Wilton is in right now." Mak didn't crack a smile at her clever comment.

Mak knew John would treat this as confidential and she didn't have to worry about him snooping through this stuff. Harper, on the other hand, was a nosey little thing. She was just learning to read, too.

"Let me guess—this is you distancing?" John asked.

"Yeah. I'm just doing my own due diligence while Wilton is off doing his." Mak scanned the pages again. Then she picked up the second file of info she had requested. She'd bought file folders. The tab she'd written said, *Trevan Collins.* She opened the file and thumbed through it.

"Having another difference of opinion?" John leaned his body against the door frame.

Mak nodded.

"You're having a lot of those these days," John

commented as he watched Mak lay out more papers on the bed.

"Yeah. This is personal for him. I don't think he can see anything objectively."

"But you can?" John asked gently.

Mak shrugged. "I'm not sure. I'm just following my gut."

"What does Sikes think of all this?" John wondered.

"Haven't talked to him about it yet," Mak admitted. She shuffled a few papers around and stared hard at them. She let out a small gasp. There was an incarceration date that matched for both Beth and Trevan. "Underage drinking," she read aloud in a whisper. A thought occurred to Mak. She remembered the file she had requested from Higgins the other day had been Davey Stinnert's.

"John, can you hand me my purse?" Mak asked pointing to the chair in the other room.

John spotted it, grabbed it, and brought it to Mak. Mak grabbed the folder out of her purse and thumbed through Davey's file.

"Aha!" Mak reacted after finding a similar report for the same date. So, Beth, Davey, and Trevan were all connected in some small way after all. And it went back to their childhood.

"Mak, about Sikes—"

"It's not my story to tell!" she interrupted him impatiently. She knew her frustration had nothing to do with John's questions and everything to do with her indecision about what to tell Sikes. *Tell him, or not tell him, that is the question.* For now, Mak was entertaining herself just fine by requesting and attempting to analyze these background checks. She would have requested a file on Wilton's brother, but she thought that might throw up too much of a red flag. Unless… She'd bet Captain Higgins could quietly get her that file as well. This is the exact town where his life was ended after all. They had to have the file in the archives.

They were quiet for minutes, each one lost in their own thoughts. Finally, Mak, never one for long silences, broke it.

"I'm sorry." Mak closed her files and walked to John. "You wanna go get a cowboy hat and Western clothes with me?" Mak looked at her husband, but her mind was still processing the connection between Beth, Trevan, and Davey. She made herself walk out of the room and shut the door.

"Western clothes?" John asked, his eyes doubtful. "Like boots and Wranglers?"

"Sure!" Mak answered.

"I want a cowboy hat!" Harper's voice sounded excitedly from the couch where she looked up from the TV.

Mak laughed and sat down beside Harper. Harper jumped on Mak's lap.

"Ooomph!" Mak grunted.

"Harper—easy! You know you have to be careful with your mom!" John reprimanded their energetic daughter.

"Actually, I feel pretty good," Mak said in wonderment. "That didn't cause any pain."

"That's good news," John said. Still, he shot Harper a look. "You still can't jump on mommy!"

"Ah, man!" Harper grumbled. "Can I get a cowboy hat?"

John looked from Mak to his daughter. "When in Arkansas... I guess we better."

"Yay!" Mak and Harper shouted together.

A half hour later found them at a local Western store. Mak had taken a pile of clothes into the dressing room with her and Harper. She came out with a long-sleeved, button-down shirt with lace on the front, a pair of bootcut jeans with bling on the back pockets, and an off-white cowboy hat.

"Try on this cowboy hat, Harper." Mak had tossed the hat to her daughter.

"It's a *cowgirl* hat, mama!" Harper had corrected Mak.

Harper had her own matching cowgirl hat in her size and a pretty, flowered top.

John joined the girls just as Mak put her foot into the most comfortable boots she'd ever worn. There was a pretty design woven through them, most of which would be covered by her boot cut jeans.

"Wow, I could run in these. They're called Ariats. They're as comfortable as tennis shoes!" Mak said as she walked around the aisle in them.

"Those are pretty, mama!" Harper said. She promptly found a pair of her own cowgirl boots and tried them on.

"Very nice," John said. He held his own set of clothes.

"Very expensive!" Mak gasped as she caught sight of the price tag.

John shrugged. "Well… we are on vacation, after all."

"Oh yeah?" Mak smirked at him. "Maybe someday we can go on a vacation where I don't have to work."

"You are the one choosing to work." John grabbed his own pair of boots and put them on. He groaned like he was in heaven. "Wow! These are nice and comfortable!"

"Look at our boots!" Harper cried. "We're a cow family!"

Mak laughed as she gazed at her own boots. She sat back down next to John. "These are on the list of things I never thought I'd buy in my lifetime."

"You could really run down a criminal in those babies," he whispered as he pointed to her shoes.

"Let's hope I don't have to," Mak whispered back.

As they waited in line to pay for their rodeo gear, Mak watched Harper crawl under clothing racks and giggle when anyone walked too close.

"Think Wilton could send for Anna and Anna could have a sleepover at the grandparents on the night of the rodeo?" Mak asked.

Harper wasn't too far away to hear Mak's words. "Anna!" she shrieked.

"Well, you better move fast on that one," John said. "This rodeo is coming up quick."

Mak picked up her phone and texted Wilton.

Mak: *Think your mom would be up for a playdate/sleepover for Anna and Harper this weekend?*

Wilton: *Seems quick but I can ask.*

Mak: *Great! You in for the rodeo?*

Wilton: *Umm… you were serious about that???*

Mak sent Wilton a picture of her new Ariat cowgirl boots in response.

Wilton: *Just wow. SMH!*

34

WILTON

Stephen checked his watch for the fifth time. Beth was officially a no-show. He cursed and felt his pulse beat faster in frustration. He left the coffee shop on quick feet and got into his car. He wouldn't let Beth blow him off. He drove to her duplex, half expecting to see her car in the driveway. It wasn't.

"Hmm, might be a waste of time to knock on her door," Stephen mumbled. Still, he turned off the car and went to the front door. He knocked but noticed it was dark inside. There was no movement coming from inside the house.

He supposed if the house was dark and empty, no one would care if he looked in the windows. Stephen looked around, then casually went to the side window and attempted to see in. It was dark and only confirmed what he thought. There was no movement inside.

Stephen felt a tingling sensation crawl from his neck down his spine. He felt the outline of his gun through his jacket and turned slowly. Was someone watching him?

"Guilt," Stephen muttered. "That's the feeling of guilt." Still, he felt spooked and quickly walked back to his car.

"Okay, maybe she's not ghosting me. Maybe she's working late."

He started his Tahoe and backed out of the driveway. As he drove slightly out of his way to pass by the bank where she worked, he began to feel concerned.

Stephen hit a drive thru and was about to pull up to his parents' house when his phone rang. Without thinking, and assuming it was Beth, he quickly grabbed his phone. He was so startled by the name on his display screen that he dropped the phone. He eased his car into his parents' driveway, shut off the engine, and grabbed the ringing phone from where he'd dropped it.

Stephen answered the phone. "Alyah."

"Stephen? Hi, how are you?" Alyah's voice sounded chipper and upbeat. Almost suspiciously so. Too upbeat.

"Alyah? Are you okay?" Stephen's heartrate doubled when a thought occurred to him. He hadn't heard from Alyah since Mak's accident. She was calling him for a reason. And he wasn't foolish enough to hope it was romantic.

"Hey, yeah... I'm okay. But I wanted to check on you. How are you?" Alyah's voice lost its perk and now she sounded more authentic, more concerned.

"I'm okay. Got a lot going on at the moment." Stephen scratched his head. "Though, I'm guessing you called me for a reason..."

"Umm, yeah. Listen, I thought of you today because, well, you know I work for the Attorney General up here. We see bolos and APBs all the time. I saw one come across the desk a few weeks ago. I didn't think much of it until I became part of a conversation at lunch today when his name came up."

"Whose name?" Stephen asked. But he knew before she answered.

"Mickey Upton," Alyah breathed.

"Ah yes, that makes sense. We just learned he's a former

senator. What's the gossip on him?" Stephen wondered. He relaxed his grip on his phone. Alyah wasn't in danger after all.

"Mickey Upton is dangerous, Stephen. The senators at the table today were expressing surprise that he hadn't ended up behind bars. He was not only dismissed from his position as a senator, he left Washington, DC, in total disgrace. There was enough question of what happened that he wasn't re-elected for another term."

"What happened?"

"He found himself in the middle of this scandal. There were lots of rumors that he had a network of girls and—"

Stephen heard her take a long, shuddered breath before she continued.

"He was running an escort business of sorts. Like hooking women up with other prominent people—important people. Then he was using that to blackmail those people in power." Alyah paused like she had more to say.

"Do you know where or how he got the girls?" Stephen asked, realizing that the more they understood about Upton's process, the better chance they would have to catch him.

"That's the thing, Stephen. They were rumored to be underage," Alyah dropped her voice. "Then a girl disappeared. Everyone thought she had been murdered. But there was no body and no evidence. You just need to know... This guy is really dangerous, Stephen."

Stephen nodded. This didn't surprise him. What did surprise him was why Upton wasn't behind bars for this. "That's awful, but it doesn't surprise me. We have eyewitnesses that name his involvement with kidnapping and a possible sex-trafficking ring."

"Oh my gosh! This is the case you're working, isn't it?" Alyah gasped.

"It's a continuation of the case we were on when you

came to visit me, yes. It's why I called to warn you to be careful and stay on guard," Stephen admitted. "But I didn't know about Upton's involvement, or that he was a former senator. Do you know why he wasn't convicted of any of this back then?"

"No, but I can look around," Alyah suggested.

Stephen wanted to tell her *no*. He wanted to warn her to stay as far away from this as she could. But it would really be helpful to know more. His emotions and logic warred within him.

"Stephen? Are you still there?" Alyah's voice broke into his thoughts.

"Listen, Alyah. Above all, I need you to stay safe. I want to tell you to drop it and stay away. But the other part of me thinks we could really use whatever information you find. Can you be discreet?" Stephen asked.

"Of course," Alyah agreed. "I'll let you know if I find anything."

"Thank you," Stephen said, expecting to hang up the phone.

"Stephen?" Alyah sighed.

"Yeah?"

"Are you okay?"

"I'm fine."

"No," Alyah dragged out the word, cutting through his trite answer. "How are you, really?"

Stephen dropped the act. "I've been better. There's a lot going on here, but I'm handling it." He paused and thought about Beth. He thought about Anthony Gerritt's murder, about Trevan Collins, and then his brother, Greg. He suddenly felt overwhelmed and tired. He had no business getting involved with anyone at this point in his career. It had only dragged these women into his messes—which seemed to be getting bigger by the week.

"I miss you," Alyah admitted. "Are you seeing anyone?"

Maybe it was a moment of weakness for her, but Stephen knew no good would come out of admissions such as these. Not from her. He couldn't handle her wishy-washy emotions right now. He was barely handling his own.

"Look, Alyah, I'm sorry. I have to go." Stephen hung up the phone before she could respond, trying to squash the guilt over his reaction. If he was being honest, he was dealing with more than the cases in front of him. Her voice, even over the phone, when she was so far away, did strange things to his heart.

He shook his head as he grabbed his fast-food bag, got out of his car, and headed to his parents' house. Alyah was a door to his past he needed to keep shut. The sooner he moved on from her, the better. Maybe that needed to be his new stance on relationships in general.

Before he reached the door, Stephen caught movement out of the corner of his eye. He whipped around and drew his gun in one quick motion. There, standing on the sidewalk twelve feet away, stood David Stinnert.

"Hey!" Stephen yelled, but David was already running.

Stephen dropped his food bag on the porch, holstered his gun, and jumped down the two stairs in one leap, landing flat-footed on the ground. His parents' house was on a slope and the momentum threw him forward. Stephen stumbled and landed on his knees. He was up in a flash and gave chase, but David already had too far of a lead on him.

Stephen sprinted, but David jumped a fence that led into a small, wooded area. By the time Stephen got there, the moonless night cast too many shadows. With the lead David had on him, Stephen knew he wouldn't catch him now.

As Stephen walked back to his parents' house, trying to get his heart rate back under control, he couldn't help but think of all the times lately that he had felt himself being watched.

So, David Stinnert was stalking him. He could remember the last time a criminal stalked him. It hadn't ended well. But then, David wasn't really a criminal after all. Why would David stalk him?

Stephen could think of several reasons. None of them were good.

35

BETH

Beth felt like she was floating on a dark sea of unconsciousness. Here, her critical brain argued with itself. *What were you thinking anyway, Beth? Did you really think you could control both sides?*

In the beginning, when she first tracked down Stephen Wilton's phone number and called him, she was thinking if anyone could help her out of this mess, it was him. Only, Beth hadn't been honest with Stephen because she never felt like she could trust him. She couldn't. It had been the theme of her life. Beth could not trust anyone but herself.

When Lacy went missing, Beth thought her life was over. She knew why they had taken Lacy. They—the Corruptors, her childhood tormentors—had targeted Lacy. They had given her a place to live and kept Lacy close until the moment they chose to make her vanish. It had all been to keep Beth in line. The same way they had used Lacy to control Beth when Beth was in high school.

If you don't do this, Beth…

If you don't do that, Beth…

You have a daughter to think about, Beth…

She regretted not allowing her parents to legally adopt Lacy. But keeping Lacy as hers was the one thing Beth had clung to like hope for the future. Beth was Lacy's mother and as soon as Beth had her life together, she'd planned to take Lacy and start her own life somewhere far away where no one would find them. But that had never happened.

Beth opened her eyes, which felt gritty and raw. There was only darkness that surrounded her. A big, empty expanse of nothingness to gaze into. Her head hurt—pounded in a way that made her feel sorry for people who got regular migraines.

Beth reached up to touch the tender spot at the back of her head, but found her arm was stuck—both of them were pinned to her sides. She moved them with more determination and felt a pinch of pain. She yanked harder, thinking maybe she was tangled up in blankets or sheets. But she could hear a soft *clank, clank* noise. That's when she stilled and let the cold, hard sensation of metal under her arms and around her wrists sink in. She rolled her wrists to discover there was not much wiggle room between her and whatever was holding her in place.

Pure horror occurred over the realization that Beth was handcuffed to a chair in a room that smelled dank and moldy, like wet earth. Being held in a tiny cellar so dark she could not see or make out figures in front of her sent her into a panic. She knew where she was, which accelerated her anxiety. She'd never been here as an enemy, only as an ally. She knew what the Corrupters did to their enemies. Unbidden, a picture of Trevan popped into her mind.

"Help!" she screamed. Her words echoed and bounced around the tavern-like cave room. "Someone, please help me!"

Then she waited and listened to the way her words landed flatly. There was no sound. She moved her feet, surprised to find them unbound. That was going to be a big blunder for her captor. Maybe this was one gigantic mistake. One she could fix immediately.

Beth was an overthinker. She always had been. She had taken time—countless hours of her days, which had turned into weeks and months—to process and contemplate where she had gone so terribly wrong in her life. She didn't believe in playing the victim like the others in her group did—the Delinquents. Life had dealt her a terrible hand, and she had been trying ever since to make the best of it. There was a point where she had accepted her fate and had determined who she was, choosing to embrace the dark path fate had her on. She wasn't special and neither were the others. If they had all accepted it the way Beth had, maybe they wouldn't have fought it so hard. Maybe they would still be alive.

Beth had figured out how to play the game. She had allowed herself to be a pawn in an army that had grown much bigger than herself over the years. At the same time, Beth kept an eye on her group.

We've got each other's backs, they used to say. They'd made pacts to always protect each other first and foremost. Protecting the siblings was secondary. All she had to do was stay in control of all the moving pieces. It was a dangerous balancing act. One that Beth had perfected.

Until the day Trevan Collins admitted that he'd found an incriminating photo, stolen it, and given it to Stephen Wilton. Greg's little brother, Stephen Wilton, had grown up to be a cop. Then he'd become a US Marshal. Beth didn't think she would have to protect Stephen anymore. In fact, she'd fantasized that Stephen could save her—save them all. But Stephen Wilton was a liar. The very worst kind. He pretended to be a good guy. But he had his own secrets. Beth knew Lacy was alive because Upton had told her. The one thing Stephen had promised to let her know was if anything developed with Lacy. But Stephen didn't keep that promise.

Stephen hadn't killed Anthony Gerritt. Beth knew a lot of things thanks to Upton and the recent group meetings she and the others had been forced to attend. Anthony Gerritt had his own agendas and had become egocentric. Gerritt wanted to take over everything. But when Lacy escaped and the other women were rescued, the brunt of that mistake fell on Gerritt. When Gerritt was taken in for questioning and the cops immediately released him, everyone knew Gerritt had made a deal. Because Gerritt only cared about himself, he would do anything to remain free. Even become an informant. That was the last straw. They took Gerritt out before he could take down the rest of the organization.

Beth had been faithful to the Corrupters. Which is why she was sure her being tied up in this prison was a mistake. She just needed to explain the mix up.

"Help!" Beth screamed loudly again. Only this time, she didn't stop screaming. She screamed as loud as she could for as long as she had it in her. She yelled obscenities and threats.

Finally, she heard loud echoey footsteps against the epoxy floor. She knew what the floor was made of because she had been here before. When the Corrupters called them in, this is where they met. The *tap, tap, tap* of shoes on the ground stopped a few feet in front of her. Then, Beth heard a loud click before a hot light flooded down on her.

"Hey!" she squealed in protest, blinking rapidly at the sudden intake of bright light burning into her retinas. She couldn't see who was in front of her, but this person was going to regret treating her like this.

"Shut your mouth! Stop screaming, sit still, and wait for your sentence!"

Beth didn't recognize the voice, but she wasn't surprised.

Upton loved to send idiots to complete his tasks. Only, this guy was about to go down.

In a deadly calm voice, Beth cleared her throat and spoke. "I think you have the wrong person. Better go double check your instructions, because I'm with Upton."

Beth felt it before she saw the hand smack the side of her face so hard her head flew to the side. Pain and heat radiated over her cheek bone. Tears stung her eyes and threatened to fall. She willed them back in. She would not show this man weakness.

"Turn off the light and hit me again. I dare you!" Beth said through clenched teeth, anger evidence in her voice. She didn't feel fear, only a deep determination to live.

The light turned off, and after blinking a few times, Beth could see the outline of a tall, muscle-bound man standing in front of her. When he came close enough again, Beth shot to her feet, picking up the chair off the ground. Using the element of surprise, she spun the chair with all her power and slammed it into the muscled man, throwing him to the ground. She stood in front of him, arms still bound to the chair, and used a free foot to kick him in the stomach. She reared back to kick him in the face when a voice interrupted her.

"That's enough," a deep, angry voice snarled in the darkness, drawing out his syllables with a slight southern drawl.

"Upton. Nice of you to show up. You know you can skip the binds if you want an audience with me," Beth sassed, her heart pounding in her chest from the rush of adrenaline and activity.

Loud clapping echoed as Mickey Upton stepped forward. "Impressive."

"What the hell, Upton! What is this?" Beth spat out. She still stood with the chair bound to her.

"Surely you of all people can understand the need to be

sure the people on the team are loyal," Upton's lips pulled up in a sneer.

"Loyal?" Beth was instantly mad. "Let me tell you about loyalty. I've done nothing but your bidding since I was sixteen years old. I've sacrificed everything. Not to mention, Trevan... Who brought you that photo?"

"Yes, you brought the photo to me because I asked you to *after* I had Trevan followed and learned where it ended up. Let's talk about that photograph and the person who had it." Upton pulled out a folding chair from a dark corner Beth had not been able to see and sat calmly across from Beth. "Please, sit down."

"I'd rather stand, thanks," Beth said as defiantly as a teenager. Though she could admit to herself that standing with a chair attached to her was getting uncomfortable.

"My confusion about your loyalties began when I noticed the US Marshal was sharing your bed. Tell me what reason you would possibly have to buddy up with the very enemy who has the authority to take us all down?" Upton drummed his fingers on the chair in a nonchalant way.

Beth wasn't fooled by this laid-back act. She'd seen Mickey Upton kill a man in front of her with his bare hands for defying him. Not to mention that she was fairly certain Upton had killed Trevan.

Beth reluctantly put the chair back on the floor and sat up tall, ready to spring up and move fast again if she needed to. "You know what they say about keeping your enemies close."

"You're lying," Upton hissed. He drew a gun.

"A gun?" Beth asked. "That's your weapon of choice for me? Is that how you killed Trevan?"

"That wasn't me," Upton said.

"I call BS on that," Beth argued boldly, looking Upton in the eye.

Upton shrugged. "You should worry about yourself right now. I only have one reason to keep you alive."

Beth gasped. She could see it in his eyes. She knew what he was about to say. "No."

"It's the only way to know you're truly loyal to me and no one else. We'll exchange you for Lacy. See, you and this US Marshal cavorting together doesn't sit well with me. I can understand if you like him. Maybe he's nice on the eyes, maybe he's good in bed, but I think it's more than that. I think you were looking for someone to protect you."

"That's so 1950s of you, Mickey," Beth sneered with more venom than she had in her. "Maybe you don't realize women can protect themselves these days."

Upton rolled his eyes and guffawed his disbelief.

Beth felt anger surge through her. She leaned up with challenge in her eyes and sweet sarcasm in her voice. "Tell me again, how did Lacy get free?"

Upton moved fast. He was on Beth before she had time to comprehend his intention. Beth's head snapped back as Upton's fist landed between her eyes. Beth blacked out and came back to consciousness in time to feel the pain explode in her jaw as Upton followed his first hit up with a powerful hook to her face. Beth's chair flew to the side and landed on the floor. Beth's hand was pinned under the steel arm of the chair, with all her weight on top of it.

The pain in her hand was so sharp and overwhelming, Beth instantly felt nausea rise. She threw up the contents of her last meal before she passed out.

One last thought flitted through her mind. *What I wouldn't give to go back to the beginning. Well, not the beginning... to six months ago, when the nightmare amped up... When everything spiraled out of my control.*

36

BETH

Six Months Ago…

Rhythmic, frantic thumping sounded at her front door, waking Beth up out of a solid slumber. Rain pattered loudly on her roof. Thunder erupted, and a bolt of lightning illuminated outside her windows. Beth squinted at the clock. It was two fifteen in the morning and still dark outside, save the flashes from the storm.

For a minute, she lay there wondering if it was the rain that had woken her. But then she heard it again. Knocking at the front door. Fear shot adrenaline into her veins, and she jumped up. No good came of phone calls or door knocks after midnight.

Beth rushed to the door. She looked out her peephole to find Trevan Collins pacing on her doorstep, wearing a black hoodie and looking over his shoulder. Beth opened the door and pulled him in quickly. She crossed her arms over her t-shirt, thankful she'd worn sweatpants to bed.

Trevan slammed the door behind him, wordlessly handing her an envelope. She opened it and pulled out a picture. Her hands trembled as she touched it. It was a picture of the night Greg was killed. The background was blurred. *Thank God,* she thought.

"Where—where did you get this?" Beth whispered, fear downloading into her heart. She looked around to be sure her blinds were closed tight.

"Doesn't matter. I'm taking it to Greg's brother—"

"Why?" Beth hissed. "Why would you do that?"

"I can't do this anymore. High school was one thing. We were young and dumb. We thought we didn't have a choice. We know better now. Wilton deserves the truth." Trevan paced around like a trapped animal, leaving wet footprints on her Pergo flooring, the whites of his eyes showing up in the dark as he looked around wildly.

"No!" Beth protested. "Wilton can't help with this. No one can. Does this have to do with the meeting?"

"Yes. That meeting changes everything. The Corrupters left us alone for years. But now..." Trevan shook his head. "All of those men together in the same room, coming together for the worst kind of evil and trying to pull us into that? Peddling drugs was nothing compared to this. I can't be associated with that. Can you?"

Beth felt tears spring to her eyes. "No, but this isn't the solution." She shook her head and tapped the photo. "This will get you killed."

"Maybe it's better than the alternative." Trevan's chest rose and fell. His eyes pinned Beth with a meaningful stare.

Beth shuddered, knowing exactly what he meant.

"Wilton might be the answer to fixing this whole messed up situation. I'm giving him this photo. I just thought you should know my plan."

She had no time to argue or talk him out of it. Trevan left her staring at the closed door for minutes after he disappeared through it. There had been no stopping him.

When she'd met Stephen that first time in the coffee shop, she had been as surprised as he was over their instant connection. She hadn't anticipated the attraction she'd felt, nor did she expect Stephen to ever trust her. So few people had. But Stephen did, and that had shocked Beth. It was in that moment she remembered her promise to Greg and to the others—to keep each other safe and the siblings protected. She owed it to Greg to protect Stephen and keep him close.

At the point that Stephen came back to her with hearts in his eyes and zero information about Lacy, Beth had tried to gain back control of the situation, but it backfired. When Upton had called Beth.

There's an envelope with sensitive information that I need you to find and bring to me. Upton had commanded.

That's vague, Beth had responded. *What's in the envelope?*

It's a picture of a crime occurring, Upton hedged.

How did this photo come to exist? Beth had gathered her courage to ask.

Uh-uh, young one. You don't get to know the whole story. Just your piece of it.

I see, and how is this my piece? Beth had kept her voice neutral and felt nauseated asking the question.

Upton had laughed. *I think you know exactly what I'm talking about and where it is. You have twenty-four hours to procure and deliver it. Otherwise, bad things will happen to the one you love.*

Beth had always done her best to protect herself and Lacy, but all those efforts had failed. Without the knowledge that Lacy was safe, Upton still owned Beth. She had no choice but to comply. He was right. She did know where that envelope was. It hadn't been hard to steal.

"Here!" she'd flung it at Upton the next day. "If this doesn't prove my loyalty to you, I don't know what will. Release Lacy."

Ever so slowly, Upton had taken the picture out and gazed at it, his face expressionless. Then he looked up at her with those dark, dead eyes. "Where did you find this?"

"It doesn't matter," Beth responded. "This proves my loyalty. Now let Lacy go."

Upton smiled. "How does this prove your loyalty?"

Beth gritted her teeth, thinking fast, using her relationship with Stephen. "I found this in US Marshal Stephen Wilton's car."

"Good girl," Upton purred. "Do you know how he got it?"

"No," Beth snapped.

"How do I know *you* aren't the one who gave this to him?" Upton challenged.

"I didn't!" Beth put a hand to her chest, horrified over his implications. Then she replayed his words. *Good girl.* Upton had asked her a trick question to check her honesty. "But you already know it wasn't me, don't you? Do you follow us around?"

"I do like to keep tabs on my workers." Upton's lips curled into an ugly, arrogant smile.

"Well, I've passed your test. Release Lacy."

Upton eyebrows shot up. "Given your involvement with the marshal, I'm surprised you don't already know…"

"Know what?" Beth asked, her heart sinking. Stephen had information he hadn't given her?

Upton smiled. "She escaped. Your Lacy is already free."

Beth was relieved but horrified at the same time. If she'd known Lacy wasn't a hostage anymore, Beth would have had more of a choice. She wouldn't have had to retrieve Upton's evidence. He had preyed on her assumption that Upton was still holding Lacy captive.

Her anger turned to Stephen. If he'd told her the full truth, not hints and riddles, Beth could have avoided this. She was so tired of being played as a pawn. She'd been at

Upton's beck and call yet again but this time for no reason. That was Stephen's fault. Not knowing for sure if Lacy was alive had been frustrating, a source of resentment Beth had harbored against Stephen from the beginning. But this—knowing he'd kept it from her—had doomed their relationship.

37

WILTON

Stephen stared up at the ceiling long past midnight as he wondered what would make Beth agree to meet with him but then not show up. She could have said *no*. Most likely, Stephen had been pushy, and Beth only said *yes* to get him off the phone. Stephen was no stranger to rejection. Far from it. But this—Beth ghosting him—gave him a bad feeling.

Maybe he would drive by her work tomorrow to make sure she made it in. Perhaps her car was in the shop, and she was using other ways to get around town. Since she kicked Stephen out, he really didn't know what was going on in her life. With this new tentative plan, Stephen finally let himself fall asleep.

The next morning, he woke before the alarm on his phone went off. He showered, grabbed coffee, had a quick chat with his parents, then headed out the door. It was after nine and Stephen knew what time Beth would be at work, so he drove straight over.

He frowned when he noticed Beth's car wasn't in the parking lot. He debated driving to Beth's home to see if she had called in. But something made him turn off his car and walk into the bank. Casually, and with a friendly smile, Stephen approached the bank teller.

"Good morning," she greeted, looking a little frazzled.

"Good morning." Stephen gave her his most charming smile. "I'm looking for Beth Donovan. Is she available to help me?"

"You and everyone else. I've been fielding calls for her all morning," the woman grumbled quietly. Then she quickly masked her expression into a blank one, looked contrite, and answered with professionalism. "I'm afraid Beth isn't available at the moment."

"Oh?" Stephen checked his wristwatch and put on a puzzled look. "That's odd. I had an appointment with her for 9:30 a.m. If it's okay with you, I'd be happy to wait. I think I'm a few minutes early."

The woman's mask slipped again, and she looked over her shoulder. "Look, Ms. Donovan isn't available because she didn't show up for work today. I'm sorry about your appointment. Is this about a loan? Maybe someone else could help you?"

"She didn't show up to work?" Stephen didn't have to pretend his surprise. "She seems more reliable than that. Is she sick? I would be happy to reschedule when she's well."

"Mister, I don't know if she's sick because she failed to let us know she wasn't coming. You know what I know. Now, is there someone else who can help you?" she repeated with a clenched jaw.

Stephen shook his head. "No. Thank you. I'll try back tomorrow."

Stephen left and sat in his car for minutes. What now? He started his Tahoe and drove by Beth's house. He frowned. There was no car in the driveway. He kept driving and found himself at Mak's Airbnb.

Without much thought, Stephen stalked to the door and knocked rapidly. He could hear loud music coming from within. He rapped harder on the door. When no one answered, Stephen turned the doorknob and walked into loud pop music and John cooking at the stove.

"Come on in," John invited, noticing Stephen when he looked over his shoulder.

"Stephen!" Harper squealed while jumping on the couch.

Harper and Mak were having a loud, animated dance party in the living room.

"Should you be dancing?" Stephen asked Mak, feeling concerned.

"What?" Mak yelled.

Stephen found the eyes of an amused John. "Should she be dancing?"

John smiled. "Ask her. She got good news today. It's omelets, mimosas, and a morning dance party to celebrate."

Stephen shook his head and wandered into the living room.

"You have to dance if you come in here," Harper sang.

Stephen took two quick steps backward.

Mak laughed and finished off the song before she turned the music down.

"John says you got good news?" Stephen asked.

"The best!" Mak grinned. "I've been released. Cleared to go back to work."

"Wow!" Stephen was surprised. "Congratulations!"

"Thanks!" Mak said as she grabbed a glass of bubbly orange juice. "Mimosa?"

"Umm, sure," Stephen agreed. He didn't feel much like celebrating because Beth was missing. In fact, that's why he'd come over. He needed his partner's advice. He was at a standstill—with everything. The case of who killed Trevan and framed him, the cold case of who killed his brother, and now Beth's disappearance.

"John's making you an omelet. Do you like bacon, ham, cheese, and onions?" Mak asked.

"Yeah, that all sounds good." Stephen eyed a closed door he assumed was a bathroom and headed toward it. "I just need to run to the restroom." His hand was on the doorknob and turning before Mak called out.

"Second door on the right."

But Stephen was looking into the spare room and what was covering the bedspread. File folders lay open and old handwritten records had been pulled out and were laying side by side. He saw the familiar names—Trevan Collins, Beth Donovan, Davey Stinnert, and Greg Wilton.

Stephen slowly reached down for his brother's file. He thumbed through it. He scanned the report detailing his brother's death. None of it was a surprise. The report mirrored what he'd been told his whole life. Eyewitnesses reported hearing an argument in the park. They testified to seeing Davey Stinnert with a gun in his hand. One of them even went as far as to say Stinnert pulled the trigger. But the eyewitnesses' names had been sloppily redacted. Big, ugly black sharpy had drawn over their names. Stephen picked up the paper, turned it over, and held it up.

"Damn," he muttered. He had hoped he could see their names through on the other side. There was so much information here. It would take days to go through it.

"Stephen!" Mak's voice snapped at him.

Stephen looked up.

Mak was standing in the door with her hand over her mouth and her eyes big. "I didn't mean for you to see all this."

"Well, now I have." He looked back down at his brother's

file and thumbed through it. It was surprisingly light for someone who everyone claimed was a big troublemaker. But then, Mak had pulled some information out. He looked up at her, silently waiting for an explanation, surprised by the calm he portrayed when his emotions were jumping all over the place.

"I wanted to get some facts and process this objectively," Mak admitted. She stepped into the room.

"Because you think my emotions have my judgement compromised," Stephen stated this as a fact.

Mak shrugged. "Your brother was killed. David Stinnert takes the fall, who knows why. Trevan gives you an envelope with incriminating evidence about his death. Then Trevan gets killed." Mak crossed her arms over her chest.

"And Beth?" Stephen asked, picking up an incident report with her name on it. He scanned the report. "Underage drinking?"

"There's more." Mak took the page from Stephen's hand and lined up four similar reports. "All of them—Beth, Davey, Trevan, and Greg were busted for underage drinking on the same night. See." Mak pointed to a date on each of the reports.

Stephen followed her finger. He stood silent as he slowly scanned one report, to the other, then the other. Until minutes had crawled by.

"Stephen, I'm sorry I—"

"Shh!" Stephen interrupted her. He moved his finger to the signature line on all four reports. "Look at that."

Mak leaned forward and peered harder. "It's a pretty messy signature—" She gasped suddenly. "Obediah Pottstaff!"

"It might be time to visit our new sheriff friend and have a conversation," Stephen decided.

"Soon," Mak agreed. "Wait, you're not mad?"

"Oh, I'm not happy." Stephen finally looked her in the eyes. "You did this without me. We're supposed to be partners. It feels like you went behind my back."

Mak had the decency to look ashamed.

"Where did you get all of this?" Stephen asked.

"Most of it came from our office. But I got Greg's file from Higgins," Mak stated.

Stephen pulled out Beth's file and thumbed through it. "Huh, she was a little troublemaker, wasn't she?"

Mak shrugged. "Seems like childish stuff. Stealing from the grocery store, egging someone's house, you know, stupid kid pranks. Thank God no one was watching me this closely."

Stephen's eyes snapped up to Mak. "Say that again."

"Thank God no one was watching me that closely."

Stephen grabbed each file and shuffled through them. After a few minutes went by, Stephen fanned out all their reports, side by side. "They all have a minor infraction or two, all before this one incident, right here." He tapped Beth's underage drinking report.

"So, this scared them all straight?" Mak suggested.

"Wait," Stephen pulled a page from Beth's folder. "Until she was pulled over for a DUI six months ago. Beth isn't a drinker."

"So, you think something happened that made her drink and drive?"

"Not sure. I came over here to tell you that she's missing, by the way. Beth is." Stephen put the papers back in their appropriate folders and laid them back on the bed.

"What do you mean, missing?" Mak tilted her head to the side.

"I mean, I can't find her car. She's not home and she no-showed work today. Not sure where else to check," Stephen admitted.

"Do her parents live around here? Would she go there for any reason?" Mak scratched her head.

"They do live around here, somewhere. I've never met them. She didn't talk about them a lot. But good call. Maybe I can find their address and drive by."

"Why are you looking for Beth?" Mak asked.

"She promised to meet up with me last night but ghosted me. It might have made me angry, so I went looking for her. She wasn't home." Stephen didn't mention his creepy encounter with David Stinnert.

"You could try using that stalker app she downloaded to your phone," Mak suggested as she led the way out of the room.

Stephen stopped short and stared at Mak. "I completely forgot about that." He pulled his phone out. He had planned to delete the app but hadn't. "What are the chances that she stayed connected on her phone..."

Stephen found Beth on the app. "Gotta go." He rushed toward the door.

"Want me to go with you?" Mak asked.

"No."

"Bathroom is the next door down if you still need it," Mak pointed down the hallway.

"Right," Stephen followed where she pointed. When he came out, John was holding an omelet on a paper plate for him.

"Breakfast to go?" John asked.

"Yeah, thanks!" Stephen's stomach grumbled. Gratefully, Stephen grabbed the plate and headed back to the Tahoe. On a whim, he pulled up his app and took a screenshot of Beth's location. There was a little caution symbol by Beth's number that said *low battery*. Stephen didn't want to lose her trail if her phone died.

From what Stephen could see on this app, Beth wasn't at

her parents. It was a remote location on the outskirts of town. Stephen remembered the area from growing up around here. He also remembered that area had always given him creepy vibes, but he never knew why. He hoped today would not be the day he discovered the answer.

38

WILTON

Stephen was standing in an open field with wheat that brushed against his ankles each time the wind blew. Beth's red compact car was parked off a dirt side road. But there was something fishy about her car. It was parked at a precarious angle—half on the road, half off. The front left tire was in the ditch. The right front tire was on the side of the road. Both back tires were on the road as well.

"Maybe her tire went flat?" Stephen mused. He walked around checking the tires. Nothing was amiss. He scanned the side of the car. He stood in the wheat field studying the car. Nothing was out of the ordinary there either. There was nothing visible that would have made her pull off the road.

It had taken Stephen an hour to track down Beth's phone, and it had led him here. To her abandoned car. His heartrate spiked two times—once when he identified her car and a second time when he realized she wasn't in it.

"Her phone must be in her car." He stepped forward and peered in the windows. Her car was clean. No sign of a struggle. No purse. No phone. He walked all the way around the car again, peering in.

"Okay." Stephen pulled out his phone and checked the app again. There was an option to get directions. Despite the caution sign that said the battery was at 15 percent, Stephen followed the map that popped up on his phone. He circled the car several times before he dropped to his knees and peered under the car.

There, lying face down in the dirt under her car, was Beth's phone. Not too far from that were her car keys. Stephen's heartrate tripled. Did Beth get pulled out of her car, struggle, drop her things, and get pulled into another vehicle?

Stephen opened the driver side door and sat down. He put the keys in the ignition, turning it far enough to check her gas gauge.

"Half a tank. She didn't run out," Stephen said, which might have been a logical reason why she would take a ride with someone else.

Stephen took out his phone and called Captain Higgins.

"Stephen," Higgins greeted him curtly.

"Hey, Higgins. Sorry to be the bearer of bad news, but Beth Donovan is missing," Stephen stated.

His statement was met with a brief silence. "What do you mean, missing?"

"I mean, I thought she ghosted me last night when we were supposed to meet for coffee. I drove by her house last night and today. I didn't see her car. Then I went into the bank where she works but she no-showed today—"

"Do I need to say this is sounding—"

"Stalker-ish. Yeah, I know how it sounds. But, I pulled up Life 360—"

"What?" Higgins roared.

"Would you please just let me finish?" Stephen requested tersely. "Beth put an app to track me on my phone when we were together. It backfired when I found out about it because

I can track her, too. Well, I found her car, her phone, and car keys all on a side road in the middle of nowhere. She's not here. Her car looks abandoned. I don't have a good feeling about it." Stephen ran his hand through his hair.

"What's the nearest town?" Higgins asked.

"I was heading toward Weableu," Stephen admitted.

"Son, that's not the best area," Higgins' voice held hesitation.

"Tell me about it," Stephen agreed.

"Well, you have any leads? Is there anything that tells you which direction she went from there?" Higgins asked.

Stephen let out a growl as he looked around and found acres of wheat fields in every direction he could see. "No. No clue."

"What's your plan?" Higgins asked.

"Drive on into town and ask around, I guess."

Higgins was silent.

"Let me guess. You don't think that's a good idea."

"You know as well as I do that folks around there are mean and suspicious. It's a meth town. They don't like police or law enforcement poking around. Even if they saw Beth, do you think they'd tell you?" Higgins challenged.

"Good point," Stephen was sweating. It wasn't from the warmth either. At the moment, Beth was officially gone.

"Now, what I can do is put out an APB and talk to the police station there in Weableu." Higgins rustled paper around.

"And her car? What do we do about that?" Stephen wondered. "I almost want to leave it and the keys where they fell on the off chance she returns and needs a quick getaway—"

"Or if she returns from a ride she voluntarily took down the road with someone," Higgins inserted. "Maybe we can get back out there and dust for prints. Do you have a piece of clothing of hers? Maybe we could take the dogs out and have them sniff around."

Now it was Stephen's turn to be silent. He turned away from Beth's car and stepped back up onto the main road. From his slightly higher vantage point, Stephen scanned the fields.

He understood with clarity what Higgins wasn't saying. They needed to consider all possibilities. Was Beth's body lying discarded somewhere in those fields?

39

WILTON

It took less than an hour for a search party crew to show up. While he waited, he'd taken a walk around the perimeter himself. The sun was warm, and he felt anxious about what they might find. Stephen was impressed that Captain Higgins had moved that quickly. They had agreed to keep this mission quiet and limit it to a team of detectives and dogs to stay off the radar of the drama-loving town nearby.

Stephen had called Mak after his conversation with Higgins. For Mak, Stephen had a special request. When Higgins pulled up, Mak was the first to hop out of the passenger car she'd ridden in with Higgins. She approached Stephen with a jacket in her hand. It was one that belonged to Stephen that Beth had worn more than once.

"I see you'll ride shotgun with Higgins," Stephen muttered grumpily.

Mak waved the jacket at Stephen. "You're welcome."

"Yeah." Stephen took the jacket and held onto it until the K-9 unit showed up. He remembered the last time Beth had worn this.

Stephen had smiled at Beth, who had emerged from the

bedroom wearing jeans, knee-high boots, and Stephen's heavy jacket with flannel lining. The jacket hit her petite frame mid-thigh.

Is it really that cold out? Stephen had teased her.

The look in Beth's eye had told Stephen he needed to tread lightly. *Yes! Nights can be deceptively cold.*

We're just going to dinner, Stephen had answered. He'd grabbed his car keys off the table by the door.

You don't want me to wear it? Beth had pouted, suddenly looking so unsure.

I'm sorry, Stephen had replied as he pulled her into his arms. *It looks great on you. Much better on you than it does on me. Please wear it.*

Beth had snuggled into his arms before they'd walked out the door.

The pain of that memory, knowing what they had hadn't been real, was a present-day reminder of what Mak had told him not so long ago. He did have terrible judgment when it came to women. But none of that mattered. They just needed to find Beth. He hoped they wouldn't find her today. Not here in these fields.

Higgins approached and handed Stephen a dust kit. Stephen thanked him as he took it from the captain's hands. Stephen surveyed the group of them—Mak, Higgins, and four detectives all stood in front of him, looking to him and awaiting his orders.

He cleared his throat. "I walked the border around these two fields and think we need to work the length of each section. Let's split up into teams, four in one and three in the other. Comb the whole area. The K-9 unit will be here any minute. That should speed this search up a little. Let's get to it."

They divided up and began walking the fields. Stephen hadn't a clue where to go from here if they didn't find her.

But his apprehension over finding her was worse. When the K-9 unit pulled up, Stephen greeted the officer and watched as he gave a dog the jacket and let him sniff.

From there, Stephen watched as the dog meandered close to Beth's car and whined a little. Stephen still had the keys in his pocket, so he popped the trunk, just in case. He breathed with relief when the trunk was practically empty. In the back was a blanket and a small set of tools—nothing out of the ordinary.

The K-9 officer steered the German Shepherd away from the car and let him loose in one of the fields. He stood with Stephen and watched as the dog walked, sniffed, walked more, then ran, not seeming to pick up Beth's scent.

"You must really think this girl is in trouble to go to these lengths," the K-9 officer said.

"Just covering my bases," Stephen responded as he pulled out the dust kit and started dusting for prints on the door handles, the steering wheel, and inside the car, hoping the officer would get the hint. Stephen had never met him. He thought he recalled Higgins calling him Miles.

"This personal for you?" Miles asked, still standing near the car, his attention on the dog in the field.

Stephen swung his full attention to the K-9 officer. "I'd like to think we'd do this for anyone who goes missing and leaves their car abandoned on the side of the road."

Miles shrugged. "Just seems like a lot of manpower when there might be a perfectly logical explanation."

Stephen gritted his teeth, thinking about the information he and Mak had uncovered that morning. "It's part of an ongoing investigation."

Miles shrugged. "Okay."

Stephen finished up with the dusting and pointed to the field opposite the dog where Mak and Higgins were looking around. "I'm gonna join the search."

The K-9 officer nodded and walked toward his dog.

Stephen detoured and put the fingerprint kit back in his Tahoe.

"Bout time you showed up." Mak grinned in a good-natured way.

"Hey." Stephen fell in step beside her.

"What's up?" Mak was still walking forward slowly, her eyes roaming the area as she went. She seemed to have established a rhythm already.

"Am I doing that thing I do?" Stephen asked quietly. "Am I putting my personal business over all else and dragging everyone else along?"

Mak stopped walking abruptly and swung her startled eyes to Stephen. "I dunno. This sounds like a logical plan to me. How would you feel if we didn't look, and all along, she was lying right here—"

"Yeah," Stephen cut Mak off, not wanting to hear the word *dead.*

Mak crossed her arms over her chest and squinted at Stephen against the streaming sunlight. "I'm not a detective, Wilton. Never was. But I've done my fair share of sleuthing to figure out which way the criminals went. I agree with you. This doesn't look good. The angle of the car. Almost looks like she was forced off the road. Her cell and car keys found under her car seems like they were dropped suddenly. Like she was surprised and then grabbed. No way would she willingly leave without those things."

"That's what I thought, too," Stephen admitted, checking the time on his phone. Hours had passed since he'd found Beth's car and called it in.

"Not to mention the connections we made this morning. Not only did she know your brother, Beth also knew Trevan. Plus, she's Lacy Donovan's sister. It's like at the center of every puzzle is Beth holding it all together."

"I don't know about that." Stephen still felt reluctant to acknowledge Mak's point. But Beth knew Davey Stinnert, too.

"Yeah. If Beth disappeared, you can bet there's a reason, and it's not a good one." Mak turned her gaze back to the field and started searching again.

Stephen wordlessly joined the search. After hours, every detective, the K-9 officer, Higgins, Mak, and Wilton all admitted defeat. With no other course of action or lead to speak of, they got in their cars and headed back home relieved that they hadn't found a body but frustrated by the lack of resolution.

"I'll ride back with Wilton." Mak waved to Higgins.

Shocked, Stephen watched Mak sit in the passenger seat and buckle herself in. Too tired and lacking the energy to mess with his partner, Stephen wordlessly started the car.

It was a half hour before Mak broke the silence. "You okay?"

Stephen shrugged. "Just frustrated. All investigations keep dead-ending."

"Wilton, I've been thinking... This has gone too far. I really think we need to tell Sikes what's going on," Mak asserted.

Stephen was silent for a minute. Then he turned to Mak with a smirk. "Did it take you a half hour to get up the nerve to tell me that?"

Mak threw up her hands. "Well. You're very touchy these days!"

"Touchy?" Stephen repeated.

"Yes."

"What good can Sikes do for us here? We may have our jobs back, but we are still investigating something that wasn't issued to us from the marshal's office. I think we need to tread lightly." Stephen got serious again.

"I think we need to loop him in. You just got out of trouble. I'd hate to see this put you back in it." Mak looked out the window.

"Well, don't stop now. I assume there's a theory rolling around in your head," Stephen stated.

"You'll probably call it fiction again," Mak said, glancing at him.

"No, I'm all ears. What you got?"

"If something happens to Beth—and I'm not saying it will or putting bad things into the universe—I'm afraid you'll take the blame again. Going back to the theory that someone is working hard to frame you." Mak untied her unruly ponytail and worked to smooth her hair back, then retied it. "I'm really trying not to step in your territory, but I think the best thing you could do right now is to be proactive with Sikes."

Before Stephen could answer Mak, his phone rang. Incredulously, he picked up his phone and showed Mak the screen. "Speak of the devil!"

Mak put her hands up defensively. "I had nothing to do with it!"

Stephen pushed a button to answer through his car. "Wilton."

"And Mak," Mak chimed in.

"Someone want to tell me why I just got an anonymous phone call stating they have Beth Donovan, and they want to make a trade?" Sikes spoke without preamble.

Stephen felt the air leave the cab of the Tahoe. He gasped in surprise as Sikes' words confirmed his suspicions that Beth had indeed been taken. "What do they want to trade?"

"Lacy Donovan."

40

BETH

As Beth slowly came back into a state of consciousness, she was aware of a few things. Someone had righted her chair, and she was sitting upright again. Her head was flung backward, and her neck felt like it was stuck in this unnatural position. The pain in her neck as Beth slowly straightened it paled by comparison to the pain in her hand. She attempted to flex her fingers, but a jolt of pain zinged through her hand and traveled up her wrist.

Beth gasped and moaned aloud. She peered hard into the darkness. It was so hard to see anything in front of her. She stared, willing her eyes to adjust, but it was as black as Beth's soul.

Hot, desperate tears welled in her eyes as she contemplated how her life had come to this. Once the tears formed, there was no blinking them away. They rushed down her face in a torrent of sadness and pain. Emotions Beth had stuffed deep since her teenage days came flooding out of her. Her whole body began to shake.

Beth cried for her lost childhood. For that little girl in her who was forced to grow up way too quickly. For her teenage self, who had lost her innocence far too early, making choices she could not undo and living with consequences that were far too steep. She'd seen life and death played out in front of her, but she'd never allowed herself to mourn.

Sobs erupted from somewhere deep inside of her as more emotions surfaced. Guilt and shame slammed into her as the terrible things she had done over the years played out like a bad movie on repeat. She'd had a child when she had been a child herself, and she'd shirked her responsibilities. She'd worked for the Corrupters, selling drugs to other teenagers. She'd let Lacy walk right into danger and hadn't even been able to save her. And now, Lacy was in danger again. All because of Beth.

When her body was spent and there were no more tears left to cry, Beth took a few breaths, ragged at first, then deeper. The tears dripped down her face, to her chin, and onto the collar of her shirt. She sniffled in an effort to stop her nose from dripping. Despite everything that had happened in her life that had brought her to this point, Beth had never felt so powerless.

That's when she heard a *tap, tap* on the wall.

"Hello!" Beth yelled. "Who's out there?"

Her yell was met with momentary silence. Then a loud banging on a wall to the right of Beth answered her question. Beth shrieked in response. It sounded so close. Like it was coming from the other side of a wall. A wall was separating her and whoever was making that noise.

"Hello?" Beth called out a little quieter this time.

She was answered again by two quick knocks on the wall.

Beth could tell she was alone in this room. But on the other side of the wall... what unspeakable terror must be there separated merely by drywall and plaster?

"Oh God, he's got women down here!" Beth whispered, the horror of that realization curling her toes. The Corrupters took women, right? Even though Beth had never been a part of that, she'd known on some level. It was why Greg had lost his life. Greg had been protecting her.

When the Corrupters decided running drugs wasn't enough, they had requested that Beth bring them girls from her school. She had refused. The day Greg died, that gun had been pointed at Beth's face. Then, it swung to Greg when he stood up for her. He'd been killed because of her, and Beth hadn't even lived a life worthy of his sacrifice.

Then, they'd taken Lacy. Though Beth had never been completely clear on the reason behind that, she'd assumed they had taken Lacy to prove they could get to her anywhere at any time. They needed to keep Beth in line. To control Beth. Just like the old days.

Beth attempted to stand and move with the chair like she had before, but her captors had learned their lesson. Beth's feet were now tied to the legs of the furniture. Defeated and in pain, Beth embraced the darkness. She was familiar with the void.

"This is what I deserve," Beth whispered as she closed her eyes against the endless nothing. "All of this. I deserve this pain. I was born bad, I did bad things, and I'll die bad." She couldn't even protect the one person who should have been the most important person to her—Lacy. Lacy didn't ask to be born to an irresponsible fifteen-year-old child. Not that Lacy would ever know that truth. Beth would likely take that secret to her grave.

What was that saying? You're only as sick as your secrets. Well, Beth had deemed herself the most aggressive form of cancer.

"Wherever Lacy is, let her stay put," Beth sent the request to the universe. "I hope she never learns the truth about her no-good birth mother."

41

MAK

Mak stared at the computer screen in front of her where they were on a Zoom call with Sikes, who was back in Kansas City. It wasn't as fancy as the big-screen Sikes liked to project on the wall back in the marshals' office. Still, it was functional. Just like this small conference room in the Police Station of Little Rock where she sat with Wilton on one side and Higgins on the other. To Sikes, it might look like they presented a united front. But Mak felt anything but united.

Mak cleared her throat and laid the files on the table she'd picked up on the way to Higgins' office. "The purpose of this meeting is to get on the same page. All of us. In doing so, we hope to brainstorm solutions to the situation we find ourselves in."

"Well, Mak, we need to do it quickly because Beth's kidnappers gave us twenty-four hours to decide. We're down to twenty-two hours and forty-five minutes," Sikes cut in.

They'd made a phone call to Higgins after Sikes broke the news. Beth was officially missing and this ransom was their confirmation.

"Okay, the purpose of this meeting is to get on the same

page and find a solution to bring Beth home, keep Lacy safe, and we have a day to do so. But first, Wilton has agreed to share some information with you that we hope will shed a little background information that we suspect might play into what's happening with Beth," Mak dictated.

"Go on," Sikes requested.

Wilton sat up straighter. "Over eighteen years ago, my brother Greg was murdered—"

"Shit, Wilton! Sorry. I didn't know," Sikes exclaimed.

"Not many people do, and I'd like to keep it as quiet as possible."

Sikes nodded.

"At Booker's funeral, Trevan Collins, an old friend of my brother's, showed up and gave me an envelope with strict instructions not to seek him out. Inside the envelope was a photo of a man with a gun to Greg's head minutes before Greg was killed." Wilton held up his phone displaying a picture of the photo, enlarged the screen, and pointed to the date and time stamp in the corner. "This photo and time-stamp proves the boy who confessed to killing Greg and served time for his murder was not the man who murdered my brother. The man in this picture, whoever he is, is my brother's murderer. Following?"

Sikes nodded again.

"Now, Trevan Collins has been murdered. The original of this photo was found at Trevan's duplex with my fingerprints all over it. The theory is that someone took it from my car, where I'd been keeping it inside an envelope. But my finger-prints aren't the only ones on the envelope."

"Who else?" Sikes asked.

"Beside Trevan? Beth Donovan and Mickey Upton," Mak informed.

Stephen shot her a look and Mak looked instantly sorry.

"Whoa," Sikes said.

"Beth Donovan, Lacy's sister, and I were seeing each other at the time." Stephen held up his hand to stop all comments on that. "She likely found the envelope and photo or put her fingers on it because I had it under the passenger seat of my car."

"Or she took it to Trevan's duplex." Mak crossed her arms over her chest.

"You think Beth killed Trevan?" Sikes gasped.

Stephen opened his mouth to protest but Higgins beat him to it.

"Now hold on a minute," Higgins interjected. "That's part of an ongoing investigation and we need to hold all speculation. Just the facts, please."

"Right," Mak said.

"Beth told me she knew Trevan in school, but they weren't friends even though they lived near each other. She also dated Greg in high school. Davey Stinnert—Greg's professed murderer—was also in the same grade as Beth and Trevan. Mak was able to prove that Trevan, Davey, Beth, and Greg associated with each other because of a police reports they each had in their files for the same date, time, and location and signed by Sheriff Pottstaff. The charge was underage drinking." Wilton ran his fingers through his blond curls.

"I fail to see the connection between—" Sikes began.

"It's there, sir," Mak interrupted. "Greg was murdered. Trevan was murdered. Beth has been kidnapped. The only one alive and not accounted for right now is David Stinnert. All we know about him is that he didn't kill Greg."

"He's not exactly unaccounted for," Wilton admitted. "He's been skulking about. I've seen him watching me. I chased him down last night, but he got away."

"Hmm." Higgins made a note on a steno pad.

"So, you think the same person who killed Greg killed Trevan and now has Beth?" Sikes asked.

Higgins opened his mouth to speak but Mak rushed ahead. "It's a theory and the only one I have right now," Mak spoke quickly.

"It's gotta be Upton," Sikes stated. "We know he's in the area. You guys got eyes on that build. He's around somewhere, and we suspect he's holding women again."

"Let's not count out David Stinnert," Wilton stated. "Just because he didn't kill Greg doesn't mean he's not mixed up in this somehow."

"So, find Stinnert and Upton. I think it's high time we bring Upton in for questioning," Sikes suggested. "Let's try to find Beth before we have to answer kidnapping demands."

"Stinnert we can find. Upton has not been so easy," Wilton mused.

"I actually have an idea about Upton," Mak chimed in. She pulled the rodeo flier out of her back pocket and unfolded it. She held the flier up to the camera so Sikes could see. "This is a really big event in this area. The contractor on the night build told us Upton is planning to attend opening night. Maybe Upton will show up and he might be entertaining some big, important people."

"Why would he do that?" Sikes asked.

"Because he's a former senator," Higgins answered. "A disgraced one with his hand in the pocket of others who might be doing his bidding."

Sikes whistled. He shuffled around his files. "How did we miss that?"

"Alyah called me the other day to warn me that Upton is scary dangerous. The politicians sitting around gossiping about him remembered some pretty bad things," Wilton admitted.

Mak turned to Wilton with an inquisitive look. "That was nice of Alyah to go out of her way to help us."

Wilton shrugged, but Mak could see the heat creeping up his neck.

"The rodeo sounds like a good idea. In the meantime, I suggest pulling in Jonas Petry and Mike Bacon to let them know about the ransom and try to come up with a plan. Hold the line." Sikes put the Zoom on mute.

The room was silent as the three of them waited.

"Wonder why Sikes is pulling in Petry and Bacon? He can't be entertaining the idea of bringing in Lacy, right?" Mak broke the silence.

Stephen's eyes widened.

They were in a no-win situation. A life for a life was not a possibility here. They needed to keep both Lacy and Beth safe. This was starting to feel out of control.

42

WILTON

After a quick break, the team was back together with Jonas Petry and Mike Bacon now added to the meeting. Stephen's stomach churned. Beth was missing. No matter how they ended things, Beth was still a person Stephen cared about.

Sikes re-started the meeting. "Approximately two hours ago, we got an untraceable phone call stating that Beth Donovan is being held captive and we have twenty-four hours to respond to the ransom."

Stephen's eyes flicked to the time, thinking about the time difference where they were. It was a little past three in the afternoon.

"What's the ransom?" Jonas Petry asked, sitting up straighter and coming closer to the screen. Even across the computer, Stephen could see the way his jaw clenched.

"They will release Beth Donovan in exchange for Lacy Donovan," Sikes announced.

"No effing way!" Jonas exploded.

Stephen saw Mak's eyebrows raise. He understood the reaction Jonas had, but the outburst was uncharacteristic of the agent. Still, when Stephen thought back to the last case, remembering how much Jonas had bonded with Mrs. Lablanc in a short period of time, he concluded Jonas must bond easily with people he was protecting. Stephen could understand that.

"Well, Jonas, the purpose of this meeting is not to hand Lacy over, but to come up with a win-win to keep Lacy safe and get Beth back. Think of this like a brainstorming session. We have twenty-two hours to come up with a solution. Let's throw everything out there."

"A look-alike?" Mak tossed out. "We find an agent or law enforcement female to pose as Lacy. We demand to see Beth first, before we send the agent out, and make the exchange in an open field. At the last minute, swarm and grab the women and Upton."

Thinking back to the case where Booker was killed by a sharpshooter, Stephen shuddered. "We can't take any chances. If they think for a second that we're playing games or playing bait and switch, I think they'll kill Beth. In fact, I think their main goal is to eliminate Lacy. Remember the sharpshooters in New York?"

"I remember," Mak said. They all shared a moment of silence on Booker's behalf.

"I agree. Putting Lacy anywhere in their vicinity will end in a blood bath. Not to mention, what's to keep them from killing both Beth and Lacy?" Jonas asked directly.

"I'm talking open field with no trees and nowhere to hide," Mak interjected. "A place where no sharpshooter could get to them."

"It's not like they're going to drop Beth out of the sky. Someone will be with her. That someone will likely have a gun and kill Lacy the minute Lacy is within shooting distance," Jonas argued.

"Then we don't let Lacy within shooting distance," Mak stated.

"How the—" Stephen turned inquisitive eyes to Mak.

"I like your idea of dropping out of the sky. What if we bring Lacy in a helicopter, we drop in the middle of said open field with agents loaded inside, ready to shoot at the first sign of trouble," Mak suggested.

"In the meantime, both Lacy and Beth are right in the middle of the gun fight," Jonas snorted. "Are we actually considering these nonsense ideas? I refuse to put Lacy in the same town, let alone in the same field."

"We are throwing out all ideas," Sikes stated with a warning look on his face.

"How about trying to find Beth before a switch even takes place. Why are we here wasting time? Why aren't you out there looking for Beth right now?" Jonas practically shouted.

"We did, actually," Stephen admitted, looking miserable.

"What?" Jonas snapped.

"We found her car abandoned on the side of the road before the ransom call came in. We pulled together a team and dogs to comb the area with no luck. The town closest to the site is known as a meth town. It's small and dangerous. People shoot first and ask questions later simply because you're a stranger and look suspicious. We were regrouping to come up with a better search plan when we got the call," Stephen explained.

"Maybe *we* can put sharpshooters out there?" Mak suggested. "So we have backup in case things start to go south."

"That's enough," Jonas snapped. "Over my dead body! It's my job to protect Lacy. I just never thought I would have to protect her from my own team!"

"Chill out, man," Bacon spoke for the first time, elbowing Jonas.

"No!" Jonas snapped. He addressed the team directly. "How about this for an idea. Go do your job!"

"Jonas—" Sikes started.

"It's my job to keep Lacy safe, and I'm doing it. Your job is to track criminals and save those they harm. Beth's life is not interchangeable for Lacy's. You have twenty-two hours. Good luck. Use them wisely because Lacy will not be your solution here."

Jonas' screen went black.

Silence filled the room.

"Geez," Mak breathed. "I've never seen Jonas like that before."

Stephen nodded but he agreed with Jonas. "He's right. This is on is. We need to find a different solution without involving Lacy."

"There's always the rodeo," Mak said.

Stephen snorted. "Mak, do you really think for one minute that Upton will show up in public when he has a warrant out for his arrest?"

"Does he know there's a warrant out for him? This is the biggest rodeo in the tri-state area," Mak interjected.

"Right, a big rodeo where big names, such as politicians show up," Stephen finished sarcastically.

"We can't burn time here," Sikes stated. "Do we think Upton will show up or not?"

"If he's in the area, I think he'll be there. I think his underground sex trafficking ring only flourishes if he wines and dines his potential investors," Mak stated firmly.

"Wouldn't he do that in private?" Sikes asked.

"Not necessarily. Anthony Gerritt was all about appearances. Upton is a former senator. If Upton told his contractor he was going, then I think the chances he'll be there are pretty good. Then we could just follow him around and hope he leads us to Beth." Mak looked hopeful.

"I agree with Mak," Higgins said. "These events tend to

be about who's who and who flashes the most money around here."

"What do you think? Wilton, you in?" Mak asked.

Stephen shook his head. "No, I'm going to keep working on a new angle. There has to be something I'm missing. But text me if you get a lead on Upton, and I'll come join you."

"I'll go to the rodeo," Higgins announced.

"You will?" Stephen whirled on him.

"Sure. I love a good rodeo, and if Mak is right, she'll need backup." Higgins stroked his beard, which looked like it could use a trim.

"Alright, we're going to the rodeo," Mak said as she got up and started gathering the folders. "Seven-thirty at the Conway Arena, Higgins. Don't be late."

Higgins tipped an imaginary hat.

As they ended the call, Stephen rolled his eyes. He couldn't imagine sitting at a rodeo knowing Beth was somewhere out there. Was she safe? Had they hurt her? His stomach tightened as he thought of what would happen if they didn't find Beth in time.

43

LACY

Lacy wasn't one to eavesdrop. In fact, she prided herself on always minding her own business. But Jonas wasn't making it easy. He had been yelling at the computer. She knew he and Bacon were talking to the other marshals. Lacy told herself she was only eavesdropping because the women looked so concerned. Lacy needed to make sure everything was okay for their sake.

Only, what she heard made her blood chill.

"Over my dead body!" Jonas yelled.

Lacy put her ear to the bedroom door where Jonas and Bacon had been meeting. She could hear them that way. Though, she was having a hard time understanding what had happened.

"No! How about this for an idea. Do your job!" Jonas commanded.

"Jonas—"

"It's my job to keep Lacy safe and I'm doing it. Your job is to track criminals and save those they harm. Beth's life is not interchangeable for Lacy's. You have twenty-two hours. Good luck. Use them wisely because Lacy will not be your solution here."

"Hey, calm down," Bacon said.

"No! This goes against all my training. Shame on them for even bringing it to us!" Jonas huffed.

There was a pause. Lacy could tell that Bacon was trying to reason with Jonas, but she couldn't hear what he was saying.

"Compromised? Compromised! If anyone is compromised here, it's them! What does our mission statement say about this?" Jonas asked rhetorically. "Assuring the safety of endangered government witnesses... Not putting them in harm's way! I have half a mind to quit this job right here and now!"

Bacon spoke quietly again.

"Find another way!" Jonas barked. "I swear to God—" Jonas stopped talking abruptly.

Quiet filled the air.

Lacy had to move quickly because the bedroom door opened abruptly.

Jonas and Bacon stormed quickly through the house and out to the deck, where it looked like Bacon was trying to calm Jonas down. Maybe they realized the women could hear them in the house because the two men took steps into the yard, getting even further away.

Lacy could see Jonas waving his arms wildly. Bacon was standing with his arms crossed over his chest, nodding solemnly. Lacy didn't know Bacon very well. He mostly kept to himself. But she did think his quiet nature made him a good listener.

She sat down on the couch and tried to puzzle out the conversation she had heard. What did *Beth's life is not interchangeable for Lacy's* mean? Something must have happened. It sounded like Sikes was asking Jonas to do something that had him pretty mad. Only, Lacy had never seen Jonas mad.

Normal things that might set a person off who had been cooped up too long didn't bother him. When Lacy lost her temper, Jonas always remained calm.

Which could only mean one thing. This was about her. Sikes wanted him to do something. But what? Bring her in? They all knew she would have to testify eventually. Maybe she needed to reassure him that it would be fine. They would take necessary precautions, and she trusted him.

Lacy got up and walked to the back door. She watched as the conversation finished, and Bacon stalked back into the house. The women were sitting quietly on the couch huddled together like normal. Lacy shot them an encouraging look.

"It'll be okay. I'll be right back," Lacy murmured to them.

When Bacon came in, Lacy moved to go outside.

"I'd give him some time if I were you," Bacon warned her quietly.

Alarmed, Lacy looked out at Jonas, who was pacing on the grass. She shot Bacon her best confident face. "I'll be fine."

"Your funeral," Bacon muttered.

For a minute, Lacy froze. Her heart seemed to stop in her chest. She had been held captive under the earth and when she thought of death, it instantly took her back to that dank, dark place where she didn't know if she would make it out alive.

Bacon hesitated, seeming to realize his mistake. "I'm sorry, Lacy. Bad choice of words. Just... just be aware that he's angry."

Lacy nodded but went out the door. It was warm out and the sun felt good on her skin. Her bare feet sank into the plush grass, and she watched as her toes sank from her view. She slowly approached Jonas.

Jonas looked like a bull. His eyes were wild, he was huffing air out of his flaring nostrils, and his energy had him moving back and forth, like he was wearing a path in the ground under him.

"Jonas, what is it?" Lacy asked, timidly.

Jonas shook his head back and forth. He seemed like he was trying to come up with the solution to the world's biggest problems. He stopped pacing and turned to her, a look of defeat in his eyes. "I'm not strong enough."

"What?" Lacy shook her head.

"I can't even consider what my boss is asking me to do," Jonas said through gritted teeth.

"This is about me, isn't it?" Lacy asked. "And Beth."

Jonas finally looked her in the eyes. She saw fear. He nodded.

"Something has happened?" Lacy stated.

Again, Jonas nodded.

"I'm stronger than you think," Lacy coaxed. "Please, tell me. What is it?"

"They want Beth to—" Jonas' voice cracked.

"Beth? What about her?"

"Beth has been kidnapped," Jonas admitted.

Lacy gasped. "No!"

"Yes."

"But what do they—" Lacy stopped talking. She knew. The words fell into place. Beth had been taken because they wanted to exchange her for Lacy. Lacy was the one they really wanted. "I'll do it."

"What?" Jonas asked. "No, you don't understand what they're asking. There's no way we are going to—"

"Exchange me for Beth?" Lacy finished.

"Wave you around like bait." Jonas reached to put his hands on her shoulders but pulled them back and tucked them into his pockets. "They want to put you out there, dangle you long enough to get them to release Beth, then as you're walking toward them, we grab you both and take the criminals down."

"Could it work? Do you have a good plan?" Lacy wondered, her brain working to comprehend the possibility.

"Even the best plan is not one hundred percent. There's too much risk involved. They could insist we meet outside. There could be unseen sharpshooters waiting on rooftops, apartments, or in the woods. They want you dead. And if you get close enough, they are going to move heaven and earth to make it happen." Jonas raised his eyes to the sky.

"She's my mother," Lacy said quietly, her eyes looking off in the distance.

"What?" Jonas looked back down at Lacy in confusion.

"Beth is not my sister. She's my mother." Tears filled Lacy's eyes.

"Awe, hell, Lace. Don't cry." Jonas patted her shoulder. Lacy knew he wanted to pull her into his arms. "I'm confused. Did I misunderstand? All this time... I thought Beth was your sister."

"So did I. I don't have confirmation, but I put it together the other day. I was meditating and saw a repressed memory. Or maybe it was one I was too young to understand. I never questioned why Beth was fifteen years older than me. I just thought I was a whoopsie baby. But it was Beth. I believe she had me, but my parents raised me like I was their daughter."

"You didn't tell me." Jonas looked hurt. "That must have been hard to make that connection being so far away with no contact."

Lacy nodded. "I've been processing it."

Jonas looked like he wanted to say more, but Lacy cut him off before he could.

"I'll do it," Lacy said decisively. "I'll go in her place."

"No!" Jonas crossed his arms over his chest.

"I said I'll do it," Lacy argued.

"And I say it's a stupid idea that will never work."

"What if the marshals come up with a foolproof plan?" Lacy asked. "I trust them."

"Nothing is foolproof." Jonas ran a hand through his hair. His eyes fell on Lacy. "I can't lose you. Do you understand me? You are the single most important person in my life. I would take a bullet for you. I would die for you!"

Lacy couldn't breathe. The thought of Jonas dying to give her life wasn't an option. She would never put him in danger like that. But as she gazed at him, she understood that he was saying something much deeper. Something neither of them were supposed to acknowledge.

Lacy put a hand on his forearm. "I feel the same way."

Jonas' eyes widened. For a moment, no one said a word. They just stared at each other.

"Come on," Lacy tilted her head toward the house. "We'll find a way."

Jonas followed her back into the house.

But as Lacy walked, she wondered if she was referring to getting Beth released or pursuing this relationship with Jonas.

44

WILTON

The police department was practically empty when Stephen left that afternoon. In fact, the sun had started to set. He found Higgins around the corner from the building outside with a cigarette dangling from his fingers.

"You're smoking?" Stephen asked with a smile playing at his lips. The Higgins he knew back in the day didn't smoke. He'd been too buttoned up. He followed the rules too hard core.

"Hell, Wilton. What are you doin' sneaking up on a man like that?" Higgins growled.

"Closet smoker, eh?" Stephen found a bench and sat down while Higgins leaned against the building. "It's like I don't know you at all."

"Nah, I don't smoke much. But desperate times call for vices," he said as he flicked the ash toward the ground.

"Wait, you're really stressed about this?" Stephen looked up at Higgins.

Higgins shrugged. "We have a time clock. It's not moving in our favor. We've got nothing. I'd give Mak's idea with Upton a twenty percent chance."

Stephen sighed. "Mak is creative. Sometimes those crazy ideas of hers pan out. Just be glad she has a plan this time. She usually rushes in and worries about the details later."

"Reckon that's what got her hurt, right?" Higgins drawled.

"Yeah, yeah it did," Stephen agreed.

"Some people learn from their mistakes." Higgins speared Stephen with a look as he flicked the cigarette butt to the ground and put it out with his toe.

"Oh, come on, don't go all TV dad on me," Wilton objected.

"Maybe someone needs to." Higgins regarded him seriously. "I know what you're thinking, and going off lone wolf to try to save the girl by yourself has never worked well for you."

"Someone needs to go do the real work," Stephen bristled. "We don't have time to play around at a rodeo."

"I agree," Higgins said. "But I don't think we're going to *play*. We don't have anything else at the moment. Might as well follow this."

Stephen fell in step with Higgins as they walked to Higgins' vehicle.

Higgins unlocked the truck and put his hand on the door handle but paused. He looked at Stephen. "Do the right thing and let us know where you go and if you get yourself in a bind, son," Higgins said. He waited for Stephen's reluctant nod and pulled himself into his truck. He started it up and drove away.

Stephen stood watching until Higgins' taillights disappeared, thinking how much nicer Higgins truck was than the one he'd owned before. Stephen guessed the raise Higgins got must have been a good one. He turned and walked to his car. The truth was, Stephen had no idea where to start. He supposed he'd drive back to the town where they'd found

Beth's car and try to stay as inconspicuous as possible while he looked around for any missed clues or signs of which way she went.

Dusk had settled when Stephen made his way to his Tahoe. Wearily, he opened the door and sat in the driver's seat. Before he could even start his car, the passenger side door opened and shut. Stephen froze, his hand immediately reaching for his gun.

"I wouldn't do that if I were you." The man was dressed from head to toe in black. A black hood was drawn over his face. But what drew Stephen's attention was the shotgun in the man's lap that was pointed right at Stephen. "Slowly take your gun out and place it right here on the center console."

Stephen kept one hand up and pulled the gun with his other hand. He placed it between them. The man immediately threw Stephen's gun on the floorboard. Stephen looked up into the man's eyes.

David Stinnert stared at him from under the hood of his sweatshirt.

"Now drive," David commanded.

Stephen could feel his phone in his pocket. He put his vehicle in drive and slowly pulled out. He palmed his phone in his left hand and dropped it straight down between him and the seat. He managed to unlock the phone and pull up the last name in his text. It was Mak. He swiped across his text keyboard.

"What do you think you're doing?" David reached out and yanked the steering wheel, causing the truck to swerve dangerously.

Stephen dropped his phone, which landed face up, illuminating the floorboard on the driver's side. He grabbed the wheel and straightened it out. "Don't ever do that again." Anger lined Stephen's dark tone.

"Give me the phone. Now!" David shouted as he pulled the shotgun up, angled at Stephen's chest.

Keeping his eyes on the road, Stephen lowered his body down just enough to grab his phone. His thumb hit *send* as he handed it to David.

"One more tricky move and I'll blow your head off!" David shouted.

A bead of sweat formed on Stephen's forehead. As he chanced a glance at David's erratic eyes darting from Stephen to the gun and back to the road, Stephen truly believed David might shoot him.

45

MAK

Mak tapped the toe of her brand-new Ariat boots, then forgot to be anxious as she studied the pretty turquoise design. But as she tipped her head, her cowgirl hat fell forward.

The sound of John's laughter had Mak peeking up from underneath the brim of the hat. "What? I totally look the part!"

"Yeah, but you're so fidgety, anyone can tell you're nervous," John teased.

Mak scoffed. "I don't get nervous. It's more like pent-up excited energy."

"I see." John lifted his eyebrows like he didn't see at all. "How about me? How do these bootcut jeans make my butt look?"

Mak let out a bark of laughter and smacked her husband's butt. Then she spied Higgins walking their way. Here she thought *they'd* be late dropping off Harper at Stephen's parents' house. "There he is!"

Higgins was in similar western gear, but his clothes looked like they were a regular part of his weekend wardrobe. His boots were scuffed, the knees of his jeans looked worn, and his flannel shirt looked like it had seen better days.

"Hello!" Higgins greeted as he walked up.

"Hey, Higgins! This is my husband, John," Mak introduced the two men and watched them shake hands.

"Thanks for showing up looking less like a—"

"Like a cop?" Higgins finished her sentence quietly.

"Yeah," Mak smiled.

"Not my first rodeo," Higgins quipped.

"Right. Well, it is mine, so you get to show me around." Mak waved a hand toward the event.

The three of them went into a large arena with a dirt floor and stadium bench seating. The smell of popcorn and burgers greeted them when they entered, and Mak spied a concession stand.

"You want anything to eat?" John asked.

"Nah, just a beer for me," Mak requested.

John quirked an eyebrow at Mak again.

"Just one and mostly to fit in. Doubt we'll get any real action here tonight anyway. This really is a long shot," Mak admitted with a sigh.

"Yep, a beer for me as well," Higgins decided.

They went through the line, got what they wanted, and turned to survey the crowd.

"Already filling up," Mak said as they stood scouting for empty seats. Maybe she should have thought twice about general admission, but the entrance price had given her sticker shock.

"There's your long shot right there," Higgins took a swig of beer and ticked his cowboy hat to the right.

"Holy crap!" Mak breathed. Mickey Upton stood shaking hands with two other official-looking men, all of them sitting in a glass skybox in an elevated luxury seat beside the announcer's box.

"Are they wearing suits?" John's mouth fell open a bit.

"Suits and cowboy boots," Higgins answered, like it was a normal occurrence.

"That hat looks like it cost more than my yearly salary!" Mak's eyes were big as she checked out Mickey Upton's gear. She hadn't known much about western wear until today, but she was pretty sure she'd seen a price tag on a cowboy hat just like the one on top of Upton's head. It was more than she spent on her entire wardrobe for the year.

"I think I see a few seats close to his box." Higgins pointed a finger and started walking. His gait was slow and nonchalant. Mak matched his pace, acting as if her heart wasn't beating out of her chest.

"You gonna start a big scene?" John ducked and whispered into Mak's ear. His hand was on her back, propelling her forward.

"No. We stick to the plan." Mak followed Higgins up a few rows to seats where they had a great view of the exit doors where Mickey Upton was entertaining his guests. Two large secret service men stood guarding the doors and scanning the crowd. Mak pretended not to notice them. Trying to arrest Upton would certainly cause a scene right now. Perhaps that was why Upton was hiding in public.

"And what is the plan?" John asked.

Mak wiggled her phone at John. "I text Wilton for backup. Higgins and I nonchalantly follow Upton while you head back home. Whether we quietly shadow them or cause a scene tonight is up to the disgraced politician."

"I won't wait up. I have a feeling you'll follow Upton until he's apprehended," John surmised.

"Right." To Higgins, Mak asked in a low voice, "Who's that with Upton?"

"One is a state senator, I believe. Not sure who the other

man is. Looks like Upton kept some of his ties from his congress days," Higgins gossiped.

"What's with the suits? Who does he think he is, the president?" Mak tried to joke but her stomach rolled at the implications of Upton having ties in senate. This ring could be bigger than she thought.

They found their seats, but before they could sit, an announcer requested they remove their hats and stand for the National Anthem. Mak watched as the entire stadium obeyed, and everyone got quiet.

After a pretty, tall blond sang, everyone sat, and a rodeo clown commandeered the crowd. Mak's attention was divided as she kept Upton in her sights and simultaneously watched as an angry bull charged out of the gate and rushed straight for the brightly dressed clown, who kept tripping over his own feet.

She took out her phone, kept the angle at the arena, discreetly zoomed in her camera, and took a clear picture of all three men without attracting any attention. She needed to know who was with Upton.

Huh, she thought to herself, feeling fidgety. *I wonder why Wilton hasn't texted.* She'd texted Stephen that Upton was here about fifteen minutes ago.

She kept looking down at her phone as an hour crept by. Still no response from Wilton. They couldn't afford to lose Mickey Upton. They might not get another chance like this again. With or without Wilton, they had to make a move. Only, what was keeping Wilton from responding?

"Did Wilton say why he bailed out tonight?" Mak asked quietly to Higgins.

Higgins shook his head. "No but if I know him like I think I do, he's going to try to find Beth on his own. He told me he didn't want to sit around and waste time here."

"Yeah, what a waste," Mak smirked as her eyes darted to

Upton. Regardless of Higgins' explanation, something didn't sit right with Mak. Why wouldn't Wilton at least respond to the text she sent? Maybe she needed to get on that Life 360 app with him. Wilton always had a plan. But if he had one now, he certainly wasn't sharing it with them.

"You're fidgeting again," John said as he put an arm around Mak.

"It's Wilton. He's not responding." Mak jiggled her phone.

"Wilton's a big boy. If he gets himself in a bind, I'm sure he can get himself out," John said as the show rolled into intermission.

"He goes dark when he thinks it's his fault," Higgins said as he stood. "Nothing you can do about it. I had to just let him go to fight it in his way."

"He thinks this is his fault?" Mak asked.

Higgins nodded. "Guarantee it." He tapped his head. "Lot of guilt happens with that man. Guilt motivates him, but it also makes him isolate. Partnership is hard for him."

"I didn't know..." Mak noticed movement from the box where Upton and the two men stood. She pondered Higgins' words. They made a lot of sense. "Let's move out."

"Plan?" John said, his jaw clenching.

"Depends," Mak said. "If Upton goes to the bathroom, you two follow him. If he leaves, Higgins and I move out."

They followed the men from a distance, which was easy because the crowd moved so slowly. *They seem like a herd of cattle,* Mak thought to herself.

Just as the men disappeared into the restroom, Mak's phone buzzed. "Thank God," Mak stated. She looked down to see two words.

Wilton: *Mak, I'm...*

46

WILTON

As Stephen drove, he felt hyperaware of all his senses. He could see the final colors of the sun disappearing behind the clouds. The faint outline of the moon was slowly taking its place in the sky. There was a stuffiness inside the car as light warmth pushed through the otherwise cold vehicle. Stephen could feel the ridges around the steering wheel and noticed his hands were going numb from gripping it too hard. His foot felt heavy on the gas pedal as he drove without knowing where he was going.

Stephen could smell his own deodorant as his body broke out in a sweat. He could hear the faint sound of the country music he had been listening to on the radio this morning, which he'd turned down to take a phone call. Out of the corner of his eye, a man dressed in black sat in his passenger side. Not just any man. It was David Stinnert with a shotgun sitting on his lap and pointed at Stephen.

"Where are we going, David?" Stephen asked.

"Just drive. I'll tell you where to turn."

"You taking me out of town?" Stephen tried again.

"No, no, no. Stop talking. I'm going to talk. It's my turn. I'm going to tell you a story," David's voice rose in agitation.

Stephen's heart beat faster. He didn't know David. Even when they were kids and he called him Davey, Stephen hadn't really known him. He lifted his fingers up in surrender, his thumbs still gripping the wheel. "Okay, David. Talk."

"Your brother was my best friend—"

"Then why—" Stephen interrupted.

"No!" David yelled. "You say nothing!"

"Okay," Stephen said, his heart racing as he wondered about David's mental state. "I'm sorry."

"Your brother was my best friend. I would have done anything for him. We were friends before the others. Before Trevan, before Beth, before Jacob..." David looked straight ahead, out the windshield, his eyes no doubt seeing the past.

Stephen didn't know who Jacob was, but he knew better than to ask.

"We had a pact. Just the two of us—me and Greg. We took care of each other, we took care of my sister, and we took care of you. When the others came along, we taught them the same thing. We all took care of each other and we looked out for the siblings. We all had someone to protect— to lose. It worked until the day Greg died."

"Who killed him? What happened? Why did he die?" Stephen blurted out the questions in rapid fire.

"That's not the story I'm telling!" David shouted. He clutched his gun tighter.

Stephen shut his mouth, kept his eyes trained on the road, and nodded.

"I'm talking about you. About Lacy. About my sister— Arielle. Trevan's brother moved away with his dad in a divorce. He was safe. Everything we did, we did to keep you safe. We knew if they didn't like what we did, they would go after you. It was bad enough that they had us. We couldn't let them get to you too," David sniffed.

Stephen chanced a glance at the man and saw a tear roll down his cheek. David seemed like such a contradiction. Stephen couldn't get a good read on him. Was David stable?

"I'm telling you about the night they killed Greg. Because you deserve to know..." David continued.

Stephen took a deep breath to attempt to slow his breathing but said nothing this time.

"They requested—" David's voice broke. "Beth to start bringing them... girls. Girls from our school. We'd done everything else they requested. We did it to keep you safe. All of you. But that night, Beth refused. She was adamant. They had crossed the line. Drugs was one thing. Girls was another. They threatened to take Lacy and Arielle and you. They put the gun up to Beth's head. But Greg was a hero. He pushed Beth out of the way. He told her to run. She tried, but she didn't get far. They grabbed her and made her watch. Greg just stood there in her place. He didn't flinch when they put the gun up to his head. When they pulled the trigger, he took it. For all of us."

"Did you take the fall for his murder to protect these people?" Stephen asked quietly.

"No! Don't do that. Don't make it sound like I was some hero. I wasn't. I was a coward!" David shouted. "I did it because I knew I would be next. I knew they would think I was proving my loyalty. But really, where else did I have to go? I thought prison would protect me from them. There was nowhere for me to go. The worst part? When I confessed, everyone believed me. You and your parents were in that court room, and you sat there and said nothing. You didn't know any better. But your parents *knew* me. They'd known me since kindergarten.

"A part of me died that day. The way everyone just

accepted it... I knew my life was over then. I didn't want to live in a town with people who thought I was capable of such things. I thought—" David's voice broke, and for a minute, he just cried, then he sat trying to catch his breath. "I thought they'd leave my mom and sister alone."

"What happened to them?" Stephen asked.

"Dead, man. They both died. Car accident. That's what people said. But it's not what happened. You shouldn't have come back here, Wilton. Now you're gonna die, too."

"Who did this, David?" Stephen asked. "Who killed them? Who killed my brother?"

"No! That's not the deal. I don't trust you. You're police! I can't tell you that!" David yelled.

"Okay," Stephen kept his voice quiet as if David hadn't just told Stephen that Greg's death was all Stephen's fault.

Greg had been protecting me, Stephen thought. His soul withered, reflecting on the dark night that had settled outside. There were holes in David's story. So much that didn't make sense to Stephen. David hadn't said who *they* were or how he and Greg had gotten mixed up with them. He wasn't clear on what the teenagers were even doing for these people. Stephen wondered what had happened to these bad people after David went to prison. The only thing he could surmise from David's ramblings was whoever had killed Greg had been using threats to their loved ones to coerce them to do their bidding. David had said drugs. Were David, Greg, Beth, and Trevan dealing drugs and running money for these thugs?

Now, David was making Stephen drive farther and farther from town. "Where are you taking me, David?" Stephen tried.

"Just drive. I'll let you know when we get there. I can't have you calling for backup."

Stephen tried to make sense of David's words. But the

truth behind what David said about him and his parents in the courtroom hit Stephen hard.

You sat there and said nothing.

So now, David wasn't going to let Stephen say anything. Stephen would bet David was taking him out of town to make him disappear.

47

———

WILTON

The car had fallen silent. Stephen wanted to deny David's words, but he couldn't. His mind reverted back to a night when Stephen found out Greg was going to a football game and their parents refused to take Stephen.

Come on, take me with you, Stephen had begged Greg.

No! Greg replied harshly.

Please, come on. I won't embarrass you. I promise! Stephen tried again.

Stop it! You're staying home! Greg had whirled around to look Stephen in the eyes. But what Stephen saw there didn't make sense. It wasn't anger or frustration. It was fear.

You promise me, Stevie. You promise me that you will stay here, where you're safe, and everything is okay. Greg had put his hands on Stephen's shoulders and shook him.

Stephen didn't say a word. He'd never seen Greg like that. It was just a football game. Who actually cared if Stephen went or not?

Greg shook him harder, rattling Stephen's teeth. *Promise me!*

Okay, okay, gosh! Stephen agreed.

Hey, Greg! Davey Stinnert tapped on the door. *Time to go.*

I love you, man. You just gotta—Greg had turned to Davey and shouted through the screen door, *Hang on.*

I gotta what? Stephen had asked.

Keep your head down. Get good grades. Be good. Don't be like me. Then Greg had opened the door and left with Davey.

Stephen had felt so jealous that night. Why didn't Greg want him around? Was he too uncool of a little brother? If what David said was the true, Stephen could surmise that Greg had been trying to protect Stephen that night, not exclude him.

That constant need to protect had gotten Greg killed.

The sound of a shotgun pump brought Stephen back to the present. His mouth ran dry.

"What are you—"

"Pull over. We're here," David said, holding the shotgun higher. He had the barrel aimed straight at Stephen's face.

48

———

MAK

The minute Mak had gotten that text from Wilton, she'd flashed her phone at Higgins, showing him the two-word text as they sat back down after intermission.

"What do you think it means? Do you think he got distracted?" Mak hissed.

Higgins had just grunted.

"I don't have a good feeling about this," Mak said, texting Wilton again.

Mak: *We've got eyes on Upton. Following him when he leaves. Need backup.*

Mak: *Text for updates…*

The rodeo ended, everyone leaving their seats all at once, merging into one mosh pit of people trying to exit the stadium. John had already kissed Mak good night and left early to grab Harper.

Mak and Higgins casually walked through the now empty bleacher seats to close the distance between them and

Upton's suite where he was still talking with the two men. They kept one eye on the box while watching as the crowd inched along. When the men finally exited their suite and it looked like the three men, along with the two security details, would follow the crowd like sheep, they walked right in front of Mak and Higgins, then turned abruptly.

Mak immediately noticed where they were headed. There was a back door. One that looked off limits to the crowd, but accessible to the box where Upton had sat. Her mind moved faster. Higgins had parked out front, but Upton and his men were going out back.

She tapped Higgins and tilted her head. "Give me your keys."

"No, I—"

"I'll drive. We don't have time to argue. You follow them. I'll go get your car. I'll meet you around back. Don't let them drive off without us. Do whatever you need to do. Stall them."

Higgins tossed her his keys. "White Ram 1500 TRX. Parked it three rows back on the left aisle."

"I know what you drive, Higgins." Mak grabbed the keys and ran through the bleachers until she had no choice but to join the crowd as it bottlenecked its way through the exit. She climbed over the railing and jumped over, jostling a woman in the crowd.

"Hey, watch it!" The woman gave Mak a dirty look as she adjusted her hat.

"Sorry," Mak grinned apologetically before pushing her way out the door. The cool air blasted her lungs as she burst outside and ran toward the spot Higgins had directed her. She easily found his truck. She eyed the line forming as people pulled out to leave the arena.

She unlocked Higgins' truck and jumped in. She quickly chose the path with the least number of cars and slowly moved inch by inch toward the exit. Only, she wasn't going to exit yet. When she could turn around the building, Mak yanked the wheel and hit the gas.

"Zippy!" Mak said with appreciation as the truck jumped forward. She pulled behind the arena in time to see Higgins leaning casually against the back of the building with a cigarette dangling out of his hand. He immediately squashed it under his feet when he saw Mak.

He threw open the door and got in, quicker than Mak would have imagined a man his size and age might do. He pointed to where Upton and one of the men were ambling to a car parked a few feet away.

Mak sighed in relief. "You smoke?" Mak turned disapproving eyes at the captain.

Higgins snorted. "If I wanted a lecture, I would have stayed married to my wife. Anyway, it's how I stalled them. Acted like I didn't have a light and asked if they did. Then I struck up a conversation. Gotta say, it made my skin crawl being that close to Upton without arresting him."

"Upton didn't seem to recognize you?" Mak asked.

Higgins shook his head. "Not even a flicker in his eyes."

"Huh, so he doesn't do his research like Gerritt did," Mak mused, remembering how Anthony Gerritt had known everything about them and their families. She watched as the man with secret service got into a black Porsche SUV, while Upton and the other man got into a sleek white and black remodeled Chevelle. Mak whistled in appreciation. "What year do you think that Chevelle is?"

Higgins took off his cowboy hat and tossed it in the back seat. He scratched his head. "I reckon 1969 or 1970."

"Man, would I love to race that thing," Mak said as she waited until the Chevelle fired up and drove forward. She followed at a distance.

Higgins looked horrified. "You wouldn't dare."

Mak looked at him and laughed. "I've been down a race-track or two. What do you have under the hood of this thing?"

"A hellcat. Don't get any bright ideas," Higgins grumbled. "Got it to celebrate my long overdue promotion. Do you know this is the first new vehicle I've bought since I joined the force?"

"Nice. What year is it?" Mak asked, her eyes intent on the Chevelle as she drove a distance back.

"2021," Higgins answered. "Had a healthy savings and a new promotion. I don't buy new. Don't like losing value the minute I drive off the lot. Can't do it. Never could."

"A hellcat, huh?" Mak grinned wickedly. "A six-point-two-liter supercharged HEMI V8. Where were you planning on driving this thing?"

"Home and the station. Not in a car chase. Hear me?" Higgins asked sternly.

"Yes, sir, loud and clear. Waste of talent, if you ask me," Mak stated. She took a turn when the Chevelle did, still staying back.

"Few things bring me joy, Mak. This truck is one of them. Don't make me regret handing over those keys." Higgins switched the subject. "Any word from Stephen?"

Mak shook her head. "Nothing. I'm worried. That man tends to get himself shot—"

"Oh, I'm aware." Higgins frowned. "He ever tell you when he got shot in the chest?"

"What? No!" Mak gaped at Higgins.

Higgins nodded and pointed to his heart. "Thought he was a gonner. He got lucky, if you call it that. Bullet punctured a lung. He was in a medically induced coma, and he didn't wake up for quite some time."

Mak gasped. "How long?"

"Almost a year," Higgins told her.

Mak's mouth hung open. She fell silent. She had a healthy respect for her partner and the comment about him getting shot had been a joke. Though she decided she wouldn't joke about such things moving forward.

She took several more turns and followed for what seemed like twenty minutes when the Chevelle finally turned down a blacktop road that was wide enough for two cars to fit side by side, but it looked like a private drive.

Just ahead, the Chevelle braked and came to a full stop. Mickey Upton stepped out of the car. He approached their vehicle with his hand on the gun he was wearing on his belt.

"We've been made. Here goes nothing," Mak muttered as she pulled the truck up beside Mickey Upton.

49

WILTON

"Lower the gun, David." Stephen slowly stopped the car and turned off the ignition. He put both hands in the air. "Killing a law enforcement officer won't solve your problems. It will only complicate them."

"If you only knew," David snorted. "Get out of the car."

Stephen put his hand on the handle and pushed the door open. He put his hands back up in the air. He looked around, a sense of dread settling in the pit of his stomach. They were in an open field, not unlike the one where they'd found Beth's car. But Stephen could see nothing but land for miles. No trees, no farmhouses, no roads with cars to drive by and spot them.

"Where are we?" Stephen asked.

David had made it around the car and put the butt of the shotgun against Stephen's back. "Walk."

"If you're gonna shoot me, just do it, man." Stephen took a few steps, waiting for the man to pull the trigger. There would be no coming back from a shotgun at close range. In this moment, Stephen could almost feel his gunshot scar pulsing. But no, that was his heart beating so hard, it seemed to be trying to escape his chest.

"Straight ahead."

The shotgun prodded him forward. He was looking at nothing but open field. Confused, he walked. He had no other choice but to obey. He had no plan. He felt completely out of control.

Silently, Stephen willed his brain to work, to solve this puzzle that was his life and figure out how to get out of this mess still physically intact. Then the clouds seemed to clear, and the moon shone through, illuminating what lie ahead.

A rock quarry with steep, hollowed out cliffs was looming ten feet ahead.

"Good God, David. You're gonna drop me off a cliff? I think I'd prefer you shoot me first."

"Stop," David commanded.

Stephen watched as David backed up, gun still trained on him. He could hear David muttering under his breath as he leaned down and attempted to move what appeared to be a trap door.

A trap door in the ground that looked like the rest of the ground around it. It reminded Stephen of the last case they were on. The one with Anthony Gerritt. These criminals seemed to use the same ideas over and over. *Like a business model.* Stephen shuddered at the thought.

Stephen watched as David struggled to open the door while holding his gun. He turned to Stephen. "Open it," David commanded.

"What?" Stephen felt surprised.

"You heard me." David held the gun trained on Stephen. "Open the hatch."

Stephen put his hand on a latch that blended in with the ground. He pulled but found it heavier than he expected. He grounded his feet and pulled harder. The hatch opened.

David stepped closer. "Go down."

Stephen peered down. There was a long ladder. "Jesus, David. You're putting me in an earth prison?"

"Shut up. I'm going down too," David snapped.

Stephen took a deep breath and put his foot on the first rung. As he slowly made his way down the ladder, he looked around. It was a hollowed-out room. All he could see was a closed door with a keypad next to it. With nowhere else to go, Stephen waited until David got to the bottom.

David landed on the ground with a loud thud. He rebounded immediately, stood, and pointed the shotgun inches from Stephen's chest. Stephen was backed into a literal corner with a gun preventing him from moving.

This is it. This is the end. Stephen squeezed his eyes shut.

50

MAK

Mickey Upton walked right up to Roger Higgins' Ram 1500 TRX and peered in, his eyes so dark brown, they appeared to be black. Upton was average height but had a large, tubby stomach. He had a full head of hair that looked like it was in need of a cut, which he compensated for with a lot of product to comb it to the side. He had a toothpick hanging out of his mouth.

Higgins slowly rolled down the window.

"You two lost?" Upton asked slowly with a slight drawl to his words. He looked smug, like he was a cat who had just caught a mouse.

Mak leaned forward and smiled brightly. "Nice Chevelle! Whatcha got under that hood?" She asked, side-stepping Upton's question.

Upton blinked at Mak and assessed her cooly as if deciding whether to answer her question. Slowly, drawing out his words again, Upton responded. "V8 engine. Opted for the 396 big block Chevy."

"1970, right?" Mak shot back.

Upton nodded, his eyes still weary.

"She's a beauty! Fully restored?" Mak asked.

Again, Upton nodded slowly.

"You wanna go?" Mak grinned wickedly.

Upton took a step back and assessed Higgins' truck. He lifted an eyebrow in arrogance. "Really?"

"Sure," Mak bobbed her head. "How far does this road go?"

"A mile. You want to race the Chevelle? That's why you followed me?" Upton asked.

"Heck, yes. Dream come true!" Mak pretended to fangirl.

"Okay," Upton agreed. "Terms?"

Mak thought about it as excitement surged into her veins. She ignored the murderous look on Higgins' face. She was quickly calculating what she knew about Chevelles. Her dad had one once. It took five to six seconds to get up to sixty. But she didn't know the capability of the Ram.

"Two hundred dollars. Quarter mile. Then we'll get out of your hair," said Higgins with a shrug, his words surprising Mak into silence. "Daughter here used to race."

Mak protested. "You could have left that out of the conversation!"

Upton smiled unexpectedly. But it was quick and evil. He nodded once. "Yeah. Yeah, I reckon that won't matter. Hell, I'd pay you two hundred just to go away."

"No way!" Mak trash talked. "I'll earn that fair and square."

"Fine," Upton huffed. "I'll take your money the hard way."

"No jumping the line or starting early," Mak commanded.

Upton bared his teeth in frustration. "Look, my brother can flash a light to tell us when to go. We race a quarter mile. When I win, you pay up and get the hell off my property. Agreed?"

"No," Mak argued. "Because I'm going to win."

"Win or lose, you leave." Upton glared at Mak.

"Agreed." Mak cheerfully put her hand out.

Upton reluctantly shook it and went back to his car.

"What part of *don't even think about it* did you not understand?" Higgins gritted out through clenched teeth.

"Hey, just be thankful we're still alive. This Ram would have a whole lot of bullet holes in it if it hadn't been for my fast thinking," Mak retorted.

"Fast thinking," Higgins snorted. "More like one-track mind."

Mak shrugged, conceding his point. "How fast is this thing?"

"Zero to sixty in three point five to four seconds," Higgins answered with pride.

Mak gawked at Higgins. "And you've *never* thought about racing it…" Sarcasm laced her tone.

They watched as a tall, thin man got out with a flashlight and motioned for Mak to line up with the Chevelle. Mak drove forward and revved the engine.

The man stepped between the cars and raised his hand with the flashlight pointed toward the sky.

They heard the Chevelle rev its engine beside them. Adrenaline flooded Mak, and she went silent, adopting an intense focus.

The man dropped the flashlight and Mak hit the gas. The Ram jumped ahead quickly but the Chevelle closed the gap and rode right alongside them for a few seconds. Then the Chevelle fell back abruptly.

"What the—"

"Stopped. Slammed on the brakes," Higgins yelled.

Mak immediately let off the gas. "That means—" She slammed on the brakes and the Ram stopped on a dime, throwing them forward, but it continued to slide as the blacktop turned to gravel and dirt on account of the speed they had reached. That's when they saw what lay ahead.

"Oh…" Mak was sure choice words flew out of her mouth. Up ahead was a gigantic rock quarry. The bottom was indiscernible from the angle they were at, but they were still sliding.

Mak jerked the wheel so hard, the truck skid sideways.

Higgins gasped.

Mak shrieked. "God, help us! We're going to die!"

51

WILTON

David pointed the shotgun at Stephen. Stephen stood, eyes squeezed shut, waiting for the pain that he remembered all too well to explode in his chest. When nothing happened, Stephen peeked through his tightly closed eyes.

"Move, we have to hurry. They're coming back," David snapped.

"Who's coming back?" Stephen looked back up toward the opening above them.

"Shh!" David hissed as he turned around toward the keypad. He keyed in a number. Stephen watched, committing the numbers to memory.

The door slid open.

There, sitting in a dark room tied to a chair, was a woman.

Confusion clouded Stephen's mind. Was this where David was planning to turn the shotgun on Stephen? But the longer Stephen peered into the room, the more his eyes adjusting to the darkness, and the details of the woman came into view.

"Beth!" Stephen lunged forward.

Beth squinted at him. Her eyes narrowed. "Stephen? What are you—"

David stepped up. The shotgun hit the ground with a clatter. "There's no time. Untie her feet."

They set to the task, but Stephen noticed Beth's hands were handcuffed to a metal chair. "Do you have a pocketknife on you?"

David hesitated, then took a pocketknife with other tools out of his pocket. He handed it to Stephen. Stephen picked the lock on the handcuff. Then he turned to the other side.

Beth cried out in pain.

"What happened to your hand?" Stephen asked. It was swollen to the size of an apple.

"Chair fell on it. What are you doing here, Stinnert?"

"Coming for you. Don't be ungrateful, Beth. You can thank me later." David broke the tie at her foot.

"I had things under control!" Beth snapped.

"Looks like it," David replied sarcastically.

Beth sprang up as soon as she was free. "Listen, I can't leave here yet."

"Beth," David groaned. "What now?"

"There are other women down here." Beth pointed. "Right on the other side of that wall."

Stephen swung around, horrified. "How do you know?"

Beth walked to the wall and knocked three times.

Her knock was immediately answered with an echo of knocks from the other side.

Stephen gasped and looked for a way into the other room. "There's no opening here."

"There are other rooms," David explained. "Come on, we need to go."

"I'm not leaving!" Beth stomped her foot stubbornly.

"We need to go up to find the way into their prison. It's probably accessible from the top," David stated firmly. "Go!"

"Ugh, I can't grip with my hand." Beth eyed the ladder in front of them.

"I'll help you," Stephen offered.

Beth used her good hand to climb with Stephen steadying her as he followed behind her. David brought up the tail end.

"This was your plan all along, David?" Stephen asked as the climbed upward. "To get Beth?"

"Yes," David said.

"Why did you make me think you were going to shoot me and leave my body in the middle of nowhere?"

"I needed you to come alone. I didn't want you calling for backup. And I still don't trust you."

"If you would have told me we were going to find Beth, I would have come along, no questions asked," Stephen clarified. But he didn't think that was true. He would have texted Mak, just like he tried to do in the car. "How did you know where she was?"

"I've been here before. So has she," said David. He was holding his shotgun again. He paused at the top of the ladder and looked around before crawling out of the hole. "It's where they call us for meetings."

"You are involved in all this!" It wasn't a question. "Both of you are."

"Look, I've caused your family a lot of pain. I'm trying to make up for it," David admitted.

"They'll kill you for this, Stinnert!" Beth lashed out. "You should have just left me there."

"Yeah, but at least I'd be going out on my own terms instead of theirs. Doing something good for a change." David stood upright and offered his hand to Beth who crawled out ahead of Stephen.

That's when they saw them. Stephen's blood coursed cold through his veins. Standing not even ten feet from them was Mickey Upton with an evil gleam in his eye and a shotgun in his hand. A tall, lanky man stood beside him with a pistol pointed at them.

Upton shifted and his gaze pierced them. Everything froze. The movement slowed down. The deafening sound of the gunshot echoed through the chilly night.

The gun that was pointed right at Stephen. He dared not blink. Nor did he have time to move.

"Nooooooo!" Beth screamed. It seemed to drag out and echo through the open field.

Before Stephen had time to react, his body fell sideways. Stephen hit the ground hard, and he blacked out.

MAK

The Ram had stopped. However, they were so close to the edge of the quarry, Mak could see straight down to the bottom. One more inch and they would have gone over. Mickey Upton had just tried to kill them. Which meant one thing Mak hadn't accounted for.

Mickey Upton knew exactly who Mak was. Which begged the question, while Mak and Higgins were following Upton, had Upton been laying a trap for them?

"You okay?" Higgins asked.

Mak tried to catch her breath. She didn't know when she had lost it. Nevertheless, she took a deep breath and let it out before she answered. "You know, I've never considered myself afraid of heights, but if you could see my view from this side of the truck, I think you'd find yourself a little frozen to the seat," Mak managed.

To her surprise, Higgins laughed. His loud, boisterous sound filled the cab of the truck.

"Are you laughing because we're alive or is it a delayed sense of hysteria?" Mak asked, still refusing to turn her head and look down the quarry.

"Adrenaline dump. Some people cry. I laugh." Higgins shrugged. "Not to mention, I can only imagine how much you give Stephen a run for his sanity. That guy has a chronic need to be in control at all times. That was anything but in control."

"Right?" Mak agreed on both counts.

"How close are we to the ledge?" Higgins asked.

"Geez, Higgins. You're really gonna make me look?" Fear filled Mak's eyes.

"Hey, you got us into this mess. You need to give me all the information so I know if we need to dive out of the truck or not and if our shifting weight will push us over that ledge."

"Dear God," Mak gasped. "Could that happen?"

"I think you know the answer to that." Higgins remained still in his seat.

Mak carefully lowered her head and moved it to the side to get a better view. She followed the ledge to the back of the truck with her eyes. "Okay, here's what I can tell you. We are really close to the edge, but I believe both tires on this side are solidly on the ground. Having said that, I will need to come out your side or I'm going to end up in the bottom of the quarry."

Higgins sucked in a breath. Mak knew he was thinking about his pride and joy, this truck. "Okay, nice and easy, I need you to shift your weight over to this side of the truck. I'll open the door and lean my body out and over while you come to this side. If we put all our weight on this side, then get out, we should be clear if the truck shifts in the wrong way."

"Okay," Mak swallowed. "Let's do this." Mak followed Higgins' instructions and before they knew it, they were out of the truck and on solid ground. They walked around the truck to find Mak's assessment was dead on. All tires were on the ground but barely.

Higgins pulled out his phone. "I'll call a tow truck. But keep your eyes up. We're in hostile territory."

Mak opened her mouth to respond, but didn't have time. Her words cut off abruptly.

The echo of a single gunshot reverberated through the night.

53

MAK

Mak put her hand on her hip holster and felt for her gun. It was still there. She scanned Higgins and could see his gun was still secure on him as well.

"You don't happen to have bullet-proof vests in the truck, do you?" Mak asked.

"No, but I do have handcuffs." Higgins quickly, but carefully, opened the truck door and grabbed a few sets. He tossed one set to Mak. She quickly put them in her back pocket.

Higgins pulled out his phone and requested backup. "I'll send you a pin," he told them.

"Okay, any last words?" Mak asked as she pulled her gun and led the way toward the sound of the gunshot.

"Yeah," Higgins said, following on Mak's heels. "Don't get shot."

Mak took off at a light jog, focusing her awareness on her back. Amazingly, she felt no pain. Fresh off rehab, she didn't want to push it with a full out run. Not to mention, there weren't trees to hide behind out here. Only an open field. If they were spotted, it might be a shoot-out.

When they were close enough to make out figures in the field, but far enough to not be spotted, Mak dropped to the ground and took deep breaths to calm her breathing. Higgins lowered to the ground as well.

"There's Upton and the tall, skinny guy," Mak whispered. "Upton has a shotgun!"

"I see Beth!" Higgins breathed with astonishment in his voice. "I'll be. She's got a shotgun pointed back at them! I wonder which one of them shot the gun."

"Who's that?" Mak asked as she pointed to what looked like a pile of humans. She could see several limbs but no one definitive. It was dark enough and they were far enough away that Mak couldn't make out who was on the ground.

"I don't know," Higgins answered after half a minute of staring.

"Drop the gun, Upton!" they heard Beth yell.

"You first, Beth," Upton commanded.

Beth laughed. "Did you really think it was going to work? After all I've done for you, you lock me up like I'm one of your victims? Yeah, don't look so surprised. I heard them down there. You've got women out here, you disgusting pig!"

"Careful, Beth," Upton warned, pulling the gun up higher as if taking aim. "Don't anger a man with a shotgun."

"This isn't good," Mak said as she lifted quietly off the ground and remained in a squat. She stifled a cry when she felt a quick grab of pain in her back.

"What's your plan?" Higgins asked. He was now squatting beside her.

"Apprehend the criminals. Quickly." Mak straightened, broke into a jog, and lifted her gun.

"Which ones?" Higgins asked.

This gave Mak pause. She glanced back at Higgins.

"Beth might not be as clean as you think," Higgins warned. "Let's make sure she doesn't shoot us first."

"How far out is backup?" Mak asked.

"I'd guess a good forty minutes," Higgins replied.

"Alright then. Let's not startle anyone with a gun in their hands. Time to make ourselves known." Mak sped her gait. When she was within twenty feet, she yelled out. "US Marshal, everyone drop your weapons and put your hands in the air!"

54

WILTON

Stephen lay still. He was having a hard time breathing. He felt nothing but the heavy weight over his body, pinning him down to the ground. He could see red, viscous liquid pouring to the ground underneath him.

Is that mine? Stephen wondered. He tried to pat his body to check for holes, but he couldn't move his arms or legs. He felt no pain, but he definitely could not move. Was he in shock?

"Oh, no—" he groaned, realization dawning.

A loud, high-pitched scream broke the terrifying silence that followed the gunshot. That's when all chaos broke lose.

He heard, rather than saw Beth pick up the shotgun.

Stephen tried to move. She was going to get herself killed. He struggled. Why couldn't he move? He saw a bloody hand in his face. It wasn't his. He peeked out from underneath to see Mickey Upton a few yards away with a shotgun in his hand, aimed right at them.

Stephen tried to replay what had happened. What had seemed like slow motion had actually happened so fast. Upton had pointed the shotgun at Stephen and shot. It didn't feel like he had hit Stephen even though he was pretty close. Which could only mean one thing.

David Stinnert had knocked Stephen out of the way, taken the bullet, and his dead weight had fallen on top of Stephen. Literal dead weight, if the way David lay motionless was any indication.

Stephen peeked out again and realized that Upton was talking. What was he saying and why couldn't Stephen hear him? Then he saw it. A square piece of paper lay on the ground just past David's hand. Stephen had to work at it, but he managed to wriggle his hand out and grab the paper.

Blood marred the writing, but Stephen could make out the word, though the first letters were blotched.

...angsten

What was *angsten* and why had David written the word on a piece of paper? Dare he hope that David was still alive? He couldn't let all the answers die with David.

With a burst of adrenaline, Stephen rolled David to the side and checked for a pulse.

"Oh, no!" Stephen got his answer.

"Stephen?" Beth's voice hissed. "You okay? If so, I could use some help up here."

Stephen crouched defensively beside David.

"Toss me the gun," Stephen commanded.

"What? That's your solution?" Beth snapped.

"Yes, I'm a law officer and you aren't. Now, give me the weapon."

"Not on your life," Beth argued. The shotgun rested painfully on her right wrist, and her left index finger hovered just above the trigger.

"Fine." Stephen was going to have to take matters into his own hands. He stood up and grabbed the gun out of Beth's hands, shoving her behind him. He opened his mouth to yell to Upton to drop his weapon when he heard Mak's voice.

"US Marshal, everyone drop your weapons and put your hands in the air!"

Stephen's eyes bulged as he watched Mak and Higgins approach, seemingly from nowhere.

Upton glared at Stephen with hate in his eyes. Stephen could see him clench his teeth in indecision. For half a second, Upton seemed to weigh the odds. Then, he threw the shotgun on the ground and raised his hands.

A tall, thin man beside Upton, someone Stephen had never seen before, did not drop his gun. Instead, his eyes locked with Stephen's, he raised his pistol higher, and he put his finger on the trigger.

A gun shot rang out. Instinctively, Stephen dove for Beth, throwing himself and Beth backward. He looked over his shoulder to see Mak running toward the tall man who had dropped to the ground and was now lying still.

"Higgins, call for an ambulance!" Mak called as she raced to check the man's pulse. Then she popped up and cuffed Upton. She began reading him his rights.

Flashing lights appeared and a sheriff's vehicle rolled to a stop. Sheriff Pottstaff exited the car. He walked closer, surveyed the scene, hooked his hands on his belt buckle, and chuckled.

"Someone forget to invite me to the party?" he called out as he approached.

"Pottstaff, what are you doing here?" Higgins broke the silence. "I called in my boys for backup. How exactly did you know we were out here?"

"Someone heard a few gun shots and called it in. Thought I'd come see what was happening." Pottstaff looked pleased with himself.

"There's no way anyone heard gun shots all the way out here—" Mak began.

"You!" Beth screamed.

Everyone turned to where Beth had risen from the ground and stepped out from behind Stephen. Silence descended. Even Pottstaff looked surprised.

"You killed him!" Beth shrieked.

"Me?" Pottstaff asked as he pointed to his own chest, his eyebrows lifting in surprise.

"It was you!" Beth's voice was rising to hysteria, understanding dawning in her crazed eyes. "You killed Trevan!"

"Why on earth would I kill Trevan Collins?" Pottstaff asked calmly.

Beth didn't say Trevan's last name, Stephen thought, *so Pottstaff definitely knew Trevan.*

"You were the one who took that picture with your police body footage." Beth was walking toward Pottstaff now. "You made our lives hell growing up!"

"Beth, stay back," Mak cautioned. "The sheriff has a gun."

"And a badge," Stephen warned.

It was then that Stephen noticed the subtle movement of Pottstaff's hand. His gun was within reach on his belt.

Beth didn't stop. Instead, she broke out into a run. She didn't stop until she stood in front of Pottstaff. She pulled back her hand and slapped Pottstaff so hard, his head whipped to the side.

Before Pottstaff could respond, Higgins had his gun out and poking it into Pottstaff's back.

"Hands up where I can see them," Higgins reached around and unhooked Pottstaff's gun belt, which fell to the ground. "Mak, how about we borrow Pottstaff's car and take these two for a little ride to the station."

"Sounds good to me." Mak nodded. "Wilton, you have a ride?"

Stephen found his voice. He looked at Beth. "Yes. There are women being held on this property. Once the team gets here, we'll search the premises and rescue them. Then, we'll go back to Little Rock."

"You sure?" Mak asked, looking uncertain. Stephen knew she'd rather be helping with the women.

"Positive. Beth heard the women and can help us locate them. Not to mention," Stephen said, pointing to Beth's swollen hand, "we need to make a trip to the ER."

55

WILTON

Within minutes of Mak and Higgins driving off, Higgins' team showed up, as did an ambulance. After a brief consultation on everything Beth knew that could help locate the women, Stephen walked Beth to an EMT and showed him Beth's hand.

"Stay here," Stephen commanded.

Beth rolled her eyes and sucked in a breath as the EMT lightly pressed on her hand. "Where would I go?"

Stephen briefed the officers. Soon, flashlight beams illuminated hard to see patterns in the ground where there was a small line of missing grass that led to a hidden door. That door led to another room next to the one that had held Beth. Guns drawn, Stephen and the other officers proceeded down the ladder.

This room was built exactly like the other one with a keypad for entrance. Stephen used the code he watched David key into the other room, but he was still shocked when it worked. The door slid open, revealing four women sitting on the ground against the wall, watching the door. Stephen assumed the women had heard the commotion outside. Their eyes were wide with fear, and they seemed to be positioned as far from the door as possible.

Stephen held up his badge and illuminated it with a flashlight. "US Marshal Stephen Wilton. I'm here with the Little Rock PD. We're here to rescue you."

Upon hearing those words, the women all began crying. They were thin and weak. Getting up from the ground seemed to take too much energy and effort. The men cautiously approached and offered them hands to stand. They could walk with some assistance, but it was slow going getting them out of the underground room and up the ladder.

Once they were above ground, the women started a fresh surge of crying.

"What is it?" Stephen asked, his eyes scanning the horizon, instantly on alert for an unseen enemy. Seeing no imminent threat, he turned his eyes to the women.

"We never thought we'd see the moon again," replied one of the women.

Stephen cringed inwardly. He'd never experienced the trauma they had but was thankful theirs would now come to an end. As Stephen gingerly helped the women into protected rescue vehicles, felt their boney hands, and gazed at the skeletal frames of the women, he knew this was not a predicament Beth would leave other women in. Without having to ask her, he knew she wasn't a part of this.

As Stephen walked back to the waiting ambulance, he called Higgins and requested more manpower. They would need to search the rest of the property, and Stephen knew it would take the whole night.

Beth's hand was indeed broken and needed to be reset.

"You need to get her to the ER immediately," the EMT informed Stephen. We would but we are out of room. Stephen watched as they loaded the dead bodies of David

Stinnert and the thin man who had been with Upton, whom they had learned was a relative of Upton's.

Beth swore this was the only trafficking cell she knew of and she'd only learned of it out when she had been held against her will. When Stephen looked into her eyes and saw the tortured expression on her colorless face, he wondered if Beth was thinking about how close she'd come to becoming one of them.

By the time Stephen placed Beth in his passenger seat, it had been a long night. His job didn't always end in satisfaction, but nights like these reminded him of why he'd taken this job. He was thankful that he'd been reinstated when he had.

56

BETH

Beth sat silently cradling her bulbous hand, her thoughts far away as Stephen drove her to the hospital. How she remained stoic either spoke to her strength or the dissociation of all feelings, even physical pain. Her hand had gone numb long ago.

This wasn't over. It would never be over. The marshals had just *kicked the hornet's nest,* so to speak. What they had stumbled into was bigger than Beth. It was bigger than Upton, Allister, and Gerritt all put together. It was only a matter of time before they—the Corrupters—knew she had outed Pottstaff.

Davey was dead. She was the only one left. The last one who could turn on them and tell the authorities what she knew. She didn't know everything. But she knew enough that she had just put herself in danger by publicly standing against them, siding with the law. She had to get out of town before they found her. She was the only one who could keep herself safe.

Call it luck or a small-town quiet night, but Beth was able to get into the ER quickly and get her hand set. It wasn't pleasant, but the numbing shots were the worst of it. At first, there had been discussion about her having too much swelling to get a clear x-ray, but they were able to get a picture of the bone in her hand that had snapped. She left with a cast on her hand, which was going to be tricky to maneuver.

But nothing would keep her from her plan to get out of this town, somewhere so far away that no one would ever find her. Only then could she survive another day.

57

WILTON

The car was silent as Stephen navigated to the road away from the hospital.

Beth broke the silence. "Take me back to my car, please."

"You're coming with me to the station. I need you to make a formal statement." Stephen was all business.

"After what I pulled back there, I'm as good as dead!" Beth protested with icy resolution.

"Not true!" Stephen argued. "Beth, it's over. Don't you see? Your statement and Lacy's statement will put these guys away for life."

"You keep her far away from them. You don't understand what you're dealing with. It's far from over," Beth hissed, her eyes wild.

"Then, help me. Help us stop all of this once and for all." Stephen looked at Beth. Her eyes were dark and tired, practically lifeless. Her black hair was messy from her time underground. Only after her hand was doctored did Stephen notice the bruises on her face. Mickey Upton had hit her. Multiple times from the look of it. Upton was also the reason Beth's hand was broken. But that's all Beth would tell him.

"I'll give you what I can in exchange for my freedom," Beth compromised.

"Freedom?" Stephen asked.

Beth nodded. She closed her eyes and leaned back. "I've never been free. I don't know what that's like."

"Beth, you're not making any sense," Stephen pressed.

"I need your word, Stephen. I give you my testimony and you let me go."

"Go where?" he asked.

"Wherever I want. A place where no one will ever find me," Beth explained.

"What about testifying—"

"No deal," Beth negotiated. "My testimony now for my freedom."

"Fine." Stephen held out his hand.

Beth shook it awkwardly with her left hand. "When we were kids—"

Stephen held up a finger and grabbed his phone. He scrolled as he drove until he found his record button. "I'll need to record this."

Beth stared at the phone with suspicion.

"It's the only way I can let you go, Beth," Stephen stated firmly. "You give me a recorded testimony now and I'll take you to your car instead of the police station."

"Fine," Beth agreed.

Stephen hit record and spoke in the phone. He named Beth and stated the date and time.

Then he let Beth speak.

58

BETH

Beth took a deep breath and began her story. It was so ugly—the things she had done to stay alive. Beth had always assumed she deserved what she'd gotten. She had always been deeply rebellious. She'd had a child at fifteen-years-old. Some people change when they have a child. Sure, Beth felt protective of Lacy. But she'd mostly wanted to protect Lacy from herself.

"Bad things followed me wherever I went from a very young age. I learned that it was me. I was bad. Why else would such horrible things happen to me so often?" Beth paused, thinking of her beautiful friend, Shania Woodstone. Shania hadn't deserved what had happened to her.

"What bad things happened, Beth?" Stephen asked.

Beth chose to skip over Lacy and start with Shania. But she knew she could not tell Stephen everything. "It all started at a high school party. I was sixteen." She'd already made so many bad choices by that point.

"What happened?" Stephen asked.

"I was there, hanging out with my friend who was dating

your brother. Davey was there too. Along with another friend named Jacob—"

"Can you please state full names for the record?" Stephen interrupted.

"Yes, I was at a party with Davey Stinnert, your brother, Greg Wilton, and Jacob Greenly," Beth stated.

"And your other friend?" Stephen asked.

Beth flinched. Her jaw tightened. Tears sprang to her eyes. "Shania Woodstone."

"What happened to Shania?" Stephen asked.

"I cannot talk about that part. I signed agreements. If you pull her file, you'll see everything has been redacted. I shouldn't have given you her name."

"Okay, we can strike it from the testimony," Stephen lied smoothly.

Beth knew he was lying. What had she been thinking, getting involved with a man in law enforcement? She was thinking Stephen would keep her safe and fix her problems. But he hadn't. She believed Stephen would bring Lacy home. He had not. If she brought Stephen into her life, Beth thought maybe, somehow she would become a better person. She wasn't.

"The cops showed up and busted us for underage drinking that night," Beth started the story again. "Sheriff Pottstaff specifically, only he wasn't a sheriff then. He had—" Beth stopped and thought about her words. "He had something on us. Something worse than underage drinking. He used it to his advantage—used us to do his bidding while we were in high school."

"How did he use you?" Stephen asked.

"He made us his drug mules. We peddled drugs. Sold them, supplied them, all coming straight from Pottstaff."

Stephen gasped quietly. "Surely not Pottstaff alone…?"

"No, there were many people who came and went. High turnover. Pottstaff was our constant, our point man. Any time we got sick of it or threatened to rebel, he'd threaten us right back. We all had siblings we had to keep safe. He'd tell us he would go and recruit them to do our work if we ever left. So, we never did."

"Until the day he killed Greg?" Stephen asked.

"Pottstaff didn't kill Greg," Beth corrected.

"But you know who did?" Stephen asked.

Beth shook her head. "No. I saw the picture. The one Trevan gave you. That came from Pottstaff. He kept it sitting in his desk for years. My guess is it was his insurance for if or when anyone ever turned on Pottstaff. Trevan found it one day in his office—" This wasn't what Trevan had shared with Beth. Beth had just put the pieces together.

"Why was Trevan in Pottstaff's office?" Stephen asked.

"Because they—we called them the Corrupters when we were growing up—had summoned us again. They left us alone after high school. It was such bliss. Until six months ago when they summoned us and pulled us back in. Trevan had told me he was going to find a way out. He was going to free us all. I distanced myself from him because I didn't want to be there when he went down." Beth looked out the window with remorse in her eyes.

"And he sure went down," Stephen said. "Just like you thought he would."

"Yeah." Beth originally thought it was Upton who killed Trevan. But the minute she saw Pottstaff standing in that field, it all clicked into place. Pottstaff must have found out Trevan took the photo. He might even have known he'd given it to Stephen. It all made perfect sense. "It was Pottstaff. Pottstaff killed Trevan."

"But his prints aren't on the envelope," Stephen told her.

"Let me guess, the prints belong to Mickey Upton and me?" Beth asked.

Stephen nodded. "And Trevan."

"Obviously," Beth sighed. "This is where things get murky for me, and I have to be careful how I say this. Remember, I've been working for the Corruptors since I was sixteen?"

"Yes," Stephen answered slowly.

"Upton knew Trevan had stolen the picture. I don't know how. But I know he had Trevan followed. He summoned me and asked me to get him that envelope. I knew I was on shaky ground with Upton. See, he knew about you and me. Not to mention, I thought he had Lacy. Everything I've done for them has been about proving my loyalty and keeping Lacy safe. So, I did it. I knew where you kept it."

"You gave the picture to Upton?" Stephen asked for clarification.

"Yes. Upton is a narcissistic idiot who thinks the rules don't apply to him. He didn't wear gloves. But then, neither did I. Pottstaff would have known to wear gloves. He's a cop. He knows how to cover his tracks."

"Beth, I have to ask. Is this speculation or do you have any proof?" Stephen asked.

Beth lifted her chin with defiance. "That's your job. Get proof and incarcerate the bad guys. Only, I've yet to meet one good cop who has worked things out for the good in my life. I'm giving you direction on where to start looking."

"Is there anything else you can tell us?" Stephen asked.

"Check the bullets that killed Gerritt. Bet they will match a gun Pottstaff owns. He's Upton's clean-up man. I'd bet money that he killed both Gerritt and Trevan."

"Okay, is there anything else you can think of?" Stephen asked again.

"Your brother was a hero. He died to protect me. They

wanted me to start bringing in girls from my school. I refused. I said I would rather die. Your brother stepped in front of the gun for me."

"You were there?" Stephen asked sharply.

"That's all I can tell you about that afternoon, Stephen." Beth closed her eyes a moment.

"Can I follow up with you from time to time?" Stephen asked.

"It's best that you lose my number. You'll never find me again after tonight," Beth admonished.

They had pulled up to Beth's car. Stephen parked and turned off the recording. "You don't have to leave, Beth. We can protect you." Stephen looked into her eyes.

Beth looked away. "No one can protect me. Only I can protect me."

"There's still so much we don't know. We need you. Lacy needs you," Stephen said.

"No!" Beth held up her hand. "I'm done letting people use her to manipulate me. I'm a person. She's a person. Not objects to be controlled. She's better off far away from me. When I called you, you had one job. To bring her home."

"I'm sorry, I—"

"No, I accept that you didn't bring her home. But you lied to me about what happened to her. Upton admitted that Lacy got away. I know you saved her and got her to safety. Promise me that you will always keep her safe. And if you see her again, tell her I love her. Make sure she knows that." Beth grabbed his arm, her eyes pleading with his.

Stephen nodded and pulled out his wallet.

"I don't want your money, Stephen." Beth held up her palm.

Stephen reluctantly put the money away.

"We left everything here in case you came back," Stephen explained. "Your phone and car keys are under the floormat."

"This is good-bye, Stephen." Beth looked into his eyes for half a second. Then she pushed the door open and got out. She walked to her car and took her first breath of freedom.

Beth figured Upton would be detained at least twenty-four hours, which would give her enough time to put her plan in motion to disappear. She knew in her heart that she would never come back.

59

MAK

It hadn't taken long to get a warrant to search Sheriff Pottstaff's office and residence, but they had to use Beth's recorded testimony to procure it. It was unusual, but a judge had allowed it. Mak and Wilton had accompanied several officers from Higgins' team on the search.

They'd found more than one weapon at Pottstaff's home that wasn't registered to Pottstaff, which meant he'd bought them illegally. One of them matched the ballistics on the bullets that had killed Anthony Gerritt. The gun had Pottstaff's prints on it, too.

They had been about to leave when Wilton spotted something in the kitchen. It was a leather wrap of sorts. There, right in plain sight, was a pouch with butcher knives tucked into the loops. Still wearing his gloves, Wilton unwrapped it to find one knife missing from the set. It looked like it would be the biggest one.

"Possible murder weapon of Trevan Collins?" Mak asked, feeling the tingle of excitement. "Now, we just have to find it."

"Search the house for a butcher knife," Stephen instructed the team.

Having searched the whole house, they moved outdoors to the perimeter of his property. After what seemed like hours, just as they were about to give up, Wilton spotted a patch of ground that looked like it had been freshly dug. This made it easier to move the dirt away and unearth the butcher knife.

They knew it wouldn't have prints since the envelope left with Trevan's body didn't have any. They took multiple pictures of the location where they found it before bagging it up for evidence.

Now, Mak and Wilton sat on the other side of the glass while Higgins and another detective questioned Pottstaff. Pottstaff sat expressionless in front of two officers until Higgins put his hands on the table and leaned forward.

"Not gonna lie, Pottstaff," Higgins spat the sheriff's name. "Things are not looking good for you, but I'm going to give you a chance to confess your transgressions."

Pottstaff remained silent.

"Fine," Higgins gritted out. "Where were you on the night of June fifteenth?"

"Hmm, I'll have to have my secretary check my calendar. Why do you ask?" Pottstaff wore an expression of arrogance.

"As you know, you have been arrested for the murder of Trevan Collins."

Pottstaff looked smug. "You have no proof of that."

"I'm adding a charge," Higgins announced. "You are hereby being charged for the murder of Anthony Gerritt."

Pottstaff's smirk fell, and his eyes widened in surprise. Then he made his face emotionless again.

"So, I also need an alibi for the night Anthony Gerritt was murdered. We do have evidence for both charges, so I'd be very careful about what you say here."

"You found the knife?" Pottstaff said in wonder as if to himself.

"Interesting you should ask that," Higgins commented. "We didn't release information on how Trevan was killed or if the murder weapon had been found on the scene."

"I want to make a deal," Pottstaff said quickly.

"You are aware of what happened the last time an associate of yours tried to make a deal—oh, of course you are. You're the one who murdered him."

"I'm not admitting to that," Pottstaff said quickly, leaning back and crossing his arms.

"You haven't told me anything yet that makes me believe you have information to offer. Tell me why we should make a deal with you?" Higgins challenged.

"I know everything!" Pottstaff admitted.

Higgins pulled out his phone. From where Mak and Wilton sat, they could see it was a picture of Upton at the rodeo with the man they assumed was a senator.

A look of fear crossed Pottstaff's face. Then he masked it. "I don't know who that is."

"See, that would be of real value if you did, Pottstaff. The kind of value that would make us consider a deal. Until you come up with real information, you'll hang out in a jail cell." Higgins got up and escorted Pottstaff out of the interrogation room.

Mak turned and smiled at Wilton. "Good as got him!"

60

LACY

Lacy debarked the US Marshal jet to find an unmarked Range Rover with tinted windows waiting for them. She hadn't realized she'd paused to bask in the unexpectedly warm sunlight until Jonas protectively put his hand on her lower back. She was surprised to find she wasn't stressed out about identifying her captors. She knew with Jonas by her side, she would be safe.

They had gotten word that Mickey Upton had been apprehended. He was sitting in a jail cell beside his good buddy Boyd Allister. Now that they were both safely behind bars, Lacy was here to make sure they never saw freedom again. That identification would keep them behind bars without hope of bail. This was an important key right now given the discovery of Upton's friends in the senate. The last thing they needed was Upton or Allister getting out on bail.

The US Marshal Range Rover took them straight to the jail. There, on the other side of a glass wall in which only Lacy could see a lineup of men, she quickly identified the two men who had taken her. They'd forcibly removed her from her home and put her in an earth prison where she barely ate and all her basic needs had been stripped down to a humili-ating existence. She gladly did her part, speaking on behalf of the three other women who had suffered far longer than she had.

Once she did her duty, she and Jonas headed to the US Marshal building. Oddly, she was more nervous about this next step. Tucked into her travel bag was a folder with a load of information. It was a presentation full of research she had done, well-documented results from the women she'd shared her home with and had begun to help them heal. Though Lauren, Emma, and Isa weren't well enough to go out and function in society, they had taken some positive steps in the right direction.

As a result of her experience, Lacy had changed her online major of computer science, though she did get a thrill off helping the marshals determine the area Mickey Upton had been operating. But her passion was helping women who had vanished, disappeared from their own lives, and miraculously saved. The term she used for them was Final Girls. Lacy was a Final Girl, though barely. She counted herself fortunate that she hadn't gone through what she had for as long as Lauren, Emma, and Isa had.

Not to mention, more girls had just been discovered and saved. What Lacy had to propose was needed now more than ever. She knew it would be a long road ahead of applying for grants and vetting the right people to come alongside the mission and join the women wherever they were in their healing journey.

As they arrived and walked into the US Marshal office, Lacy was shocked as every person in the room stood to their feet and burst out in spontaneous applause. Tears pricked Lacy's eyes. She didn't feel like she had earned such a response. Not yet. But she would work hard to make sure someday she did.

She thanked everyone shyly and then followed Jonas into the conference room. She shook hands with Deputy Director Rob Sikes.

"Lacy, it's so good to meet you," Sikes stated with a wide smile. "I've heard so much about you."

"Same," Lacy smiled back as she took her chair.

"I understand you have some information you want to share?" Sikes invited.

Jonas smiled his encouragement. Lacy's nerves disappeared and her passion took over. She'd never wanted anything more than she did now. She passed out a stapled set of copies full of stats and case studies. She had ideas for an expansion of the ranch home where they were staying. She had even found some professionals who would be perfect to come in and start in-home therapy sessions.

After Lacy's presentation and walk-through of the data, Sikes sat back, looking stunned.

"You want to start a recovery house for Final Girls." Sikes looked a little dazed. "I have to admit, the thought never occurred to me. In fact, because kidnapping is not usually in the US Marshal wheelhouse, this isn't something that's ever come up before. But you're right, there is a need. Especially now. Obviously, our priority would be keeping the identities of the women confidential and protecting them at all costs."

"Of course," Jonas agreed.

Lacy nodded.

"Well, it's not something we can throw together overnight. There's no protocol for this. We're in new territory. For example, that particular ranch home is the property of the US government. Having said that, you're well on your way. I would ask you to keep working on this and looking at it from every angle while I run this up to the Attorney General. I would like to support you in any way possible."

"Great," Lacy smiled with hope in her eyes.

Jonas cleared his voice. "There's, ah, one more thing."

"Oh?" Sikes asked, curiosity evident in his eyes.

"I want you to know that my number one priority has been protecting the women the past six months—"

"Naturally," Sikes interrupted. "I have no doubts."

"Well, my heart and focus is moving in a different direction," Jonas announced.

"Oh?" Sikes' eyebrows shot up.

"When Lacy gets this center off the ground, I will be working alongside her. My loyalty is to her and this vision," Jonas stated, looking Sikes in the eyes.

"Jonas, are you putting in your notice?" Sikes eyes widened in disapproval.

Jonas shook his head. "Not yet. Unless you need me to. Because there's more. Not sure if there's a precedent for this either, but my loyalty isn't the only thing that's with Lacy. I've fallen for her."

Sikes sat back and studied Jonas and Lacy, his face impassive. "I see."

Jonas put his hand on Lacy's and straightened. "I'm in love, and I plan to put a ring on her finger."

At that declaration, Lacy's eyes grew large. She knew he had feelings for her, but she hadn't known to what extent.

"You look surprised, Lacy," Sikes said. "So, I have to ask if this is returned and consensual?"

Lacy could feel the color in her cheeks. She felt like she was asking her dad for permission to go out on a date. She found her voice as she looked into Jonas' eyes. "Yes. I'm in love with Jonas, too. Have been from the beginning. I'm surprised because while I assumed Jonas felt the same way, we never acted on these feelings or expressed them to each other. Jonas has been a consistent professional."

Sikes seemed to sag in his chair. "Thank God for that.

Well, this is also new territory, so I'll put this on my list of things to discuss with the Attorney General."

"I appreciate that, sir." Jonas stood and reached across the table to shake Sikes' hand.

"I'll get back to you when I have next steps," Sikes said. "Where to next?"

Jonas paused at the door. "It's been a long day, but we would like to go back home. Lacy doesn't want to be away from the women that long."

"Though, I would like to see Beth while I'm in the area." Lacy looked hopeful.

Sikes dashed her hope in the next second. He looked uncomfortable. "Beth took off before we could get her to agree to give us a statement in person at the station. In fact, if you do get in touch with her, we would like to remind her we can offer her protection."

"What do you mean she took off?" Lacy asked, confusion in her eyes.

"Turns out, you might have been targeted because of your sister," Sikes announced.

Lacy felt her veins flush with ice. "What?" she whispered.

"Ah, hell, Lacy. I'm afraid I have questions too, but we can't get all the answers unless she cooperates. We suspect she doesn't trust authorities and ran to protect herself," Sikes said.

"I see." Lacy's eyes filled with tears.

"Don't cry, Lace," Jonas said, patting her shoulder.

Lacy swiped at her eyes.

"Don't worry, I have a feeling we haven't seen the last of Beth Donovan," Sikes said knowingly. "Please encourage her to come in if you reach her."

Lacy and Jonas nodded as they exited the conference room with plans to drive back to the US Marshal jet and head back to the ranch, which had become home—the only home Lacy had ever really known and called her own.

298

61

———

WILTON

As Stephen and Mak were walking into the US Marshal building, Lacy and Jonas were walking out.

"Jonas! Lacy!" Mak cried. She put her hand out to shake Jonas' hand. She turned to Lacy and was surprised when Lacy hugged her. Next, Lacy hugged Stephen.

"How are you guys?" Stephen asked. "Lacy, I heard you were able to ID Boyd Allister and Mickey Upton. You are the hero of the hour."

"Well, I couldn't have identified them if you hadn't caught them." Lacy grinned.

Stephen's eyes followed as Jonas took Lacy's hand in his. Before Stephen could ask about it, Lacy put her hand on Stephen's arm.

"Have you spoken to Beth?" Lacy asked.

Jonas nudged Lacy, his eyes full of encouragement. "You can tell them."

Lacy looked shy. "It's just so new…" She turned back to Stephen and Mak. "I don't think Beth is my sister. I think she's actually my mom. She had me when she was fifteen."

Mak's mouth fell open.

Stephen's body heated from the inside. He had been seeing Beth for five months, but she'd never trusted him enough to tell him that? The puzzle pieces fell into place. Stephen had always wondered why Beth was more concerned about Lacy than her own parents. Now he knew why. And Beth hadn't trusted him enough to let him in. Pain radiated through his heart.

"I did speak to Beth," Stephen answered, thinking about Beth's hasty exit. "She's safe. It turns out she has some history with the men who took you—Gerritt and Upton. She refused protection, and I have a feeling she's far away from here by now. She's just doing what she needs to do to protect herself."

"Oh." Lacy looked down, and when she looked up, there were tears in her eyes. "I hate hearing that. I was hoping to see her."

"I have a feeling you'll see her again someday, when she feels safe. In the meantime, she asked me to tell you that she loves you—very much," Stephen assured her.

Lacy nodded.

"Where to now?" Mak asked. "We should throw a party with cake, ice cream, streamers, and music!"

Stephen smirked. "It's her thing. She celebrates everything—"

"Because today could be your last," Mak took over Stephen's explanation. "Because you never know what will happen tomorrow."

"So wise," Jonas agreed. "I actually think we're going to take the jet back home."

"Home?" Mak asked.

Lacy nodded and smiled. "I'm hoping the place we've been staying will become permanent. A home for Final Girls to recover."

"What?" Mak gasped excitedly.

"Well, let's not celebrate too soon, Lace. Sikes is looking into ways to help the transition but yes, we've done a lot of research, and we've been working with the women and putting together case studies." Jonas' eyes sparkled with excitement.

"We're looking into grants and finding experts to put in place. We just presented the idea to Sikes," Lacy summed it up.

"That's amazing, Lacy! This is a great idea," Mak exclaimed.

It wasn't lost on Stephen the way Jonas and Lacy used the word *we* and *us* and *home*. He was happy for them. But something hardened in his heart. It was time to put that dream away. For him, love had been, and forever would be, a source of pain. A distraction from what he needed to focus on—himself. Inwardly, he rolled his eyes. Mak's inner healing work was starting to rub off on him. But she was right. He needed to start taking better care of himself and that would start with his heart.

"Well, it was great to see you guys!" Stephen waved good-bye as Lacy and Jonas scooted out the door. Stephen turned his attention to the office. It was the first time he was being welcomed back without suspicion that he'd participated in criminal activity. Despite his previous bitterness and anger, he couldn't help but feel the relief of walking into his work home. Stephen still didn't have a physical home here, and he didn't think Sikes would take kindly to Stephen sleeping on a couch in the office.

Similar to the reaction they had with Lacy and Jonas, the entire office burst into applause when Mak and Wilton walked in the door.

"Wow, is that for us?" Mak asked.

Sikes came out to greet them. "Sure is. It's not every day

we get three major criminals officially off the street. Sorry we don't have a cake for you, but this isn't a bad celebration."

"I'll take it!" Mak said with a grin.

They followed Sikes into the conference room. "I understand we lost two people in the confrontation?" Sikes began.

"Yeah, one was Mickey Upton's relative and helper. The other was David Stinnert."

"Sorry Davey Stinnert didn't make it, Stephen," Mak said.

"You know." Stephen shrugged, trying to shake off the emotions he was feeling about Davey. Davey Stinnert had taken a bullet for Stephen and saved his life. "It's just one more dead end in finding my brother's murderer. It seems like someone out there is working very hard to keep that under wraps."

"I still can't believe you let Beth leave," Mak moaned. "She knows everything!"

Stephen nodded. "But I brought in her testimony," Stephen said to Sikes.

Mak had listened to Beth's testimony three times. "But why did she leave?"

She didn't feel safe with me. The words had been running continuously through Stephen's mind since she'd left. That was the real reason Beth had run.

"Unless the law has changed in the past twelve hours, we can't have someone arrested without probable cause. And witnesses can refuse our protection."

"But she knows who killed your brother. Her *not* telling is obstruction of justice."

"She didn't admit to knowing that." Stephen knew his argument was weak. Mak was right. His decision to let her go had been personal.

Mak shook her head and abruptly changed the subject. "Back to Davey... The thing that puzzles me is did he tell you why he decided to help you?"

"He said he'd done so many bad things, he wanted to tip the scales. Do something right," Stephen explained.

"What bad things?" Mak asked.

"Same as Beth, drug dealing. His false confession—taking the fall for Greg. A piece of paper fell out of his hand and onto the ground after he saved me." Stephen pulled a small white paper with a blood stain dried on the corner where it curled up. He smoothed it on the table. Mak and Sikes leaned in. The blood was marring the word on the paper.

"Angsten?" Mak tried to read out loud. "What does that mean? Is it a place?"

"I think it's—"

"Langsten," a familiar voice interrupted them from the doorway.

Stephen turned slowly to find Alyah standing in the doorway, looking beautiful in her dark skinny designer jeans, with a red blouse cutting off at her waist. She was balancing on her black stiletto heels. Her hands were tucked in to the pockets of her pants, and Stephen wondered if she was trying to hide the way they shook.

"Alyah!" Mak greeted warmly. "Hello! What a nice surprise!"

"Hey, Mak!" Alyah tried to smile back. "You look great. Much better than the last time I saw you."

"Yeah, I'm fully recovered!" Mak happily turned a full circle.

"Congratulations," Alyah said genuinely, but her words lacked enthusiasm.

As Stephen looked at Alyah, his pulse quickened. He told himself it wasn't because he had any feelings left for her, it was concern over what he saw in her eyes—the fear and vulnerability.

When it came to him, he needed to harden his heart. The last time she'd left him, the pain had immobilized him. He had run straight to Beth. His mind went to Carley and Paige. One doomed relationship after another. He didn't have the capacity for any more heartbreak. Nor did he trust his own choices when it came to women anymore. Heart aside, his instincts were telling him that Alyah was in trouble.

"You were saying?" Stephen watched Alyah closely. "About Langsten?"

"It's Senator Joseph Langsten. I am working closely with his office. I discovered some things about him—dangerous things. I have a hunch it will tie into your case. That's the reason I'm here." Alyah's eyes strayed to Stephen.

Stephen could see her disappointment as he regarded her without emotion, his wall of protection going up around his heart.

Alyah took a picture out of her purse and laid it on the table. It was a picture of Mickey Upton shaking hands with a man with silver-gray hair who might have been handsome in his prime.

"That's the guy who was at the rodeo!" Mak exclaimed excitedly. "When was this taken?"

"Two weeks ago," Alyah answered. "Found the picture in an event file."

Stephen's phone dinged and he saw the scrolling message from Bernie Miltner, his investigative photographer. He'd forgotten about Bernie working to clear up the photo of his brother's murderer.

Bernie: *Got it cleared up best I can.*

Stephen clicked on the picture he'd attached and froze in temporary shock. "Perfect timing." Stephen flipped his phone up next to Alyah's printed picture.

Mak gasped.

The four of them studied the photo on Stephen's phone. There in the photo stood a much younger Beth Donovan, Trevan Collins, and Davey Stinnert with fear-filled looks on their faces, watching minutes before Greg's killer pulled the trigger. Stephen tapped the killer's face on the screen, verbalizing what everyone else was seeing.

"This confirms it. Senator Langsten killed my brother."

"There's more," Alyah's voice wobbled. She reached into the pocket of her jeans and pulled out a zip drive.

"What's that?" Sikes asked.

"I think—I think I might have found a manifest on Senator Langsten's computer—"

"What's a manifest?" Mak interrupted.

"It's the information you'll need to take down the ring. There are maps, highway routes, names, phone numbers… It's a lot. This trafficking is far reaching." Alyah took a shuddered breath. "I think he's on to me. I think he knows I took information from him."

"What were you thinking?" Stephen exploded.

"You told me to look around and I did," Alyah raised her voice back at him. "None of that matters now. I—I think I'm in danger. Maybe we all are."

Stephen ignored the stirring in his gut and told himself it had nothing to do with the deep-rooted feelings he had for Alyah and everything to do with keeping a fellow colleague safe and getting justice for his brother.

The thoughts of his brother's killer that slid through Stephen's mind went dangerously dark. Langsten was a murderer and a predator masquerading as a United States Senator, a man with a reputation of trustworthiness who was nothing more than a criminal. Stephen's entire being hardened into rage, and he made a promise to himself in that moment.

If I get anywhere near Senator Joseph Langsten, I'll kill him.

THE END

PROLOGUE, BOOK 4

GREG WILTON

If you like *Why He Lied*, order book 4 in A Mak and Wilton Thriller series—*Why She Fled*.

Nineteen Years Ago...

Shania Woodstone was the girl Greg had spent late nights and long summer days dreaming about. With her straight brown hair that touched her waist and big brown eyes framed by thick, black eyelashes, a light smattering of freckles covering the bridge of her nose, and a smile that lit up the room, Greg was *gone* over her. Shania had heart-shaped lips that were always shiny with pink lip gloss that smelled like bubble gum. Greg only knew that because one time in the sixth grade, he and his friends had played that stupid spin-the-bottle game. Greg had gotten lucky when his bottle had landed on Shania. She had developed earlier than the other girls, and every guy wanted her.

It was more than that for Greg. He had loved Shania since she'd moved there in the second grade. It had only taken him eight years to get up the courage to ask her out. If he'd known how quickly she'd say *yes*, he would have asked her out sooner. But now, as he watched her socialize, Greg wished he'd taken her somewhere else for their first date.

They were in the old, abandoned cabin just off the stone quarry outside of town—The Cliffs, they called it—a popular party place where they'd all hung out for years. Tonight, the cabin had gotten crowded, the temperature rising exponentially with each body that shoved into the cabin. There was too much competing for Shania's attention here.

It wasn't her fault really. She'd also known these other kids at the party since the second grade. Take Beth Donovan, for instance. Beth was Shania's best friend. It was rare for one of them to be seen anywhere without the other. Beth was here with a guy named Jacob Greenly. Jacob was a year older than they were. He was harmless, but Greg knew he would get tired of Beth. Beth was pretty, but she was too high-maintenance and talked way too much.

As Greg turned from the keg holding two cups of cheap beer from the tap, he noticed Trevan Collins edging his way closer to Shania, who stood on the other side of the room next to a ratty leather couch. Trevan was a tall, good-looking kid who most girls drooled over. He'd been chosen to play varsity football tight end, the spot Greg felt sure he was going to get, leaving Greg stuck on JV. It made Trevan pretty cocky. Having beaten Greg to Shania's side, Trevan was now flirting with Greg's girl.

"Back off, Collins," Greg snapped, slightly out of breath from rushing across the room. He pushed Trevan back with his elbow and presented Shania with a drink.

"You got a problem, Wilton?" Trevan's face lost its charm as he put his shoulders back and puffed out his chest, making himself appear bigger.

Greg stepped into Trevan's personal space, imitating Trevan's stance. Trevan had already taken Greg's spot on the football team. There was no way Greg was letting him have Shania too. "Back off my girl!"

"Really? She's *your* girl?" Trevan sneered. "Maybe you should ask her what she thinks of that."

"That's enough, boys," Shania blushed as she sipped the beer.

"Tell him you're here with me," Greg challenged, his eyes still on Trevan.

"Yeah, Greg and I came together," Shania confirmed.

"Well, tell him you're leaving with me," Trevan growled back.

Greg's eyes flew to Shania's face.

Shania's mouth dropped open. "I didn't—"

Alcohol and testosterone flowing through their veins, Greg turned his anger on Trevan. He could tell by Shania's reaction that Trevan was lying. He shoved Trevan so hard that Trevan's back slammed into an old wooden cabinet.

Trevan pushed off the cabinet like a springboard and flew into Greg. Bodies crashed together and then into the alcohol stacked on a rickety card table. Two legs of the table collapsed, and bottles slid to the floor. The sound of broken glass twinkled over the loud voices of the crowd.

"Let's take this outside!" Trevan, ever the hot head, yelled. "Winner takes Shania home."

"You're on!" Greg agreed as the two tramped toward the door.

"Uh, I didn't agree to that," Shania called out. "I think I'll just go home with Beth."

Not listening, Greg followed Trevan outside where the cool air slapped him in the face. He threw the first punch. Everyone knew most fights got broken up within the first five minutes, so the winner was usually the one who threw first.

Greg's fist connected with Trevan's face, knocking him backward. Trevan rebounded quickly, light on his feet, as he threw a hook that landed against Greg's ribs. A small crowd had followed them out.

Fight, fight, fight, they chanted.

For the next ten minutes, the crowd gasped and cheered as Trevan and Greg bloodied each other's faces and punched stomachs, ribs, and any other body part that got in the way.

Then they heard a yell somewhere in the distance. "Police!"

In mass chaos, the crowd scattered. Underage drinking at parties was still a huge offense in this little town. Trevan and Greg, still locked together but now on the ground, tumbled, kneeing and pinning each other like it had become a UFC fight.

"Knock it off, guys!" Davey Stinnert was coming in quick. "Didn't you hear? Police!"

Jacob Greenly and Beth Donovan still stood in place rather closely, eyes locked on the two fighters. Beth looked a little green and Jacob stared in sick fascination.

Out of nowhere, Shania stumbled toward the boys. She giggled obnoxiously as she tried to focus. "Oh, boys!"

"Is she trashed?" Jacob asked.

"I dunno," Beth said. "I didn't even think she drank that much."

"Fine," Shania slurred. "You can both take me home."

"Uh, Shania?" Beth stepped forward. "You okay?"

"Hey!" Davey's voice was loud beside them. "Watch out for—"

It all happened too quick. One minute, Shania was bobbling after the boys, who were still rolling around on the ground dangerously close to the cliff. The next minute, Shania was flapping her arms like she was fighting for her balance.

Beth rushed forward in an effort to save her friend.

"Shania!" Beth's voice pitched upward in a scream. She

arrived just as Shania lost her fight with gravity. Beth reached out, but it was too late. Shania had pitched over the edge of the cliff.

A shrill, eerie scream was the only sound in the night, until it cut off abruptly.

For a moment, no one moved. On the ground, Trevan and Greg were frozen in an awkward embrace. Beth stared in horror with an arm still outstretched over empty air. Jacob stood beside Davey, both of them gaping like fish, eyes huge and unblinking.

Then all hell broke loose.

"Police! Everybody, freeze! Put your hands in the air!" Three police officers, guns drawn, descended on the teenagers. The flashlights they held swung from kid to kid, temporarily blinding them.

A loud wail sounded from somewhere deep inside Beth.

"I'm Officer Pottstaff." A tall, intimidating man flashed a badge. "Someone better explain what the hell is going on here!"

The two other officers stood silent, waiting for an explanation.

"She's gone!" Beth wailed.

"What?" Pottstaff snapped. "Who?"

"My friend—she just went over the edge." Beth's words were now coming out in a hysterical torrent. She pointed down over the side of the cliff. For a moment, no one spoke. Hearing Beth's words made it more real. It hadn't been a figment of their imagination. Shania had gone over the cliff. She was now at the bottom.

Officer Pottstaff stalked over to Beth, planted his feet, and shined his flashlight over the edge. He gasped and then cursed. "Who is that?"

"Shania Woodstone," Beth stammered, having a hard time getting out her best friend's name.

One of the other officers pulled out a phone and called for an ambulance.

"You!" Pottstaff shined his flashlight at Beth, Trevan, and Greg, who were now sitting on the ground, valiantly trying to hold back tears. Jacob and Davey were standing stoic, frozen in their places. "You been drinking?"

No one said a word.

Pottstaff nodded. He made some signal to the other officers. The officers swooped in and handcuffed Davey and Jacob. Pottstaff handcuffed Beth. "You have the right to remain silent. Anything you say can and will be held against you—"

"What are the charges?" Greg asked, looking like he might make a run for it.

"I wouldn't do that if I were you, son," Pottstaff said as one officer took Davey and Jacob up to the squad car. He nudged Beth to start walking. The other officer cuffed Greg and Trevan and began leading them up the hill to a second squad car.

"I said, what are the charges?" Greg asked again more loudly.

"Murder."

ALSO BY ADDISON MICHAEL

A Mynart Mystery Thriller series is ghostly suspense with psychological elements. If you like complex heroines, paranormal twists and turns, and gripping suspense, then you'll love this dark glimpse into the psyche.

> **Book 1** - *What Comes Before Dawn*
>
> **Book 2** - *Dawn That Brings Death*
>
> **Book 3** - *Truth That Dawns*
>
> **Book 4** - *Dawn That Breaks*
>
> **Book 5** - *What Comes After Dawn*

The Other AJ Hartford - A phantom on a train. A mysterious kidnapping long ago. Can she connect the dots before all her futures disappear forever? If you like good-hearted heroines, ghostly phenomena, and nail-biting high stakes, then you'll love this mind-blowing adventure.

A Mak and Wilton Thriller series is a pulse-pounding crime thriller series with a strong female lead, stimulating twists, and relentless suspense.

> **Book 1** - *When They Disappeared*
>
> **Book 2** - *When She Vanished*
>
> **Book 3** - *Why He Lied*
>
> **Book 4** - *Why She Fled*
>
> **Book 5** - *Why He Died*

REVIEW REQUEST

If you enjoyed this book, I would be extremely grateful if you would leave a brief review on the store site where you purchased your book or on Goodreads. Your review helps fellow readers know what to expect when they read this book.
Thank you in advance!

~ Addison Michael

ABOUT THE AUTHOR

Addison Michael is the oldest of six siblings. She grew up with a golden reputation and a well-hidden dark side. Writing became her outlet. Addison's dark side emerges in the crime and mystery thrillers she writes today. She lives in the Midwest and believes in writing what she knows, so her stories are often set in the Midwest region. From cabins surrounded by acres of desolate woods to rural police departments and eclectic personalities, Addison Michael captures the essence of small-town living.

You'll find the following tropes in Addison Michael thriller books:
- Cabin in the woods
- You can't go home again…
- Unreliable narrator
- Kidnapping/missing person
- Addiction/recovery
- Femme fatale
- Serial killer